An intriguingly muscul... present in a tight white T-shirt. But instead o... was a belt with a silver buckle.

"Hey." It was a low voice, kind of husky, and she finally looked up.

The owner of the chest, T-shirt and belt buckle took a step back. His skin was olive-toned, and his black hair curled over his forehead. Dark brown eyes studied her face. He smiled, and his full lips parted to reveal teeth that were white and just a little crooked.

"Hey," she managed to say, and in an attempt not to gape at the man who looked as if he'd swaggered straight off the streets of Spain or Italy, she took the cloth grocery bag from his hand and set it on the counter.

"I'm Sandro," he said quietly.

"Of course. Sandro the chef." Her cheeks were on fire, and something was wrong with her brain. She stuck out her hand, and he took it, wrapping it in his long fingers and giving it a firm shake. "Um, nice to meet you. I'm visiting. From San Francisco."

"I see. Well, I hope you're hungry."

"I'm always hungry," Jenna blurted out. "I mean, I try not to eat too much—I'm a dancer.... You know, dieting and all." This was ridiculous. Just a scant hour ago she'd given Samantha a speech about how her focus was going to be on her career, and yet now she couldn't even think straight, or talk, just because of one good-looking guy.

Dear Reader,

Many years ago, I took my first Lindy Hop dance class and fell in love. It was an all-consuming love that I was lucky to share with a lively and dedicated group of dancers. And for a year or two I had a wonderful dance partner. We taught classes at a ballroom and everywhere else we could drum up work. It was a magical time.

Those experiences were the inspiration for Jenna Stevens. Dance is her passion, so when she meets a young man who dreams of becoming a dancer, she resolves to help him. But first she has to enlist the support of his older brother.

That older brother is Sandro Salazar, the rebellious eldest son of a Basque family who owns a sheep ranch outside of my fictional town of Benson, California. Basque culture is so intertwined with the Eastern Sierra Nevada, where Benson is set, that I had to have at least one character who hailed from these traditions.

Many Basque people moved to the western United States in the late eighteen hundreds as sheepherders, and restaurants serving Basque cuisine were established along their herding routes. Sandro is a chef who dreams of owning one of these restaurants and bringing a modern flair to his culinary roots. But he has a few personal battles to fight before he can make those dreams come true.

More Than a Rancher has many themes woven through it, and one of them is alcoholism. I am familiar with this disease because I was raised by someone afflicted with it. Many people know of Alcoholics Anonymous, or AA, which teaches alcoholics how to manage their addiction. In this book, Jenna attends Al-Anon, a program that is not as well known. Al-Anon, and its youth program, Alateen, are there to support anyone whose life is affected by someone else's drinking.

AA, Al-Anon and Alateen programs cost no money and are available throughout the United States, Canada and countries all over the world. Please feel free to visit my website, www.clairemcewen.com, where I have more information available.

I am excited to share Jenna and Sandro's story with you. They took me on a complicated and romantic journey, and I hope you enjoy its twists and turns as much as I have.

Wishing you joy,

Claire McEwen

CLAIRE McEWEN

—

More Than a Rancher

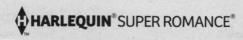

Recycling programs
for this product may
not exist in your area.

ISBN-13: 978-0-373-60871-3

MORE THAN A RANCHER

Copyright © 2014 by Claire Haiken

This edition published by arrangement with Harlequin Books S.A.

For questions and comments about the quality of this book, please contact us at CustomerService@Harlequin.com.

® and TM are trademarks of Harlequin Enterprises Limited or its corporate affiliates. Trademarks indicated with ® are registered in the United States Patent and Trademark Office, the Canadian Intellectual Property Office and in other countries.

Printed in U.S.A.

ABOUT THE AUTHOR

When Claire McEwen entered the first chapter of the first book she'd ever written into Harlequin's 2012 So You Think You Can Write Contest, she didn't place, or even final. But by some miracle, a very patient Harlequin Superromance editor asked to see her full manuscript. After much work, that rather jumbled draft became Claire's debut novel, *A Ranch to Keep,* released in February 2014.

Before writing, Claire had a career in public education, with some detours into bartending, dance teaching and leading bus tours on a Greek island. Without doubt, pieces of her past adventures will show up in future books! She is currently working on more novels set in San Francisco and her fictional Sierra town of Benson, California.

Claire always dreamed of writing books and being a mom, and she is extremely grateful to be living both those dreams. She lives in a Northern California beach town, and when not writing can often be found digging in the garden, playing by the ocean with her son or dancing with her own romantic hero, also known as her husband. Claire enjoys getting to know her readers and can be reached on Facebook, Twitter or at her website, www.clairemcewen.com.

Books by Claire McEwen

HARLEQUIN SUPERROMANCE

1905—A RANCH TO KEEP

Other titles by this author available in ebook format.

For my extraordinary editor, Karen Reid.
More Than a Rancher only exists because she was able
to see Jenna and Sandro's story far more clearly than
I did. Her insight, ideas and talent for figuring out what
I'm *really* trying to say makes my books possible.
I am forever grateful.

And for my sweet family.
Arik, who gives me endless encouragement and love,
and who is learning the Lindy Hop, just for me.
And Shane, who is always happy to join me for a dance
around the kitchen, with a smile that is pure joy.

ACKNOWLEDGMENTS

I am blessed to be surrounded by friends and family
who helped me with this book.

My brilliant agent, Jill Marsal, my sister Sally, my
husband, Arik, and my writing buddy, Lia, all joined the
fray as I wrestled my ideas into a coherent proposal.
My brother-in-law Steve, a talented cook and all-around
knowledgeable guy, helped me clarify Sandro's culinary
vision. And my dear friend, Debbie, generously shared
her experiences growing up in a Basque family of
sheepherders and ranchers. All mistakes, detours from
fact and outright embellishments are entirely my own.

***

I had the privilege of working at a lovely ballroom
with supportive colleagues and a wonderful dance
partner, who was nothing like Jenna's. The gracious
and welcoming owner encouraged my dancing, and
never gave our classes to her niece, or to anyone else.
All characters in this book, along with their flaws and
foibles, are completely imaginary.

CHAPTER ONE

WHEN JENNA'S BEST friend described the scenery in the Eastern Sierra, she'd called it *soothing* and *peaceful*. But as Jenna stood on a dirt road next to a barren pasture, staring at the pancaked tire on her beloved Mini Cooper, those were not the words that came to mind. She muttered a few of the four-letter variety instead and looked around, wondering what to do next.

Sagebrush, punctuated by beige grass, rolled along for miles eastward. To the west, beyond the highway she'd left behind a few bumpy miles ago, the Sierra Nevada sheered upward in an empty, vast wilderness of gray granite. The mountains rolled on, peak after peak, as far as she could see. Jenna and Samantha agreed on most things, but today Jenna would have to take issue with her best friend's feelings about this place. There was nothing *soothing* here. *Intimidating* was a far better word.

Sighing, Jenna walked around to the passenger side and opened the door, taking her cell phone out of her purse. No reception, of course. Not when she needed it most.

This was crazy. She should have called off the trip when her blender exploded this morning. Jenna wasn't completely superstitious, but the smoothie spattered all over her kitchen walls had felt like a sign. As if the universe was telling her to crawl back in bed, pull up the covers and stay safely home in San Francisco.

While she'd wiped up the smoothie bits, Jenna had fought the temptation to call Samantha and cancel their plans. She'd been up late last night, hosting a Latin dance party at the ballroom where she worked, and her warm bed had looked incredibly inviting. But her friend was planning her wedding and wanted help. Plus, Jenna felt guilty that she'd never even seen the ranch that Samantha lived on with her fiancé. So she'd dismissed her premonition and forced herself to load up her car and get on the road. And that was when everything started going wrong.

First was the phone call from Jeff. During that disastrous conversation, Jenna learned that there was nothing like an ex-boyfriend confessing to numerous infidelities to make a girl wish she'd stayed hidden beneath her covers all day. Jenna had pulled over, thrown up, cried, then driven to the nearest convenience store for the most massive soda she could find.

Sugar, bubbles and caffeine had worked their magic and she'd managed to continue her calamitous journey. And now here she was, with a flat tire, stuck beyond nowhere. The smoothie volcano had been a sign. And she'd been a fool not to pay attention.

Jenna opened the glove compartment and rummaged around for the owner's manual. Next time she would listen to her instincts when her kitchen appliances started erupting. This was crazy—she had no idea how to change a tire. Opening the booklet, she started reading. She hated diagrams and instructions of all kinds, but maybe if she stared at them long enough, a miracle would occur and she'd figure them out.

For an instant she was back in school, trying to focus on the textbooks while her teachers looked on in disappointment. Panic fluttered. *One step at a time,* she told herself. That was the way to get through anything complicated, whether it was a dance routine at the ballroom or a flat tire on a wrong-turn dirt road.

The manual said there should be a jack in the back of the car, so Jenna set the little book on the roof, opened the hatchback and pulled out her bags to uncover the compartment where the tool was allegedly hidden. As she moved her duffel bag, her iPod slid out and dropped to the ground. She picked it up and automatically put the earbuds in. Music was a huge part of her life. It soothed her, helped her think—and she needed all the help she could get right now.

The iPod was set to the song that she and Brent, her dance partner, were using for their upcoming competition. Jenna touched the arrow to play it. At least she could get more familiar with the rhythms while she tried her hand at auto repair.

Jenna walked over to the offending wheel, clutching the object she hoped was the jack. She set it gingerly on the ground and began reading the manual again. The words still weren't sinking in. Instead the upbeat tune vibrated through her body, and her mind drifted from the dry instructions on the page to the cha-cha routine she and Brent were choreographing.

Maybe if she just focused on dancing for a moment, it would clear her head and she'd be able to figure out how to remove this pathetic tire.

Jenna tapped her toe in time with the verse. When the chorus came around again, she launched into the spiral turns that Brent had suggested. It was fast-paced, but Brent was right. The turns fit beautifully.

Jenna did a few basic steps through the next verse and tried the turns again. Still perfect. She closed her eyes and pictured what came next. Oh, yes, a shimmy, then a body roll down…and then she heard a cough and whirled around in horror, yanking the earbuds out.

A man on horseback was watching her from a small rise several yards away. Wariness flooded Jenna as her urban instincts set in. She inched a little closer to the jack and casually picked up the handle. Weapon in hand, she felt embarrassment follow. Why had she decided to dance here, of all places?

The man walked his horse closer and she waited, shoving her iPod into the back pocket of her jeans. Then she saw a huge smile emerge from under the wide brim of the man's cowboy hat. He was laughing. Relief seeped in when she saw that he wasn't a man at all but a teenage boy with a wide, goofy grin. She set the jack handle down.

"Morning." The boy stopped laughing and rode his horse a few steps closer. The big chestnut almost dwarfed his slight frame. "You're a good dancer."

Jenna looked up at him, shading her eyes against the sun to better see his face. He had olive skin and black hair under his straw hat. His eyes were wide and dark, framed in thick lashes. His grin was friendly, not sarcastic or self-conscious like some of the more surly teens who showed up at her youth dance classes.

"Thank you," she said. "And that's a lovely horse." She stepped forward and held out her hand, the horse's silky nose brushing gently over her knuckles. Looking down its flank, she saw the big hindquarters. "A quarter horse?"

"You know horses?" The boy seemed genuinely surprised and Jenna smiled for the first time that day.

"They do have them in other places," she teased gently. "I grew up riding." The scent from the horse's strong, sun-warmed neck took her back in time to long adolescent afternoons at the stable in rural Marin County, north of San Francisco. She'd loved horses then. She'd even abandoned dance for a few years to ride as much as possible.

"Do you always dance outside?"

It was an innocent question but Jenna blushed. "My tire's flat. I was trying to figure out how to fix it, but I got a bit distracted."

"That happens to me all the time! It makes my dad crazy. My brothers, too. Well, everyone, really."

"You mean you get distracted? Or get distracted and start dancing?"

His laugh was genuinely merry. "Both." He swung a leg over the horse's back and dismounted gracefully. "You look like you could use a rescue."

She did need rescuing, but usually the damsel in distress had a handsome prince coming to her aid, not a kid. Just her luck. "I could absolutely use a rescue. I must've turned the wrong way off the highway. Is this your land? I'm sorry if I'm trespassing."

"Don't worry about it." He waved his arm around

in a vague gesture that encompassed the gigantic landscape around them. "It's my family's ranch."

"Really?" Jenna asked. "Does that make you a cowboy?"

The boy grinned and pointed to his hat. "Well, I've got the gear. But we mainly have sheep. Shepherd doesn't sound quite so good, though." He walked his horse a little ways off the road to where a patch of weathered brown grass grew between the sagebrush. He left it to nibble and came back toward her, his eyes on the Mini. "That's an awesome car."

"It's great for San Francisco—that's where I live," she told him. "It fits into the tiniest parking spaces."

"Not so great for out here, though." His smile was infectious and softened his words.

"Obviously not! I don't know what I was thinking. Well, I do, actually. I was lost." Distracted *first,* then lost. Distracted by a phone call from her traitorous, cheating boyfriend. *Ex*-boyfriend, she reminded herself with a twisting feeling in her heart.

"Where were you headed?"

"My friend's ranch. I think I turned off too soon. Or maybe in the wrong direction."

"Well, I can help you get going again. But you need to be careful out here. No more off-roading."

"Point taken." Jenna smiled. She liked his teasing—he seemed like a sweet kid.

The "kid" didn't even look at her manual. He just grabbed the jack and started cranking up the car.

Jenna felt silly. He changed the tire as if it were the easiest chore in the world, and she hadn't even been able to figure out *if* the jack *was* a jack.

In no time, he had the flattened tire off and was pulling her spare out of the trunk. "Can I ask you something?" He suddenly looked shy, more of an awkward teenager than he'd seemed before.

"Of course," Jenna answered.

"Are you a dancer? A real dancer?"

Jenna looked at the boy in surprise. "Well, I'm not sure what you mean. I dance, I teach, I compete—does that make me a real dancer?"

He grinned. "Yes!" he answered emphatically as he set the spare tire in place and picked up a bolt.

"Well, this might make you change your mind about that—I'm a *ballroom* dancer," she said.

The boy's eyes widened. "You mean like on TV, on that celebrity dance show?"

Jenna couldn't help it. His words were so unexpected she started to laugh. "I'm sorry.... It's just not what I expected! *You* watch dancing? Ballroom dancing?"

"Yeah! I watch all the shows. I try to learn stuff off of the internet, too."

The excitement in his voice was palpable and Jenna was amazed. She would never have pegged this boy, who looked so at home in this rugged country, to be a fan of television dance programs. "Do you study dance?" she asked.

He shook his head regretfully. "We have line dancing, Western dancing, that kind of stuff. But no dance school around here." He glanced around as if worried someone might hear him. "Even if there was, I probably wouldn't be allowed to take classes."

"Why not?"

"My family doesn't exactly approve of boys—" he made quotation marks in the air in front of him "—waltzing around in tights."

"Oh, it's like that, huh?" Jenna asked softly, studying the teen's profile. His focus was back on the tire but his mouth was a grim, frustrated line. "If it's any consolation, my family's still trying to get me to go to law school." She truly felt for him.

"Really?" His expression brightened at that. "Are you gonna go?"

"No," she answered. "I'm a dancer, even if they don't see it."

"That's how I feel!" He had the spare on now and was staring at her, eyes wide. Jenna realized she was probably the first person he'd ever met who understood that. She wished there were something she could do for him. If he lived in San Francisco, she'd give him her card and encourage him to come to the ballroom for lessons. But out here? Somewhere beyond the tiny town of Benson? There wasn't much she could do.

She moved her bags to the backseat and the boy loaded the flat tire into her trunk.

"I can't thank you enough," she told him. The flat tire had been just one more bad event in a terrible day, but right now she was almost glad it had happened. She liked this kid.

He blushed and looked away. "It's no big deal," he said.

"I never got your name."

"Paul."

"Paul, I'm Jenna. I wish there was more I could do to help you get started dancing, but I'm only here for the weekend. But when you're looking at videos, make sure they show real technique, not just where to put your feet. The instructor should show you exactly how to place your arms and legs, your torso, your head. They should talk about the shape of your hands—even what part of your foot hits the floor first. Go slow and pay attention to all that."

Paul nodded, his face serious. He was obviously taking in every word. "I'll do that. Thanks, Jenna."

He stuck out his hand and she shook it awkwardly. "Do you know where you're going from here?" he asked. "Want me to set you in the right direction?"

"That would be great. It's Jack Baron's place? It's off of…" Jenna tried to picture the name of the street, scrawled on a piece of paper in her car.

"I know it," Paul said. "He's a friend of my

brother's. Head back to the highway and go south about a mile and a half before making a right turn. The road will take you back behind the town, then out toward the mountains. There's a driveway off to the right that heads uphill. Take the left fork on that driveway and you're there."

"I'm lucky you came along." More than lucky—profoundly relieved. "Good luck, Paul. And thank you again for the rescue."

"Glad to help." He tipped his hat in her direction and went to get his horse. Jenna watched him go. Kids were her soft spot. Especially teenagers. Maybe when she finally got her own dance studio, she'd create some kind of program for kids like Paul, living out in the country with no support for their dreams. They could train with her for the summer and stay with host families. Kind of like foreign exchange students but an exchange from rural to urban.

She looked around at the landscape that in some places looked more like a moonscape. The sun was getting high and a dry heat was building, baking the sagebrush and filling the air with its spicy scent. If this was Paul's home, then a chilly summer in San Francisco really would be like a stay in a foreign country. And as for her, a city girl, this rocky pasture felt even stranger than that. An alien world, Jenna decided as she got into the driver's seat and started the engine. And she was ready to get back to nice familiar planet Earth.

She turned the car around and started back on the rutted dirt road she'd somehow thought would lead her to Samantha's ranch. Knowing now what it could do to her tires, she crept along, heart pounding. Watching Paul had given her some idea of what to do if she had another blowout, but she was already riding on her spare.

Gratefully, Jenna saw the highway getting closer. Motion in her rearview mirror had her glancing back. Paul was riding behind her, a little ways off the track to avoid the dust her wheels kicked up. She smiled. What a good guy—making sure she got back to the main road safely. This was why she loved working with young people. No matter how murky or dismal the future might seem, they always gave her hope.

Meeting an aspiring dancer out here was such an odd coincidence. Jenna remembered the way Paul's face had lit up when he talked about dance. Maybe she'd ended up in the middle of nowhere for a reason—to encourage him in his dream. If that was the case, then she'd been wrong about the meaning of that exploding smoothie. Maybe today was somehow meant to be.

CHAPTER TWO

"WHERE WERE YOU?" Samantha came rushing out of the beautiful log-and-glass house and down the stone steps. "I was thinking about calling the sheriff!"

"Sorry to worry you," Jenna apologized, getting out of the Mini and giving her friend a huge hug. "I had a small mishap on the way, but everything's fine."

Jenna held her friend at arm's length, admiring her glossy black hair and the way the mountain sun had sprayed tiny freckles across her porcelain skin. Samantha was wearing green to match her eyes—eyes that looked happier and more relaxed than Jenna had ever seen them when her friend had lived in San Francisco. "You look wonderful!" Jenna exclaimed. "Being engaged suits you!"

Samantha laughed and waved her hand with the huge emerald ring on it. "Can you believe it? In three months I'll be married. Who would have thought?"

"I would." A deep voice, ringing with its customary humor, had both women turning to where

Samantha's fiancé, Jack, was approaching from the barn, two border collies trotting at his heels.

"Jack!" Jenna smiled in delight.

"Red!" Jack grinned, teasing her with the nickname he'd given her in honor of her hair. It was amazing how fast, how perfectly, Jack had fit in with his fiancée's best friends. Jack wrapped her in a hug and squeezed her so hard he lifted her off the ground. "Thanks for coming out here and entertaining Sam for a few days. I hope you're up for a lot of bridal magazines and seating charts."

Jenna realized she hadn't thought this through. How was she supposed to muster any enthusiasm for weddings when she'd just been so royally betrayed? She plastered a smile on her face. "I'm not surprised about the charts!" Jenna forced out a playful wink, but it must have come out more like a grimace, because Samantha looked momentarily alarmed. "What else would we expect from Miss Organization?"

Samantha shrugged sheepishly and Jack went over to put his arm around his future wife, kissing the top of her head. The love in his expression was so vivid that jealousy bit its sharp teeth into Jenna's heart. How incredible to have a man look at you as if you were the only thing that really mattered. Would anyone ever feel that way about her? At this moment, it seemed pretty unlikely.

Shaking off that dream, she pasted on another

smile. "We can't just sit around reading wedding magazines! I have a competition in a month and you promised me lots of exercise!"

"Excellent. We'll exercise *and* talk about weddings."

Jenna hoped she could. Knowing how much heartache she was carrying around right now, she'd probably burst into tears the first time she opened one of Samantha's magazines.

"I'm just glad you're here, Jenna," Jack said. "As much as I can't wait to marry this woman, I could use a break from debating the merits of lace versus tulle!" Jack hugged Samantha even closer as he teased her. "I'll be hiding in the barn this weekend. Doing manly things."

Samantha looked up at Jack with a radiant smile and then turned and held out her hand to Jenna. "Come see the house." She pulled her friend close and put an arm around her. "Jack, if you're so into manly things, would you mind bringing Jenna's bags in?"

"Yes, ma'am." Jack tipped his hat to his wife in mock subservience.

Jenna loved Jack. He was more of a big brother than her own would ever be. Maybe she was a little jealous of Samantha and Jack's love, but she was genuinely happy for her friend. That happiness was what she needed to somehow keep her focus on this weekend. Her woes and heartache would have to wait until she got back to San Francisco on Sunday.

She followed Samantha up the steps and walked across the planks of the broad porch. It was furnished with wooden rockers and a porch swing. "This place is beautiful!" It really was. Another thing to focus on besides Jeff. "Look at the views!" Pine trees and mountain meadows rolled out to one side of the house. Pasture unfolded on the other. And the granite crags of the Sierra Nevada gave a majestic backdrop to all that beauty.

"I promise, it was Jack I fell in love with." Samantha gave her a wink as she pushed open the heavy front door. "But I have to admit, I really like his house, too."

Jenna gasped when they walked inside. "I can see why!"

A massive great room with a slate floor opened in front of them, surrounded by floor-to-ceiling arched windows that let in the light and framed the spectacular scenery outside. A river-rock fireplace rose on one wall.

Samantha led the way upstairs and Jenna tried not to envy the bedrooms filled with light and huge four-poster beds, the bathrooms Zen-like with limestone and more slate. When she saw the fitness room, bigger than her entire studio apartment in San Francisco, Jenna did a few pirouettes across the floor and stopped in front of the large mirror on the wall. "I think I'm in heaven! I may never leave!"

Her friend grinned. "I'd like that very much. Stay forever. There's certainly room."

She looked at Samantha in the mirror they were both facing. "You know me—I could never leave San Francisco."

"And how is San Francisco?" Samantha asked.

"Still the same amazing city by the bay." But even Jenna could hear the sarcasm in her voice.

"That good?" Samantha asked gently.

Jenna had promised herself she'd be cheerful for her friend, no matter what was going wrong in her own life. Samantha deserved a supportive, happy maid of honor. "Oh, you know, when is life perfect, anyway?"

Jenna turned away from the mirror, picked up a five-pound weight from the rack and did a few biceps curls. Glancing at Samantha, who was leaning against the wall watching her with a concerned expression, Jenna lifted the little barbell and pointed to her biceps with her free hand. "Look at those guns!"

Samantha smiled at the joke but Jenna's attempt at diversion didn't work. "Stop pretending everything's fine. You always do this."

"Do what?" Jenna switched the weight to her other hand. "What do I do?"

"Pretend you're happy when I can tell from a mile away that you're not."

"I don't want to bring you down," Jenna admitted. "This should be a joyful time for you. You're getting married."

"Let me guess. Jeff?"

"Now known as He Who Cheats with Groupies."

Samantha's hand went to her heart. "You're kidding."

"Nope. Wish I was." Jenna did a few more curls to distract her from the knots in her stomach—the knots that had been there for a week now.

"What happened?"

"I went to his show last weekend. I thought I'd surprise him backstage with a cake for his birthday. But someone had beat me to it—and her gift wasn't cake."

"He didn't…" Samantha paused, eyes wide. "They weren't…"

"Let's just say her present didn't involve clothing." Jenna set the weight back on the rack.

"No." Samantha crossed the floor in a few quick steps, pulling Jenna into a hug. "That is so unfair. Awful. I am so sorry, Jen."

Jenna's voice came out muffled against her friend's shoulder. "I finally talked to him today. He called while I was driving out here. It turns out that wasn't the only time he's cheated." The comfort in the hug was going to make her cry again and she didn't want to. She stepped back.

"Unbelievable." Outrage had Samantha pacing the room. "First my idiot ex, and now yours? What is wrong with these men?"

"I don't know. But until I figure it out, I'm going to avoid them." She couldn't believe she'd missed so many signs with Jeff. If she'd been paying attention, she might have thought more carefully about what he might be doing all those nights on the road.

"But if you just avoid them, then you'll never meet a good one." Samantha paused, a dreamy expression flitting across her face. Jenna knew she was thinking about Jack. "And some of them are *really* great."

"I'm starting to think you got the only good one." Jenna hoped her words weren't actually true, but at this point, post-Jeff, it seemed like a distinct possibility.

"You'll find someone." Samantha put a hand on her arm. "You're beautiful. Look at you!" She turned Jenna gently until they were facing the mirror again and picked up a lock of her hair. "Long red curls, huge blue eyes, amazing figure. You look like a miniature Rita Hayworth!"

Jenna laughed. "Emphasis on *miniature*." Samantha was about five foot eight. Next to her and four inches shorter, Jenna felt dwarfed.

"Stop that! It will work out, I promise."

"Not until my radar gets better, it won't. I *choose* these guys who cheat. Jeff always had other women hanging around after shows, but I just figured it was part of him being a musician. And when Brent and I dated, he didn't technically cheat, but only because I broke up with him right before he was about to."

"And has Brent started circling yet? Now that he knows you're single?"

Jenna smiled. "You mean with his 'I made the biggest mistake of my life letting you go' speech? Not quite yet, but knowing my luck, he will soon."

"What would happen if you ever dated him again? I mean, it was sweet and romantic when you were in love *and* dance partners…." The dreamy look was back. Now that Samantha was engaged, she wanted everyone to have their own happily-ever-after.

"He'd probably last about two weeks before he started looking over my shoulder for his next conquest. He just likes the chase. He isn't and never was in love with me. Maybe I'm his backup plan for when he's done playing the field."

"Well, either way, he's an idiot, too," Samantha declared.

"It's okay. He's a good dance partner. And I'm not in love with him, either, anymore." But she had been—very much so. The decision to keep working with him after he'd broken her heart was one of the hardest she'd ever made, but the smartest for her career. They really were good together and had two national championships to prove it.

A deep weariness hit Jenna in a crushing wave. She didn't want to talk about Jeff or Brent or any other guy who'd left her. "Let's get outside so you can show me this ranch of yours. Can I see your grandmother's house? Where it all began?" Samantha had inherited her grandparents' ranch last year, which was how she'd met Jack and fallen in love, leaving San Francisco to be with him.

Samantha giggled. "*Where it all began.* I like that. Maybe we should apply to make it a historical landmark."

Jenna felt relieved that her subject change had worked. "It should be! The site where the extremely urban Samantha Rylant fell in love with mountains and a cowboy. It *is* kind of historic!"

They headed downstairs. Once outside, they walked down a narrow, rocky path that took them to the old ranch house. Its weathered white paint and sagging porch made it the complete opposite of Jack's stone-and-glass modern home. Samantha took out a key. "We're using it as my office and a guest house for friends and family." She showed Jenna through the old rooms with their high ceilings and quaint wainscoting. Her office was so perfectly organized that it looked like one of those catalog photos of a home office, complete with neatly labeled baskets.

Jenna had never understood how Samantha had been able to live out here in the old, empty farmhouse by herself for days at a time. It seemed spooky to be alone in a house that had been closed up for years and was situated so far from everything. But now she got it. There was a cozy, comfortable feeling in the old home, such an air of happy history that Jenna couldn't imagine *not* wanting to stay there.

Samantha locked the front door behind them and they started back up the path. Maybe the clean alpine air was exactly what Jenna needed. She inhaled huge lungfuls as they wandered through the ranch, trying to take in the purity of it and exhale all her anger. She just didn't want to feel it anymore. Beyond the barn, they passed a few smaller corrals and started up a gravel road to the upper pastures, closer to the mountains.

Without a flat tire to worry about, the weathered ranch buildings and quiet pastures inspired serenity. The age-old mountains with their miles and miles of wilderness put her soap-opera troubles into perspective.

Samantha stopped by the wooden pasture fence. "Maybe we just need to set up some guidelines. You know, parameters to make sure you weed out the bad ones."

"When you say *weed,* you're not talking about plants, are you?" Jenna quipped.

"Men, of course!" Samantha had a look in her eye that Jenna recognized. It was her friend's let-me-organize-your-life look.

Jenna leaned back against the fence to face her well-meaning friend, mourning the tenuous peace she'd found right before Samantha had spoken. "Did you really need help with wedding planning?" she asked. "Or did you get me out here because you wanted to fix things for me?"

Samantha laughed. "I *do* need help with the planning! But guess I did have a feeling, when we talked on the phone, that things weren't going well. You always get hyper-cheerful when things are bad. Like you're trying your hardest to pretend they don't exist. So I figured I'd steal you away from your troubles for a weekend."

"I don't know if you can truly steal me from my troubles, Sam. They're in my genes, I think! I mean, my mom puts up with my dad's cheating. I'm a natural hereditary magnet for infidelity."

"That's ridiculous. Maybe you're just too nice. You tend to believe the best about everyone."

Jenna smiled ruefully. "You are very kind. But that's the old Jenna. The post-Jeff version of Jenna is going to make sure to believe the worst."

"No!" Samantha said laughingly. "I like my sweet friend. Don't let one flaky musician change you."

"Well, I have to do *something* different," Jenna said. "Obviously my old ways aren't working."

"So let's think of a plan that will keep you safe from cheaters." Samantha was all business now. "Okay, this is the first guideline—no one who has been unfaithful. What do you think?"

Jenna smiled reluctantly. "That seems pretty obvious, so yeah."

"And maybe you should rule out musicians. All those groupies are just too tempting."

"Okay, no musicians," Jenna agreed. After Jeff she had no problem giving up *that* particular category of men.

"You know," Samantha said, "you do seem to go for these artsy types. Which makes sense because you're an artist, too. But what about trying something different? San Francisco is full of all kinds of high-tech semi-nerdy, semi-creative types these days, right?"

"Well, yeah." Jenna could feel the resentment in her stomach. "They make tons of money and they're driving up the rents on all the apartments like you wouldn't believe!"

"But that doesn't mean they're bad people. Someone like that might be perfect for you. Maybe another guideline should be—"

Jenna didn't mean to cut off her friend, but the scrutiny of her love life was too much. Maybe she was just too raw after Jeff. Maybe it was a little too close to the advice her parents insisted on handing out at every opportunity. So she interrupted. "Okay, so no cheaters, musicians or artsy types. But mostly, I think I'm just going to take a break from being in a relationship."

"But—" Samantha began.

"Sam, you're in love. And it's amazing! You found an awesome guy and you two will live happily ever after. And I know you want me to have the same thing. And who knows? Maybe I will someday. But right now I think this whole thing with Jeff was a sign."

"A sign?" Jenna could see Samantha trying not to laugh. "You think *everything* is some kind of sign!"

"Not everything. But Jeff's cheating is clearly a sign that I shouldn't be in a relationship right now. I need to focus on my work and my dancing—without worrying about men."

"Okay, okay." Samantha bit her lip and studied Jenna closely, characteristically unsatisfied with her inability to make everything better. "I'm sorry if I overstepped." She turned to look at the horses. "I'm just happy, Jen," she said quietly. "And I want you to be, too."

"I *am* happy," Jenna said, moving so she stood next to Samantha. She looked at the horses grazing and the mountains unfolding behind them. The sun had sunk below the peaks and just the crags at the very top were lit up golden. A breeze shuffled through, chilling her skin. "When I'm dancing, I'm happy."

"Well, that's good to hear. You dance a lot, so that means you're happy a lot." Samantha must have felt the chill, too, because she shivered. "Let's go in. I forgot to tell you, Jack has something really amazing planned for dinner."

With one last look at the peaceful pasture, Jenna turned to follow her friend back to the house. For the first time in a week, she felt as if she was walking on solid ground. It might be hard to help plan a wedding right now, but Jenna was glad she was in this beautiful place, with the love and support of her best friend. There was comfort here, and she was grateful for any scrap of it she could get.

CHAPTER THREE

"JACK'S OPENING A RESTAURANT?" Jenna stood in front of the mirror in the elegant guest bathroom, staring at the dark circles under her eyes. She took another sip of the cappuccino she'd begged Jack to make her.

"Investing in it." Samantha looked up from her exploration of Jenna's makeup bag. "You always have the best stuff. Sparkly mascara? And look at this eye shadow—it's turquoise!"

"Well, you know how ballroom dancers are. We love our makeup. The more outrageous, the better!" Jenna yawned, trying to cover it with her arm. She picked up her lip liner and repaired her ruby-red lips. She rarely went anywhere without makeup, and bright red lipstick was one of her essentials. It made her feel like a 1940s movie star.

Samantha set the bag down. "Anyway, his friend, who's going to be the co-owner and chef, wants to come cook us all dinner and try out some stuff for the menu. But I think you're too tired. I'll tell Jack to reschedule."

"No, don't," Jenna said quickly. "I don't want to cause a hassle when you guys have set this up already."

"We can do it another night."

"The poor chef has probably been prepping food all day." Jenna dabbed some concealer under her eyes. "There. I'll just cover up the evidence and be good as new."

"If you're sure," Samantha said. "I promise that tomorrow we'll spend the entire day in our pajamas. You can sleep in, we'll look at magazines and then we'll go to bed as early as you want."

"Deal," Jenna said, adding on a little blush before turning around. "So let's go down to dinner. Here I was, thinking life on the ranch would involve some barbecue at best, and you've got a fancy chef coming!" Jenna laughed. "Your life is never dull, Sam."

"Jack keeps it interesting, always." Samantha smiled as she spoke.

Jenna drained her coffee cup and hooked her arm under her friend's. "I promise that tomorrow, when we're in our jammies, we'll talk all about your wedding." Maybe after a good night's sleep she'd be able to do it without falling apart. They started down the stairs. "So who is this mysterious chef, anyways?"

"Someone Jack knows from when he lived in New York. It turns out he grew up out here and moved back recently. He's really excited about the restaurant. Can you imagine, four-star cuisine in Benson?"

"Will there be anyone to eat it? This town's like

a postage stamp. Smaller. It's like the *glue* on the back of a postage stamp!"

"Jenna! It's not that small. There are all kinds of people who live outside of town. They'll be thrilled to have a great place to eat. Plus, we get a lot of tourists."

"Well, I'm impressed. Jack the restaurant entrepreneur. Is there anything that fiancé of yours doesn't do?"

"Well, I don't cook." Jack was waiting for them at the foot of the stairs with a glass of sparkling wine for each. "Or at least not well. So tonight we get to try out a few of the dishes my partner, Sandro, has been planning for the menu."

Jenna took the glass he offered, trading him for her coffee cup. "You might not cook but you do provide excellent drinks!"

He laughed. "Thanks, Red. I aim to please."

A knock on the front door had the dogs jumping up suddenly from their bed by the fire, huffing and growling. "Quiet," Jack commanded, and went to answer the door, the dogs following on his heels.

"He's great, isn't he?" Samantha said, looking after him and sipping her wine.

Jenna felt the nip of jealousy for the second time today and shoved it down hard. "He *is* a great guy," Jenna assured her. She walked over to an end table and set her wineglass down. "So let's go help him out."

A blast of cold air preceded Jack into the room as he wrestled with the bags of groceries tucked under his arms. Jenna grabbed a bag stuffed with vegetables right before he dropped it, brought it into the kitchen and set it on the granite countertop.

As she turned away, she came up against a chest. An intriguingly muscular chest. It was wrapped up like a present in a tight white T-shirt. But instead of a bow, there was a belt with a silver buckle. A picture of a cowboy on a bucking horse was etched into the silver and Jenna stared at it for a split second before a tanned, lean arm reached around her and set a bottle of wine on the counter. "Hey." It was a low voice, kind of husky, and she finally looked up.

The owner of the chest, T-shirt, belt buckle and arm took a step back. His skin was olive-toned, and his thick black hair curled over his forehead and down to his collar in the back. Dark brown eyes under black brows studied her face. He smiled and his full lips parted to reveal teeth that were white and just a little crooked.

"Hey," she managed to whisper back, and in an attempt not to gape at the tall man who looked as if he'd swaggered straight off the streets of Spain or Italy, she reached out and took the cloth grocery bag from his hand and set it on the counter behind her.

"I'm Sandro," he said quietly.

Of course. Sandro the chef. Couldn't Samantha have warned her that he was absolutely gorgeous? She was probably so in love with Jack that she hadn't even noticed. "Stevens. I'm Jenna. I mean…I'm Jenna Stevens." Her cheeks were on fire and something was wrong with her brain. She stuck out her hand and he took it, wrapping it in his long fingers and giving it a firm shake. "Um, nice to meet you. I'm a friend of Samantha's. Visiting. From San Francisco."

"I see. Well, I hope you're hungry."

"I'm always hungry," Jenna blurted out. "I mean, I try not to eat *too* much—I'm a dancer.… You know, dieting and all." This was ridiculous. Just a scant hour ago she'd given Samantha a speech about how her focus was going to be on her career, and yet now she couldn't even think straight, or talk, just because of one good-looking guy. Where were Samantha and Jack? This was awkward.

A noise at the door made her turn in relief but it wasn't her friends. A boy shouldered in through the kitchen door with a chest cooler clutched in his hands. It looked heavy. "Sandro, you dick! Didn't you know you could park in the back, right by the door?"

"Paul! Manners, bro," the tall man commanded.

Paul? The boy set the cooler down by the door and turned around. The bright smile Jenna recognized from earlier today lit his face.

"Jenna!" He bounded toward her and then stopped, as if not sure what to do next.

Jenna stuck out her hand and he shook it. "Good to see you again, Paul. What are you doing here?"

"Helping my big brother. The master chef. I was hoping I'd see you!"

"How the hell do you two know each other?" Sandro's voice was gruff with suspicion.

"Manners, bro," Paul reminded him, and Jenna saw the sassy teenager in him and couldn't help smiling.

"We met today, on a dirt road," she told Sandro. "I had a flat and Paul changed it for me. It was really very kind of him. I'm not sure what I would have done if he hadn't come along."

"Well, nice to know he's good for something." There was pride in Sandro's eyes that belied his belittling comment.

"You mean besides hauling all your gear? And chopping your vegetables?" Paul was smiling at his big brother's needling. Clearly these two had a close relationship.

"Hey, I'm paying you a good wage."

Paul sighed. "Yeah, you are, actually. I guess that means I'd better get to work. Great to see you again, Jenna." He disappeared out the door and Sandro and Jenna watched him go.

Sandro stood so close that Jenna could feel heat radiating from him. "He's a nice kid, your brother. I can't tell you how helpful he was today."

"Good." Sandro looked down at her and she noticed again how full his mouth was and the dark, sooty way his lashes rimmed his eyes. "Though I gotta ask. Paul was down in our southeast pastures all day. It's the most remote area of our ranch. How'd you end up on a dirt road out there?"

"You were on a dirt road?" Samantha's voice came from behind her and Jenna turned to see that her friend and Jack had both entered the room and were staring at her with similar expressions of surprise. "Was this the mishap you mentioned earlier?"

"Well, yes, but—"

"Jenna, you could have been lost for days out there!"

"Well, I wasn't." Jenna could feel her face getting hot again. The last thing she wanted was a scolding in front of Sandro, whom she barely knew, and who probably already thought she was nuts after her garbled introduction. He had stepped away and was unpacking groceries directly behind her. She swore she could feel the air move every time he did.

"How did that happen, anyway, Red?" Jack wasn't laughing yet, but she could hear it behind his voice.

"Um…I had a little trouble with the map."

"Upside-down again?" Samantha asked.

There was a snort of barely contained laughter behind her. Jenna glanced back and saw Sandro's shoulders shaking with mirth.

"Maybe," Jenna answered, grinning despite her embarrassment. Samantha knew her too well.

Sandro walked by her to put a bottle of white wine in the refrigerator, more composed now. "Ah," he said mildly. "So this is a common problem?"

"Okay, so I can be a little directionally challenged!" Jenna admitted. "Can we change the subject?"

"Jenna's a really great dancer!" Paul was closing the back door behind him with his shoulder, his arms wrapped around a cardboard box. He obviously wasn't aware that Jenna was already the subject of conversation.

"And how would you know *that?*" Sandro turned from the refrigerator and looked from Paul to Jenna, concern etching lines onto his face.

"She was dancing when I found her."

This wasn't good. Jenna felt a little too fragile to be the butt of all the jokes this evening. "Well, just a moment of practice while I got up the nerve to change my tire."

"No, it was awesome. She did these turns and then this shake-and-roll thing." Paul imitated Jenna's step so flawlessly that her jaw dropped. He'd imbued those two moves with more grace than she could ever muster.

"You were dancing in the desert? Instead of changing your tire?" Samantha pulled Jenna into a side hug. "I love you, my friend. But I will never understand you."

"Jenna's a dance teacher." Paul turned to Sandro, and Jenna could hear the excitement in his voice.

"Okay, enough." Sandro's voice held an authority that Jenna imagined must serve him well in busy restaurant kitchens. "Paul, I'm not paying you to get your groove on. And as much as Jenna's adventures are entertaining to hear about, I respectfully request that you all leave this kitchen and let us cook you something awe-inspiring."

"We're happy to stay and help prep," Samantha offered.

"No, we're good." His voice was just a little abrupt.

Jenna wondered if Samantha and Jack had noticed, but they seemed happy enough to wander into the living room and settle onto the couch in front of the fireplace. Jenna took one last look at Sandro, who had moved to the sink and turned his back to her. He was briskly pulling vegetables out of the box to wash. She gave Paul a little wave and followed her friends out of the room.

SANDRO WAITED UNTIL Paul had finished chopping the shallots. While his little brother added them to the skillet on the stove, Sandro tried to keep his voice casual. "So how come you didn't mention meeting her today?" He tilted his head in the direction of the living room.

Paul shrugged as he rinsed the cutting board in the sink. "I dunno. It happened a lot earlier on. I did a bunch of stuff afterward."

"But you changed her tire."

"I change tires all over the ranch. It was no big deal." Paul raised his eyebrows. "Why are you so curious about it, anyway?"

"I'm not curious. Just wondered why you didn't say anything, that's all. Usually you don't shut up for more than two minutes." Sandro didn't know why he was so curious. Of course Paul would help anyone he found stuck out on the ranch or anywhere else.

There was just something about Jenna that was getting to him. Maybe it was the way her bright blue eyes had widened when she'd seen him. Or the way her delicate skin had flushed so pink when they'd been joking about the map. Or maybe it was because she was a dance teacher, and the last thing he needed was someone fueling Paul's useless dreams. Dreams that would only lead him to a whole lot of heartache.

Sandro took the medallions of lamb he'd been marinating out of the cooler and put them in the roasting pan. He went to find the root vegetables he'd cut this afternoon. The murmur of Jenna's voice from the next room was distracting him in a way it shouldn't. She looked like a 1940s bombshell combined with a pixie. Her legs were slim in their pegged jeans, and the black Converse sneakers on her feet were retro and rebel all in one. They were a sharp contrast to the sweet button-up blouse she wore. Then there was the red hair, styled in an elaborate curl over her forehead and falling in perfect waves down her back. With the heavy makeup and the dark lipstick, she looked gorgeous and edgy and quirky. And that was a lethal combination for him.

Sandro couldn't afford distractions right now. His plans were finally coming together just as he'd hoped. He was going to own a restaurant with Jack, the most upstanding guy he knew. He was going to have complete control over the menu and the running of a place for the first time in his life. Getting distracted had destroyed his dreams of making it big in New York. He wouldn't let that happen ever again.

Well, Jenna was here, in Jack's house, and obviously great friends with Jack's fiancée. And she was about to come through the dining room door and eat his food. He'd just have to be polite, keep his distance and try to ignore how much he wanted to get to know her. And of course, he had to keep her from talking dance with his little brother.

Suddenly inspired, he looked over at Paul. "Hey, bro," he said.

"Yeah?" Paul stopped hacking at the garlic for a moment.

"Wanna eat here in the kitchen tonight? Maybe keep an eye on things for me? I know hanging out with a bunch of adults and minding your table manners probably isn't your thing."

Paul looked relieved. "Sure!"

One problem solved. The dancer and the wannabe dancer wouldn't get much opportunity to chat. Sandro pulled the greens he'd been sautéing off the heat, pouring in pine nuts and a shot of white wine. He stirred it all together and set it on a cool burner. They were half-cooked. He'd put them back on the heat and finish them off just before he served them.

Taking a deep breath, he wiped his hands on the dish towel at his belt. He was going to walk into that living room and announce dinner and keep in mind that whatever he'd felt around Jenna was no big deal. Just one of those odd little moments life threw at you that in the grand scheme of things meant nothing. And he'd remember, when her smile lit up the room, that he had a plan for the future, and that plan didn't include Jenna Stevens.

THE LAMB WAS quite possibly one of the best things Jenna had ever tasted—and she didn't even like lamb. Sandro had glazed it in a slightly sweet sauce and served it with a fragrant mixture of fresh herbs, garlic and olive oil. It was kind of like the chimichurri sauce they'd eaten with steak when her parents had hired an Argentine chef. Sadly, that chef hadn't lasted long—Jenna suspected it had something to do with the flirtatious glances between her father and the chef's wife—but she'd never forgotten the powerhouse flavors of the chopped fresh herbs on a perfectly grilled steak. And Sandro had re-created that, but better somehow.

Jenna tasted a slice of golden beet gleaming at the side of her plate like a coin. A tiny moan escaped her lips and she bit it back, but Sandro glanced over, an eyebrow raised.

"Okay, that was amazing," she told him, as the now familiar blush crept over her cheeks. Why did she have to moan? She was *eating* the vegetable, not sleeping with it. But it was really, *really* good. She licked a spot of sauce off her lip and then noticed that Sandro was watching her mouth intently.

He shook his head slightly and his eyes found hers. Focused. "You think so, huh?"

"Yes." She took a sip of wine to hide her confusion. He was still watching her mouth. And it hit her. He felt the same attraction she did. Even though she had no business being happy about that, it felt good. His attention was a balm for the sting of Jeff's rejection. Because despite knowing that Jeff's cheating was a result of *his* weak character, she still ended up feeling as if somehow *she* was the one lacking. She hadn't been sexy enough for him. She just hadn't been enough.

"Bet you can't guess my secret ingredient." He issued the challenge, watching her over the rim of his glass as he sipped his water. There was heat in his gaze, and something between them connected and sizzled.

Jenna knew it was wrong, but she'd felt so awful all week, and here was a chance to make herself feel a tiny bit better. A little harmless flirting might be good for her battered ego. Plus, being raised by parents who employed a private chef meant she had a good palate—she could answer him no problem.

She leaned over the corner of the table, giving Sandro a nice eyeful of cleavage in the process, and whispered, "Meyer lemon." She quickly straightened and took a sip of her wine, waiting for his response from a safe distance.

His eyes were glazed. He looked satisfyingly befuddled.

"Well?" she asked. "Did I get it right?"

He seemed uncomfortable all of a sudden. "You got one of them right...but there's a few."

"Just give me time," Jenna assured him. Of course, she wouldn't take this any further, but it was nice to know that someone found her attractive enough to go a bit cross-eyed when she was near.

Jenna glanced down the table, figuring that was

enough flirting with the chef. "Jack, this food is so good."

"We'll see if the people of Benson are ready for it," Jack said.

"What do you mean?" Jenna asked.

"Well, Sandro is talented, but the food he loves to cook isn't necessarily the food that folks in Benson traditionally want to eat. Let's just say they're a little more into the basics."

"Roast this and roast that," Sandro said ruefully. "But we're hoping to shake it up a bit. So I've made roast lamb tonight, but the raspberry glaze and the herb sauce take it up a notch. And we're serving it with a bunch of baby root vegetables instead of the usual potatoes."

"So you're trying to bring cuisine around here to a new level, without stepping too far out of people's comfort zones." Jenna took a sip of her wine. The Cabernet filled her mouth with a rich mix of flavors.

"Exactly," Jack said.

Jenna turned to Sandro. "Is that the kind of thing you cooked in New York?"

Sandro went still for a moment. Whatever he was thinking or feeling etched a vertical line between his brows. Maybe she'd gotten the wrong impression when she'd started flirting with him. He certainly didn't look pleased with her now.

Finally he answered in a casual tone, "I cooked

all kinds of stuff in New York. Worked at a lot of places." He ate a bite of lamb, making it clear he wasn't going to elaborate. Jenna noticed he'd barely touched his wine.

Over dessert, Jack told them about a meal he'd had at one of Sandro's restaurants when they'd known each other in New York. How people had lined up around the block to get a table. But it seemed to Jenna that the more Jack talked, the more remote Sandro became. Maybe it was just humility? But there was a darkness in his eyes, a bitterness in the lines of his mouth that Jenna didn't understand. According to Jack, he'd been a huge success, but he didn't look at all happy about the memories.

As Jack's story came to an end, Jenna studied Sandro covertly. He was staring into deep space located somewhere between his water and wine glasses. Well, he might be a bit of a moody person, but it was clear to Jenna that Jack's money would be well invested. Sandro had a gift, a talent for blending ingredients and flavors in new and fascinating ways that would be a huge hit. The delicate vanilla-bean flan that had finished the meal alongside a perfect cappuccino was the final proof.

She glanced down the table to where Jack and Samantha were holding hands and smiling at each other. "Nice work," she whispered, interrupting whatever dark reverie he was lost in. "Jack and Samantha look like they're in a blissed-out food coma."

Sandro looked up and smiled at her, his mood apparently lightening, and her stomach did an odd flip. "The highest compliment," he whispered back. "But you're still clearheaded. Should I be worried?"

It took a moment to follow him but when she did, she giggled. "Because I'm not comatose? No. The food was delicious. But I've got a competition coming up and no matter how good the food, I have to eat a little less of it than most people."

"Sounds like you're missing out." He winked. "Especially when you're eating my food."

"Missing out on stuffing myself? I don't see it that way. Dancing takes discipline. But the fun of it is way more than the pleasure I might get from a few extra bites of food." Jenna paused and licked some flan off her spoon, noticing how Sandro's eyes locked on to her mouth. "No matter how incredible they might taste."

THEY'D MADE THEIR way to the living room to sit in front of the fire with the last of the wine. Samantha and Jack were curled up on the couch, staring at the flames. Jenna sat on the rug by the hearth, petting Zeke, one of the collies. He'd snuggled up next to her the moment she sat down. She wove her fingers into the soft, thick fur around his neck and he sighed in doggy bliss.

Sandro had flopped into the armchair but only stayed a few minutes before disappearing into the kitchen. Jenna could hear the clattering of dishes. "Shouldn't we be helping?" she asked.

Yawning, Samantha lifted her head from Jack's shoulder. "Good luck. Sandro never lets anyone help. Maybe it's a chef thing."

"Any particular reason you want to lend a hand, Red?" Jack was looking over Samantha's head at her, grinning suggestively.

"Are you thinking that I—?" Jenna stopped, glancing toward the kitchen to make sure its occupants couldn't hear.

"Jack, stop teasing her!" Samantha sat up and elbowed her fiancé. "Give Jenna a break. She can't help it if she's so beautiful that men fall all over her. But seriously, Jen, if there was any more chemistry between you two at dinner, this whole house would have gone up in flames."

"There's no chemistry," Jenna lied to her friend, ignoring the feelings racing through her.

Jack gave Jenna a long look. "It's obvious even to a dumb guy like me that there's something there. I've known Sandro for years and I've never seen him quite like that."

"What, talking with people at dinner?"

"No," Jack replied. "That's pretty standard. This is different. For one thing, he kept staring at you."

That shouldn't have been such interesting news, but Jenna's pulse sped up at the thought. The last thing she needed was a gorgeous, moody man who lived a couple hundred miles away from San Francisco. But despite what she'd told Samantha, the chemistry she felt with Sandro was palpable. Flirting with him was addictive and she wanted more. Jack's next words felt like cold water.

"Look, Red. You gotta know this. Sandro's my friend and he's a great guy. An amazing, dedicated chef, too. And he's fine to flirt with. But his history with women… Well, let's just say there's a long, long history and it's not pretty. He doesn't take much seriously outside of cooking. Don't even think about getting involved with him. I've seen way too many women regret that decision."

There was disappointment but not surprise. Jenna had lived in San Francisco long enough to know that good-looking single men in their thirties were usually too good to be true. Mostly, she felt something close to horror. Only a few hours had gone by since she'd vowed to take a break from dating and thus avoid cheating men, and she was already drawn to one like some pathetic moth to a lethal flame.

She sighed. "You don't have to worry, Jack. He's good-looking and all, but I don't want anything new." Jenna hoped that if she just kept saying the words, they'd be true. "I just want to keep my focus on my dancing right now." A funny thought struck her and she smiled. "Even if I was interested, we wouldn't cross paths. I doubt he'll be signing up for dance lessons in San Francisco anytime soon!"

Jenna stared at the whispering flames in the fireplace, trying to force Sandro out of her mind. *Think about your dance studio,* she commanded herself. The one she was going to create now that her long, exhausting search for the perfect place had finally produced a result. Jenna pictured the old ballroom, forgotten at the back of the run-down social club. It was like discovering hidden treasure, complete with crystal chandeliers. It was going to be perfect, as long as no one else noticed it before she could pull her money together.

She'd been with Jeff the day she'd found it. Such a fun day and they'd celebrated afterward at a bar that only served champagne—one of those businesses that could exist in a busy city where people loved their wine. They'd tried a few different kinds and then gone back to his apartment and...

Ugh! Why was she thinking about Jeff? Any thoughts of sex with Jeff were hideous now that she knew he'd been sleeping with other women. She stood suddenly, her heart pounding with the enormity of his betrayal.

"Are you okay?" Samantha asked sleepily.

"I'm good," she lied. "But really tired. I think I'll just say good-night." She *was* exhausted, she realized. It had been a rough week.

She said good-night and went to thank Sandro

and Paul for dinner. Dirty dishes were still scattered around the dining room table and she grabbed a stack of plates as she went by. In the kitchen, Paul was packing groceries back into the cardboard box. There was no sign of Sandro.

"Paul, how come you didn't eat with us?" Jenna asked.

"Sandro needed me to stir the sauce and do the prep for the desserts. I ate in here. It was good, though."

"Your brother's got talent for sure," Jenna told him. "Do you like to cook, too?"

"Nah." Paul grimaced. "I mean, I'm happy to help out Sandro, but I'm not really into it."

"Me, neither," Jenna said. "I live on takeout. Way too much, probably." She scraped the plates into the garbage and took them to the sink to rinse them off.

"Can I ask you for a favor, Jenna?" Paul kept his voice low and looked behind him for a moment, as if making sure no one would overhear.

"Sure," Jenna answered.

"Would you be able to tell me…?" Paul's face reddened. "I mean, it's probably dumb, but can you tell me if I'm any good? At dance?"

"You looked pretty good when you were copying my moves in here earlier," Jenna teased.

"No, I mean *really* good, like maybe I could actually *be* a dancer."

"You want to dance? Here?"

"Yeah. Please, Jenna? Who knows if I'll ever meet a real dancer again?"

Jenna sighed as the prospect of her comfortable bed upstairs faded a little farther into the distance. "Hang on." She left the kitchen and found her purse near the front door. She rummaged inside for her iPod. As she headed back with it, Samantha and Jack looked at her curiously. "Don't ask," she said. It was just too silly that she was going to dance with a teenage boy in their kitchen.

There was an iPod dock on the counter. "What kind of dance do you want to try?" she asked Paul.

"Um…salsa?" His voice was uncertain and she could tell he was getting nervous. She found one of her favorite teaching songs, where the rhythm was easy to hear, and turned the volume up slightly, trying not to disturb Samantha and Jack's peace in the living room.

"Okay. Stand next to me. Follow my feet." She launched into a basic salsa step.

Paul watched her for a moment and then followed her moves effortlessly. He was instantly transformed. The gangly teenager was gone. Every part of his body was working together, all the moves initiating right from his center, as they should, everything fluid, connected and reflecting the rhythm. Hips swaying, Jenna led him around the kitchen and he followed.

"Okay, now a basic step in closed." She showed

him where to put his hands. "A little more tension between us. Tighten the muscles in your arm, but don't make them rigid. Follow my feet." It took only a moment for him to master the basic in closed position and then he lifted his hand and spun her in a perfect open turn. She laughed in delight.

"I got that from a video." His grin was ear-to-ear.

"I'm impressed!" It was unbelievable. Paul the baby cowboy was a natural dancer. They continued to dance in closed position. And Jenna knew for certain that *this* was why she'd ignored her intuition this morning. *This* was why she'd gotten lost in a pasture. It was because of Paul. Because Paul needed encouragement to reach his dream, and here she was, in the perfect position to provide it.

"Paul!" Sandro's tone was harsh. Paul and Jenna froze and he stalked across the room, touching the iPod to stop the music.

"What's wrong?" Jenna asked.

"Why are you getting his hopes up?" Sandro was making a visible effort to calm down, but his voice was still rough.

"We were just dancing. And he already has hope— he's that good. He just needs training!"

"What he needs is none of your business."

"Now, that's just rude!" Jenna felt her temper rising and reminded herself that Sandro was Jack's good friend. She forced herself to make her own voice calm but couldn't keep from pressing him.

"Why are you angry? Shouldn't you be proud of your brother? Excited for him?" Jenna knew it probably wasn't a good idea to get involved in the family issues of a boy she barely knew, but Paul's love of dance, and his natural ability, struck a chord with her. She knew well what it was like to come from a family who disapproved of dancing.

When Sandro spoke this time, he didn't sound quite so angry. "Of course I'm proud of him. But that doesn't mean I think he should be putting his energy and time into dancing right now. He should wait until he's eighteen to get involved in that."

Jenna stared at him, not knowing what to say. Finally she decided that the way to combat ignorance was education. "Sandro, with the right training, Paul could probably be a very successful dancer. But if he waits until he's eighteen, every other talented dancer will have way more knowledge and ability than him. Why would you want to set him up for failure?"

"If he's that talented, he'll catch up. He can wait." A muscle in Sandro's jaw twitched and his brows were furrowed. Jenna could almost feel the stubbornness thicken the air around them. It was that strong.

"That's not fair!" Paul argued. "I've told you, I don't want to wait. This is what I want. You got to cook! Why can't I dance?"

"Because there's a price," Sandro said heavily.

His initial ire seemed to have dissipated and now he just looked depressed. He picked up a bag of produce and shoved it in Paul's arms. "Go load these. And wait for me in the car."

Paul didn't move.

"Is there a way that Paul could get to a dance school?" Jenna asked. "I know there's nothing in Benson, but in Carson City, maybe?"

"It's too far," Sandro answered shortly.

"Sandro, *come on!*" Paul rested the bag of produce on the counter. "What about those cooking classes in San Francisco you're gonna do? On the weekends. I could go with you and take classes with Jenna."

"You're teaching cooking in San Francisco?" Jenna looked at Sandro in surprise.

"A weekend gig." He glared at his little brother. "It's temporary."

Jenna couldn't believe there was such a clear solution right in front of them. "It's a good idea. I teach classes for teenagers on the weekends. It's a sliding-scale fee—people pay what they can. It would be perfect!"

"No, it wouldn't. Paul needs to help on the ranch on the weekends."

"I'll do extra chores during the week," Paul countered.

Sandro opened the refrigerator with a little more force than necessary. He pulled out leftover ingredients and dropped them in the chest cooler. "I think we're done talking about this."

"Sandro, this is nuts!" Jenna exclaimed. "Why can't Paul have the same chance you did to follow your dreams?"

"He can. When he's older." Sandro shoved the lid onto the full cooler and picked it up, signaling that the conversation was over.

Paul glared at his brother. "*This* is why I didn't tell you about meeting her today! Because I knew you'd get all upset." He looked at Jenna over the groceries. His eyes were sad, his mouth typical-teenager sullen. "Thanks, Jenna," he told her. "For the dance, for the advice, everything." He pushed his way out, the back door slamming behind him.

Sandro watched him go and then looked at Jenna. He must have seen the outrage in her eyes because he set the cooler on the counter and sighed. He looked away, running his fingers through his unruly hair in a gesture of frustration. "You must think I'm a jerk."

"Pretty much," Jenna answered truthfully.

"I've got my reasons." He looked almost as sullen as Paul.

"I'm sure you *think* you do. But I wasn't kidding when I told you he's got talent. He's a natural. Why won't you let him pursue it?"

Sandro shook his head. "You wouldn't get it, Jenna. You grew up in San Francisco, right? With

Mommy and Daddy signing you up for your ballet classes and clapping at your recitals?"

She nodded. It had been true, once.

"It's different out here," Sandro told her. He picked the chest cooler up again.

"Wait." Jenna stopped him. Her heart ached for Paul. She knew what it was like to want, more than anything, to dance. "I'll be right back."

Jenna went back to the hall for her purse, found her wallet and took out a business card. On the back of it she scribbled her cell phone number and her weekend class schedule. She returned to the kitchen, relieved to see that Sandro had waited. She pressed the card into his hand. "Take this," she ordered, "in case you change your mind."

Sandro studied the card for a moment. When he looked up, he was half smiling. "There's glitter on your business card."

"It's ballroom dance. We're way into our glitter. And sequins." She tried not to sound defensive.

"Well, thanks, but I won't be calling," he told her, shoving the card into his back pocket, the hint of humor vanishing.

"Why not?" This was all so mysterious. Clearly she wasn't going to win this argument, and she wanted to understand why.

He must have seen it in her face, because the steel in him softened just a little. "Because I can see down the road for Paul and it isn't pretty. I wanted to cook and my family and my friends gave me nonstop grief for being different. I handled it, but it made me a lonely, angry kid. Eventually it made me a runaway. I don't want that for my little brother."

Jenna studied the stern lines of his face, new sympathy filtering through the irritation and frustration. Sandro might be misguided, but his motives were pure—he was protecting the brother he loved.

But poor Paul was going to have some long, bitter teenage years ahead if he wasn't allowed to dance until he left home. She couldn't do much more for him, but she had to try. "I'm sorry that happened to you, and I admire you for wanting to protect your brother. But don't you think that if you forbid it, he'll just want it more?"

There was a bag of groceries on the floor and Sandro was nudging it with his foot. Fidgeting, but possibly listening.

Jenna played her last card. "Maybe you should just let him try it. Dance training is hard. It's difficult, repetitive and sometimes even boring. Most people end up quitting. Paul will probably lose interest when he gets to know the reality of it." It was true that most people quit, but Jenna was pretty sure Paul wouldn't. She could recognize a fellow fanatic when she saw one. Paul would make dancing his life—but Sandro didn't need to know that right now.

He was watching her speculatively. For an instant she thought he'd say yes, but the moment passed and the wall was back between them. "I think I know what's best."

"Maybe." Anger rose again. Her voice was sharper than she meant it to be. "I suggest you think a little more carefully before you squash his dreams." She turned on her heel and left the room, sad for Paul and, oddly, sad for Sandro, too.

CHAPTER FOUR

"WHAT DO YOU mean you'll be in San Francisco?" Joe shoved the fence post deeper into the hole they'd just dug and gave it a kick with his work boot to make sure it was solid. Sandro glanced at his brother, all six-plus solid feet of him. Joe was a year younger than Sandro, but people always assumed he was older. With his light brown hair and broad face, he took after their father in more ways than just looks. Joe loved the ranch, had never questioned that his future lay there. He was the oldest son in every way but birthright.

Sandro poured the quick-setting cement into the battered wheelbarrow. Paul brought the hose over and let the water spurt over the dry powder. Grabbing a shovel, Sandro started mixing. "I'm teaching classes at a cooking school. It's a great gig. It'll pretty much pay for all the new appliances in the restaurant."

"Oh, yeah. The *restaurant*." Joe said the word as though it tasted bad in his mouth. "It's a big weekend, Sandro. Pops wants all hands on deck to move the sheep."

"Well, Joe, Pops has to understand that the sheep aren't my first priority. I'm trying to help out with the ranch as much as possible, but I came back here to start my own business."

"Okay," Joe said reluctantly. "I get it." He bent down with a level to straighten the post. "But why take Paul with you?"

Sandro started shoveling the concrete into the hole and Paul picked up his shovel to help. They were careful not to look at each other. "I'll need extra help. My class is completely full. If I don't have an assistant, there's no way I can pull it off." He glared at Paul, silently cursing his brother's endless arguing, two weeks of it, that had finally worn him down.

He hated to admit it, but Jenna had been right. The more he'd said no, the more Paul had insisted he *had* to take her dance classes. Sandro could only hope she was right about the other part, that Paul would change his tune once he realized how hard the training really was. He jabbed Paul in the ribs with his elbow. "Besides, he's a whippersnapper. Not much use to you out there anyways."

Paul stood up at this and punched Sandro in the shoulder.

"Easy there, little brother." Sandro grinned. "You don't want to mess with the big guns." He set aside his shovel and flexed his biceps a few times while Paul cracked up.

"Will you two stop clowning around so we can get this done?" Joe grumbled. "In case you hadn't noticed, we have a truckload of these to set in the next couple days. Besides—" he held out his own arm, enormous muscles bulging "—I wouldn't go showing off those biceps around here, Sandro. You may be the oldest but you're a scrawny bastard. Comes from spending your life in a kitchen instead of doing man's work."

"Well, it's a pity we can't all be muscle-bound meatheads like you, Joe. But given the choice, I'll take my brains over your muscle any day." He ducked as Joe's giant fist came at him in a mock swing. "So it's a done deal. I'm taking Paul to San Francisco and the rest of you mindless country boys can follow the sheep up the hills."

The truth was, Sandro liked moving the sheep. Riding into the mountains on horseback, making sure the flock got up to the summer meadows, was a hell of a lot more relaxing than teaching a bunch of pretentious San Francisco foodies how to make a decent paella. And the route to the pastures was beautiful, too. But the cash he'd make from these classes was way too tempting. And if it meant that Paul would finally stop making his life miserable and get a dose of reality to cool his dancing obsession, that would compensate for missing the ride. Hell, he'd missed it for the past decade anyway— what was one more year?

Sandro gave Paul a wink to acknowledge the success of their ruse and picked up his tools to head to the next posthole. As his spade hit the rocky ground, he used all the force he could to tame his unruly mind. Because all week his mind had been on Jenna Stevens.

And he had no business thinking about her. His life was in Benson now, not with some woman from the city. She was everything he needed to avoid—gorgeous, funny and flirty. Distracting. He'd made a choice to leave women like her behind in New York and he wasn't going to choose differently, no matter how much he might want to.

So far work had been his solution. When thoughts of Jenna's bright blue eyes heated his mind, he worked. When haunted by the vision of her stalking away after dinner that night, all righteous and fiery, he worked even harder. Since he'd been thinking of her almost nonstop, it had been a very productive couple of weeks.

But the endless work didn't get rid of the shame he felt, and it irritated him. Jenna was kind, and he'd been hostile to her when all she'd been doing was trying to help Paul. Sure, he didn't want Paul to dance, but that was no reason to be rude to her about it. There was only one logical explanation for his behavior—one which Sandro was loath to admit. When he'd walked into the kitchen and seen Jenna dancing in his brother's arms, he'd been jealous. Jealous of the fun his brother was having with her, making her laugh as she turned so easily across the floor. He'd been jealous of a fifteen-year-old kid, and that was downright pathetic.

Even more pathetic, he'd spilled his guts to Jenna about his past. And he *never* talked about that. Outside of his family and a few folks in Benson, no one knew he'd run away from home. He wasn't even sure how he'd ended up telling her. She'd seemed to genuinely want to know *why* he didn't want Paul to dance. And her compassion had somehow gotten him talking about his crappy teen years and how he'd run off. She must think he was a pretty sorry case. He wished he didn't care so much about what she thought.

He was just like Paul, he realized, as he jammed the posthole digger farther into the earth. Wanting something simply because he couldn't have it. Maybe he should just try to sleep with Jenna and get her out of his system. His stomach coiled at the thought, some uneasy combination of lust and anxiety. That was certainly what he would have done a few months ago.

But that was just one more reason why he wasn't going to do it now. He wasn't willing to go down that path again. He was different now. So he'd just keep his head down and his hands busy until his interest in her passed.

Maybe the upside of taking Paul to these lessons

was that he'd see her at work with a bunch of teen-agers. Hopefully, she'd look like every one of San-dro's high school teachers did—tired and hassled. Maybe just like Paul, he needed a good hard dose of reality—though he had a bad feeling it would take more than that to rid him of his thoughts about Jenna.

JENNA WATCHED HER mother pour herself another glass of white wine. If she was counting correctly, it was her third, and that was on top of the cock-tails her mom had insisted on before dinner. She hadn't seen her mother drink quite like this since, well, since Dad's affair came to light a few years ago. But she knew her mom drank when she was alone. Jenna got enough late-night drunken phone calls from her to know she was hitting the bottle solo on a fairly regular basis.

She looked down the gleaming mahogany table. Daniel, her older brother, was nodding off over his plate. He'd worked at the hospital last night and he was having coffee with his dinner instead of wine. Shelley, her older sister and a rising star at the San Francisco district attorney's office, was speaking animatedly with her father about a high-profile case she was working on. Her father actually looked re-laxed and happy as he listened, asking all kinds of questions about Shelley's progress.

Jenna felt a pang of envy that was so old and

familiar it was almost like a part of her body—an extra organ or limb. It had always been that way— Dad asking about Shelley's day at school, buying her expensive gifts in honor of her perfect grades, crowing to their friends about her many accomplishments.

Jenna had worked hard in school, too, clocking far more hours in the library doing homework than Shelley ever did. Yet it never got easier. It was as if her brain had trouble translating the words in the textbook into coherent ideas. So she got Cs and Bs most of the time, and those hard-earned grades were a constant source of disappointment to her father.

Jenna knew now that she was full of imperfections he simply couldn't understand. In his eyes, her dancing was an embarrassing hobby that stood in the way of real success. Her curvaceous figure and wild curly red hair held no beauty when contrasted with Shelley's slender form and straight blond locks.

"Jenna!" Her father's voice suddenly boomed down the table. "What were you doing today? Twirling around the ballroom?"

Jenna winced at the disdain in his voice. "Teaching, practicing, the usual."

"And how's John?"

"John?"

"You know, that musician you go out with?"

"Um…you mean Jeff?" Jenna shook her head in

disbelief. She'd dated Jeff for two years, and her father had met him several times.

"Yeah. That's right. Jeff. The drummer with the long hair. How's that going for you?"

Jenna hated to give him any satisfaction, but she wasn't going to lie. "We broke up." Her brother and sister didn't even bother to disguise their "I told you so" eye rolls.

"Well, good. You need to stop dating all these guys with no focus, no ambition. Shelley, Daniel, you must know some people from work Jenna could go out with. Or why don't you let your mother help you find a decent boyfriend?"

Oh, like she found you? Jenna wanted to say but didn't. *A man who cheats on his wife?*

Shelly cleared her throat. "Look, Jenna, I spoke with Ralph Clark yesterday."

"Who?" Jenna turned to her older sister, who was smiling at her benevolently.

"Ralph Clark—a lawyer at my old firm? He told me that they need an administrative assistant. He'd like to interview you."

Jenna stared at Shelley in disbelief. How was it possible they'd grown up in the same house, just a few years apart, and yet Shelley knew so little about her? She took a sip of her wine and suddenly felt sympathy for her mother. This family would drive anyone to drink eventually.

"Jenna? What do you think? Should I send you his email address tomorrow?"

She sighed. "Thanks for thinking of me, Shel, but I already have a job."

"Oh, ballroom dancing? Jenna, that's not a career—that's a hobby." Shelley was a perfect echo of their father.

"So why do I get paid, then?" Jenna tried to keep her voice calm, but she could hear the edge in it. "It's not a hobby—it's my career, and it has been for ten years now. And if you'd been paying attention, you'd know I am really good at it."

Her father's voice was softer than usual in attempted persuasiveness. "Jenna, Shelley is just trying to help you. Just go in for an interview. They'll pay well. They have great benefits. You know your mom is so worried about you living in that tiny apartment. You could afford something better with a higher salary."

"Dad, I like my apartment. I like my job. There's nothing wrong with my life that you or Shelley or anyone needs to fix!"

"Honey, we just want you to be successful. Look at your sister. Did you know she's considering a run for supervisor? She'll be mayor of San Francisco one day—mark my words. And your brother here is so humble he wouldn't mention it, but he's just been promoted to head of surgery."

"Congratulations, Daniel," Jenna said to her

brother, raising her glass slightly in his direction. He smiled at her sleepily. "Dad, I'm glad they're doing so well. But I'm also successful." She glanced around the table and saw the doubtful look on every face. "Look. I have a competition in two weeks. It's a big one. If my partner and I win, we'll be national champions for Latin dance—again. We won it the last two years, as well. Why don't you come out and see for yourself?" She realized she sounded as if she was pleading with them. Pleading for attention and acceptance.

"I'll be in Chicago for a conference," Shelley said.

"Dancing's not really my thing." Daniel rubbed his eyes wearily. Her father didn't answer at all, just poured himself another drink and looked down at the floor, as if his disappointment was so great he couldn't even acknowledge her.

When would she learn? Jenna could have kicked herself for trying. She turned her focus to her mother. "So how are you, Mom? How's your work going with the cotillion committee?"

Her mother took another swallow of wine, draining her glass. "Oh, you know…it's fine…the usual…" Her voice trailed off and she didn't seem to notice.

Well, at least the food was as delicious as always. A grilled salmon with a slightly brown buttery crust. All kinds of summer vegetables fresh from the farmers' market, lightly sautéed. Their current chef was a really talented guy. Jenna's thoughts immediately drifted to Sandro and the incredible meal he'd cooked at Samantha's. And the bitter expression on his face when he'd found her dancing with Paul. He'd probably get along great with her family.

When her mother reached for the bottle to fill her glass again, Jenna couldn't stand it any longer. Glancing down the table to make sure her father and sister were still engrossed in conversation, she put out her hand and stilled her mother's. "Mom, I'm not trying to be rude, but it seems like you're drinking a lot. And you've hardly touched your food. What's going on?"

Her mother looked outraged, but under the indignant expression, Jenna noticed something else. A puffiness that no amount of expensive makeup could hide. This wasn't the first night her mother had been hitting the bottle hard. Her heart sank.

"Jenna! What has come over you?" Her mother was going on defense. "We're having a nice dinner and I'm having some wine. That's all."

"Mom, you're having four glasses of wine. That's an entire bottle. Plus you had a couple cocktails. I'm worried about you. Is something wrong? Between you and dad?"

"You've been counting my drinks? Jenna, I'm not a child. Why do you try to treat me like one?

You have no respect for me. No respect for all the things I do!"

Her voice was rising, and Jenna's father and sister stopped talking and looked down the table at them. Her mother seemed to appreciate the audience. "You don't get to show up at this house and tell me what I should be doing! You ask *me* what's wrong? I should be asking the same of you, Jenna. Why don't you listen to us? We're family—we want what's best for you."

"Because dancing *is* what's best for me!" Disappointment had tears stinging her eyes. Her mom was so defensive about her drinking she'd attack her own daughter. "Mom, let's not fight. I asked you about the wine because I love you and I'm concerned." Jenna was using her full voice now. She figured her father and sister had probably noticed the empty bottles at their end of the table, too. Maybe they could all work together to find out what was wrong with Mom.

Her mother's voice was icy. "You may be on one of your newest health kicks, Jenna, but I happen to enjoy a glass of wine with my dinner and I don't see anything wrong with that. I'm just trying to have a nice evening with my family. I don't see why you have to come here and cause a scene."

"Mom, I wasn't—"

"That's enough." Her father's voice interrupted and it shook with anger. "Jenna, I wish we could just have a peaceful night as a family. Maybe in your life at the ballroom, with all those artsy dancers, this kind of drama is acceptable. But here in this house it's not okay."

"It's not drama, Dad. I am worried about Mom. And maybe if you spent a few minutes paying some attention to her, you'd see that she's drinking way too much!"

There was a silence at the table so solid that it felt like a wall around her. Jenna waited for her sister to say something. Or her brother. He was a doctor, after all—he should be the one bringing this up. And her father *must* be able to see how much her mother needed help.

Instead the silence seemed to go on forever before her father broke it up. "How dare you insult your mother like that?" His voice was low and mean and it occurred to Jenna for the first time that he really might hate her. Just for being her. And for being honest.

Shelley shook her head slowly, as if heavy with her displeasure. "Jenna, Dad's right. This is really uncalled for."

Jenna stood up. Her legs were shaking. She turned to her mother. "Mom, I'm sorry I offended you. I was only trying to help. I am worried about your drinking and you should be, too. And, Dad, I don't think it's drama to be concerned for someone you love. You should try it sometime."

In the hall she grabbed her backpack and coat from the maid, who'd hustled to fetch them for her, and burst into the foggy night through the giant oak front doors, then closed them behind her—grateful for the thick wood between her and the bizarre evidence of her family's denial. They truly did not believe, or didn't want to believe, that her mother had a problem. They truly believed that *Jenna* was the problem. The cold mist mingled with the hot tears pouring down her cheeks. It was moments like these, when the differences between her and her family were so stark, that she felt the most alone.

Fumbling through the jumbled contents of her backpack for her keys, she cursed herself for opening her mouth. Why did she think that her concerns would make any difference to her family? They had no respect for her or for her work; why would they respect her opinion?

She snapped open the lock on her bicycle, threw the coiled cable into her backpack and shoved her helmet on her head. She hated that her hands were trembling so much she could hardly close the buckle.

Jenna pushed her bike into the empty street of the exclusive Seacliff neighborhood and started pedaling, swiping her sleeve at the tears trickling down her face. As always, exercise was an escape. She covered the two blocks to California Street in what seemed like moments, pumping hard, not bothering to switch gears on the slight uphill, forcing herself to stand on the pedals and put all her frustration into propelling the bike forward.

She swung left and got into the bike lane, thankful that the evening traffic rush was over. She pedaled furiously, the old shame and anger that her family inspired burning like rocket fuel inside. In record time she was turning right onto Arguello Boulevard, heading toward the black shadow that was Golden Gate Park at night. Pedaling around its shadowy edge—no way would she venture into its dark groves at this hour—she cut through the Haight-Ashbury, the famous old Victorian buildings a dim blur as she rushed past.

By the time Jenna got to Divisadero Street, her anger had cooled a bit, the bitterness had tempered and she pedaled at a steadier cadence past the neon marquee of the Castro Theatre. She automatically looked up to see what they were showing, and a small thrill interrupted her gloom when she saw that it was *An American in Paris*. Gene Kelly and Leslie Caron dancing together—a heavenly duo. Jenna tried to picture her class schedule for tomorrow. Maybe she could steal a few hours and escape to the theater's vintage red velvet seats and indulge her love of old musicals. That would cheer her up for sure.

A few blocks more and she was pedaling uphill to the top of Dolores Park, close to her apartment now. She stopped on the sidewalk, her breath audible in the quiet of the night, her emotions finally calm enough to let her body rest.

Breathing deeply, Jenna visualized exhaling the last of the turbulence out of her system. It worked before dance competitions—why not now? She'd left the fog behind in the Haight-Ashbury and she inhaled the rare clear summer night, the feel of her body after exercise, the peace she felt up here on this hill, temporarily above the bustle. She exhaled anger, worry and that horrible sense of rejection her family was so good at serving up along with their perfectly cooked meals.

She inhaled the view. The downtown skyline lights were glittering. The familiar silhouettes mixed in with all the new buildings that were going up so quickly that the horizon seemed a little different each time she stopped to look. But no matter how it changed, it was always magical, always compelling her to explore it further, always making her glad she'd been born and raised in San Francisco.

Her heart calmed and her frayed nerves wove themselves back together. She looked up at the few stars bright and brave enough to appear despite the glow of the city lights. And she waited. Slowly a thought crystallized. The frustration and hurt she felt after tonight's disastrous dinner was there for a reason. It was starkly obvious. There was a lesson in what had happened with her family tonight. *She needed to stop hoping that people would change.*

She shouldn't have gone to dinner expecting her family to be supportive of her. They'd never supported her before, so what made her hopeful that they'd suddenly start?

She shouldn't have expected she could have any influence over her mom's drinking. All the literature from the Al-Anon meetings she'd attended for months, ever since her mom's drunk dialing started, clearly stated that you couldn't make someone else stop drinking.

In fact, at Al-Anon they said the Serenity Prayer, which was all about change. *Grant me the serenity to accept the things I cannot change, the courage to change the things I can and the wisdom to know the difference.* Jenna obviously needed that wisdom right now.

The only person she could change was herself. It was a lonely thought, but it was also oddly comforting. If she stopped trying to change others, it would mean less betrayal and hurt when people didn't act the way she wanted them to. It might even mean she'd have more energy to focus solely on her own life—her dancing, her performing and hopefully soon her own dance studio.

Jenna leaned on her bike and watched the sparkling lights of the city. When she owned her own business, one or two of those fairy lights would be the lights of *her* ballroom. Back in Benson she'd vowed to devote all her time and energy to pursuing that goal. She might be on her own, with no family and no boyfriend to lean on, but if the result was that she finally made her dreams come true, then maybe being alone was a pretty good choice for now.

CHAPTER FIVE

"JENNA, BRENT, CAN I speak with you two for a moment?" Marlene Dale, the owner of the Golden Gate Ballroom, looking elegant in a pale pink cashmere wrap, was standing by the side of the dance floor.

Jenna let go of Brent's hand. They'd been practicing since six in the morning and it was almost nine. Her classes would start soon anyway. "I guess we're done for now?" she asked him.

"You wore me out, pretty lady." He winked at her. Years ago it would have melted her heart. Today it was irritating. She'd been trying to ignore his lavish compliments, hoping he'd get bored or that someone new would catch his eye like a bright, shiny toy, diverting his attention. "Coming, Marlene!" Jenna called.

Brent shoved his straight blond hair out of his face. He needed a haircut and Jenna hoped he'd take care of it before their competition. "I'll go get the music." He strolled away, apparently in no hurry to talk with Marlene, and disappeared into the DJ booth at the opposite end of the room. Jenna walked

over to the tall front counter that separated the ballroom from the lobby.

Marlene looked up from the class schedule she
had open on the desk.

"Love the hair today, Marlene!" Jenna exclaimed.
Marlene's bleached-blond mane was piled up into
a near beehive. Jenna and her boss sometimes
clashed, but they both appreciated the beauty of
vintage hairstyles.

"Thank you," Marlene said, bringing her hand
up to pat her back-combed creation. Then she stood
and placed her scheduling book on the counter so
Jenna could see it better. "Nicole has approached
me again about taking on some parts of the salsa
program." She didn't look at Jenna, instead keeping her eyes glued to the book, obviously uncomfortable with what she was saying.

Jenna didn't feel much sympathy. Nicole happened to be Marlene's niece, who Marlene had hired
in a foolish act of nepotism. Now she was running
Marlene ragged with her diva demands. Despite the
fact that Nicole was still learning many of the ad-
vanced steps, she wanted to step into a head teaching role. Jenna's role, to be precise.

"The salsa program is doing really well, Marlene. Our classes are packed. Why would you want
to take us out of them?"

"Well, Nicole was thinking maybe she could

take over for *you* a bit and have a chance to dance with Brent."

Well, at least her ambition to take my place is out in the open now. Jenna bit her lip to keep from actually saying her thought aloud. She and Marlene had been having these types of conversations a lot lately, and Jenna was losing patience.

"Brent and I are partners, Marlene. We work together. Nicole needs to make connections with other dancers her age and find her own partner. That's how everyone else does it, and that's how she'll be successful in the long run."

"Well, yes." Marlene stared at the schedule, still not meeting Jenna's eyes. "But she feels it isn't fair that you and Brent have so many students."

Jenna looked away, out the wall of windows to the street. It was only nine o'clock on a Saturday morning, and Brannan Street was still pretty quiet. A few taxis meandered by, but this part of San Francisco generally slept late on the weekends. Jenna searched inside herself, trying to find some scrap of sympathy for Nicole that would prevent her from throttling the younger woman the next time she saw her.

She remembered what it was like to be new at the ballroom—young and ambitious and hungry for your dreams to come true. But unlike Nicole, she'd recognized how much hard work that took. How the glamorous moments were few and far between, and most days were spent taking class after class, attending practice after practice and teaching private lessons to stumbling beginner students—computer nerds looking for an ounce of cool or the recently divorced, seeking endorphins. It was part dancing, part counseling, and it was important work, but Nicole didn't see it that way. She snapped at her students, frustrated with their lack of skill within the first five minutes of the lesson.

And because she was so impatient with them, most of those students never came back to her. They either fled the ballroom forever in search of a less stressful hobby, or they found another teacher. Just yesterday one poor man had pulled Jenna aside in the hallway and asked if he could start classes with her because he'd heard that not all teachers were as mean as Nicole.

But how to explain this to Nicole's doting auntie? Marlene had never had children of her own. She'd devoted her life to dance and to her business. And when Jenna saw her desperation for Nicole's affection, she could tell that Marlene's choices had left her with regrets. Dance could be a magical love affair, but it could also leave you jilted.

Realizing that Marlene was waiting for an answer, Jenna turned away from the street scene out the window. "I understand that Nicole wants more students, Marlene, but people know Brent, and they know me, and they come here to take classes with *us.* If you just pull me out and pop Nicole in my place, they won't be satisfied. And it's not fair to me, either. It doesn't reward me for my hard work in building the program."

"Well, yes, Jenna, I am aware of the risks, of course. I have owned this ballroom for several years now."

Oops. She'd stepped on Marlene's toes again. It was easy to do. Jenna looked over at the empty ballroom. Where was Brent? He should be here right now supporting her, but he always seemed to vanish on some mysterious errand when these difficult meetings came up.

"Of course, Marlene. I'm sorry if I sounded pushy." Jenna tried a new tactic. "What if you gave Nicole a beginning salsa class on a night when Brent and I don't work? Then she can build her own group of students from the ground up without feeling like she has to compete with us."

Marlene stared at the schedule, considering. Jenna looked at the book and pointed to the Wednesday column. "Look, there's a seven-thirty slot available. That's a great night for teaching." And a night when she and Brent were busy with an outside gig. They were taking a break from Latin dance and focusing on the popular dances of the 1930s and '40s at a local hotel ballroom. Swing, Lindy Hop and Charleston—it was rapidly becoming one of her favorite nights of the week.

"That's a good suggestion, Jenna." Marlene paused. "And if I could ask you a favor...maybe you could mentor Nicole a bit? Help her work on her professional demeanor and create a bit more of a nurturing attitude in her classes?"

Jenna groaned so loudly inside that she was sure Marlene heard it. Nicole seemed to hate Jenna even more than all the other people she disliked. Maybe it had something to do with Nicole's obvious crush on Brent or her envy of her and Brent's success. Whatever the reason, the girl spent a lot of time and energy trying to make Jenna miserable—Jenna was the last person Nicole would accept advice from.

She had to tread carefully. "Marlene, I'd be happy to try to help Nicole. But honestly, I've noticed that she doesn't seem that fond of me."

"Oh, I'm sure Nicole is just intimidated by you," Marlene said dismissively. "Just be as nice to her as you are to your students and you'll be fine."

"I'll do my best, Marlene." Jenna's heart sank. In her experience, the nicer she was to Nicole, the worse she acted. Now Jenna was supposed to convince her to be more nurturing?

Marlene was staring at something over Jenna's shoulder. Her eyes were wide and her mouth turned up into a sultry half smile. "Can I help you?" she asked in a silky voice. Jenna glanced at her boss in surprise.

"I'm looking for Jenna Stevens?" *Sandro.* That

low voice, and the effect it had on Jenna, was unmistakable. Her nerves rippled to life, making her skin feel as if it were suddenly electrified.

He was here. It had taken a couple weeks, and she'd pretty much given up hope, but he'd listened to her. Her heart lightened and she turned around, knowing she was grinning, trying to keep the triumph she felt off her face.

"Sandro! Paul!" She held out her hand and took a few steps to shake each of theirs. "Welcome to the Golden Gate Ballroom!"

Marlene looked at her with a whole new level of respect. She might be in her fifties but the woman sure did enjoy good-looking, younger men.

"This is Marlene, the owner and my boss," Jenna said.

Much to her relief, Sandro made no cynical comments about the pink walls of the lobby or the giant portraits of the teaching staff that hung on them. Instead a perfectly behaved version of Sandro stepped forward. His relaxed demeanor and warm smile betrayed no sign of the angry anti-dancing man she'd left in Samantha's kitchen. "Nice to meet you, Marlene." He shook her hand firmly. "We really appreciate Jenna inviting us to your ballroom. My brother Paul wants to learn to dance and Jenna has been an inspiration for him."

That was laying the charm on a bit thick. What was he up to?

"We're happy to have you here, Paul. Welcome. And, Sandro, you're not signing up for any classes yourself?"

"Well, if anyone could talk me into it, Jenna could." Sandro's smile was so sweet that Marlene blushed like a schoolgirl. He wasn't wearing his cowboy hat, but his faded jeans ended in black cowboy boots and his tight T-shirt advertised the Reno Rodeo. Marlene's eyes were wide, taking in his tall frame. Who knew the glamorous older dancer had a thing for cowboys?

"We saw her dance the other weekend." Sandro sent a quick wink Jenna's way. "I can't say I've ever had much interest in ballroom dance before, but Jenna was something else. She's a credit to your ballroom."

Now he was getting carried away. Marlene might enjoy flattery but she also didn't suffer fools, and Sandro was on his way to being one. Jenna sailed forward and took Paul by one arm, Sandro by the other. "I'm just going to give my new student a tour of the ballroom before class," she told Marlene. "Excuse me."

She steered her visitors through the lobby and into the main ballroom. The building had been an old hotel at one point in its past, and the ballroom was a testament to faded glory. Jenna loved the old crystal chandeliers that had shone on generations of dancers. Plaster roses adorned soaring columns around the arched edges, and one wall was floor-to-ceiling windows, filling the room with natural light.

"Great place," Sandro said, looking down at her with that humorous smile that shook her confidence and made her let go of his arm abruptly.

"It's awesome!" Paul added. "Can I go look around?"

"Of course," Jenna told him, and watched him walk across the room to the main teaching area, where the wall was lined with mirrors.

Jenna and Sandro followed, walking more slowly. Jenna looked up at Sandro, unable to resist asking the question foremost in her mind.

"What were you doing back there with Marlene? Your flattery was very nice but not exactly sincere."

"How do you know it wasn't sincere? Your dance in the kitchen did make quite an impression."

"An impression that really upset you!"

"Well, I've had some time to think, as you suggested. I'm sorry I was so rude that night."

"That still doesn't explain…" Jenna motioned vaguely toward Marlene, who had gone back to staring at the schedule, probably trying to figure out if there were any other of Jenna's classes she could give to Nicole.

"We'd been standing by the door for a while." Sandro turned to face her, serious now. "I guess you didn't hear us come in, but I heard most of what *she* was saying. I figured she needed a reminder of what you're worth."

He could be nice. She'd had no idea. Was this really the same Sandro she'd met in Benson? She had a sudden image of Sandro crossing the Bay Bridge this morning in some old pickup truck, gazing at the fantastic view of the San Francisco skyline as he approached. Could the relaxed attitude that her home city was famous for work its magic so quickly? And now she was the one being rude. "Thank you," she blurted out. "It's nice that you tried to help."

"Seems like I owed you one."

She made the mistake of looking at his eyes. Dark chocolate, with the bitter and sweet both evident. She couldn't look away—there was too much regret and warmth holding her there.

Sandro set her free by glancing at his watch, raising one dark brow when he caught sight of the time. "Paul, let's get you set up in your tutu. I have to get to the cooking school."

Reality came back into focus. No magic here. She had to stop that kind of wishful thinking. Sandro was merely here to drop his brother off, nothing more.

"Sure," Jenna agreed, taking a step back from him and forcing her eyes away from the older brother to the younger. "Don't worry, Paul, we don't do tutus here."

Paul hadn't even heard his brother's teasing. He

was standing in the middle of the dance floor, turning slowly as he took in the grand ballroom. The smile on his face was pure wonder and excitement.

She looked back at Sandro, making sure to avoid his eyes. She looked at the line of his clean-shaven jaw instead. A firm jaw, defined and strong, and she tried to resist when her imagination took hold, conjuring the feel of it under her fingertips. "I can get Paul ready for the class. And I'm sure Marlene will be happy to help with your bill. Actually..." She looked over to where Marlene had abandoned the schedule in favor of leaning on the front desk and peering through the wide ballroom doors to get another look at Sandro. "If you smile at her like you did before, I'm pretty sure she'll give you guys a full scholarship."

Sandro glanced toward the desk and Marlene abruptly began studying the schedule again. He grinned, all arrogance, and Jenna could see why he had such legendary success with women.

"Hey, sometimes the cowboy thing opens doors. If it gives me a discount for this insane notion of Paul's, I won't complain."

He turned that same smile on Jenna and she felt its power as her skin warmed. She backed away a few steps to avoid the heat. "I'll just get Paul started, then. Good luck with your cooking classes. We'll be done here at five."

"Jenna, wait." His voice was soft and he closed

the distance between them. He glanced at Paul, suddenly the worried older brother. "Take good care of Paul, okay? This is a totally foreign world for him."

"I will," she promised, touched by his concern. "But I don't think you need to worry. He looks pretty happy so far."

"That's what I'm afraid of."

"Sandro." Jenna put her hand on his and instantly regretted it. The strength of him scrambled her thoughts. She pulled her hand back and continued. "It's going to be okay. You did the right thing for him."

"I doubt it." A shadow of emotion crossed his face. "I'm not known for my good judgment, Jenna." He seemed to catch himself and pushed whatever dark feeling haunted him aside, because the humor came back. His defense, she suddenly realized. "But it's not like the kid gave me a lot of choice. He hasn't shut up about taking your classes since you busted some moves in Jack's kitchen. Thanks for that, by the way."

"You're welcome," Jenna said, ignoring the teasing sarcasm. She nodded to where her other students were starting to file in, dropping their duffel bags by the row of chairs along the wall, some already seated, changing their shoes. "And I've got to go bust a few more now."

"And I've got to go tame Marge Simpson at the desk."

"Be nice!" But she couldn't help laughing. "I happen to love her hair! And if you say something nice to her about it, I'm sure you'll make her day."

"Your faith in me is touching."

The conversation was obviously over, but Jenna was having a hard time looking away. Sandro's smile gave warmth to the masculine lines of his face. His eyes lingered on her, too.

Neither of them said anything. Then Sandro seemed to re-collect himself, because he glanced around, breaking whatever strange spell had held them so still. "Thanks again for helping Paul." He turned to go. "See you later, Jenna."

"See you," Jenna somehow managed to mumble. There were ripples of something on the bare skin of her arms. Goose bumps? She'd go get her sweater before class.

Sandro walked toward the lobby, and Jenna watched him go. His cowboy boots clicked on the polished wood floor. With his jeans, tight T-shirt and a leather jacket slung over his shoulder, he looked out of place in the ballroom, clearly from another world. Which he was, she reminded herself, turning back toward Paul. But by praising her to Marlene today, he might also have been her guardian angel.

She shot a look over to the row of chairs where the kids were sitting, half expecting her students to be staring at her. How could they not have noticed the way Sandro had left her heart pounding at the thought of seeing him again after class? But the teenagers were oblivious, absorbed in gossip and laughter as they changed.

Only Paul seemed to have noticed. He was standing close by with a grin on his face. "I never thought he'd come around and let me do this, Jenna. Thanks for sticking up for me back in Benson."

She loved this kid. If his family ended up rejecting him for his dancing, she'd adopt him. He was that cool. She grinned back. "My pleasure. Glad you could come. Was it worth pestering your brother for?"

"It's awesome."

And he seemed to mean it. Jenna studied him for a moment. He looked like a young Sandro, with curly dark hair and those same dark eyes. He was going to have the girls in her class vying to be his partner for sure. Just like his older brother had big girls vying for him all the time, she reminded herself, glancing over to where Sandro was leaning on the front desk, talking to Marlene as if she were the only woman in the room. "Well," she said brightly, "our first class will start in a few minutes. It's all Latin dances today. Tomorrow is fox-trot and waltz. It's going to be a lot to learn. Are you ready, Paul?" She glanced down and saw the cowboy boots on his feet. "Oops! Let's go see if we can find you some shoes."

Paul flushed and she felt horrible for embarrassing him. "No, Paul, how would you know? And even if you did, where would you shop? Come on. It'll take no time at all to get you ready."

She led him over to the small shopping area in one of the alcoves under the old arches to help him pick out his dancing shoes.

CHAPTER SIX

HIS BABY BROTHER was surrounded by girls. Lots of them. They were leaning in to hear whatever joke Paul was telling, nudging each other subtly out of the way to be the one closest, giggling and tossing their hair at him.

For a moment Sandro felt sheer panic. What had he done? All these teenage girls spent so much time dancing that they probably rarely saw a boy. This was a bad idea. They'd boost his ego way too high.

Sandro winced as guilt stabbed at him. He'd wanted to spare his little brother the mistakes he'd made. Instead he'd led him straight into the same type of situation that had been a part of his own downfall. Big fish in a small pond. Inflated ego. So many women interested that he forgot how to respect or value them.

His fists curled and Sandro willed himself to stay calm. He took a few breaths and waited, but the flirting went on and Paul didn't see him. He couldn't stand it a second more. He took the first step of a run that was going to end up with him hauling his little brother out of the damn ballroom by the ear and throwing him in the truck bound for Benson. Then he felt a light touch on his arm. Jenna. Looking up at him with those huge blue eyes. Her porcelain skin glowing with exercise and happiness and calm.

"Are you okay?" she asked.

"You said you'd take care of him!" It came out as an accusation.

"I have! He had a great day." Her delicate brows drew together with concern. "What's bothering you?" She didn't say it but he could hear the *now* at the end of her question. She must think he was the most uptight person she'd ever met, but he couldn't help it. He had to do right by his brother.

"You call *this* taking care of him? Look at those girls hanging all over him. His ego is expanding as we speak."

Jenna looked over at Paul. "Really? I don't see ego. I see a kid who's happy, who spent the day doing what he loves most. With other kids who love the same thing."

"Other kids who happen to be girls."

"It's dance, Sandro. Face it, most of the people he takes class with will be girls."

"You don't get it, do you? This is how it all goes wrong! Thinking he's got it made. Thinking women come a dime a dozen."

Jenna turned and looked at him sternly. "Are you sure we're still talking about Paul?"

Sandro looked out the window of the ballroom at the busy evening street. She'd seen right through him once again. A family walked by on the sidewalk outside—a mother, a father and a couple teenage kids. He wondered, briefly, how they survived being parents. He wasn't even Paul's father and he felt sick with worry.

"It's his first day," Jenna said, softly now. "Let him enjoy the attention. Class was a challenge for him, since he doesn't know as much as everyone else yet. Let this moment help him gain his confidence."

The fear and shame that had coiled inside him started to unwind at the wisdom of her words. She really was like some kind of angel. In her pretty dress, with her hair radiating around her face in waves of red and gold, she reminded him a little of the good witch in the Oz movie. The one who showed up in the bubble. Except Jenna was way hotter.

"You're right. I just don't want it to mess him up. I really don't." He watched Paul take a girl's hand. He spun her around once, and she giggled. Sandro cringed.

Jenna remained standing next to him, watching Paul and her other students with a thoughtful look on her face. "What if we all went out for dinner tonight? To celebrate Paul's first class."

She turned to face him and for a moment he forgot her question and his worries. Her lipsticked mouth was full, so soft-looking, and serious now. Then she bit her lip and he saw that she was worried by his failure to answer.

"I'd like to, but I'm not sure I feel like celebrating tonight," he said.

"I can tell."

Sandro caught her light touch of sarcasm and he realized he'd been a jerk again, blaming her for Paul's actions.

"But what if I talk to him a bit at dinner?" Jenna continued. "I can make sure he understands what he needs to do if he really wants to become a professional dancer. That he can't let anything sidetrack him. Even my cute students."

He'd be an arsonist playing with fire if he spent more time with Jenna. But Sandro also knew there was no way he could handle Paul alone. He'd end up yelling at him and making it worse. And for whatever reason, Jenna calmed him. She helped him move away from his black-and-white way of looking at things and steered him into the much more reasonable gray. "Yes." It came out almost too firmly. Abrupt. "I'd like that. I'd like your help. I can't let him dance—and hang out with all these girls—if it's going to change him."

"If it makes you feel better, he did really well in class today. He may be playing catch-up with the other students, but I couldn't believe how fast he picked up the steps. Some of these kids have been dancing for years, with every kind of formal training, and he kept up with them for the most part. Paul's got a ton of natural talent, Sandro. You did the right thing, bringing him here."

Sandro looked back at his brother again. "I hope so. I really do." But he didn't feel hope. Just doubt and worry.

"So, dinner," Jenna said brightly, obviously trying to lighten his mood. "Where should we eat?"

He'd promised himself that seeing her at the ballroom would be a dose of reality, a way to forget about her. Instead he was going to have dinner with her. Maybe the reality was that he couldn't seem to stay away from her. "I was planning to head to a restaurant in the Mission District," he told her. "A guy I interned with in Spain opened it. Oliva."

"Oliva?" Jenna looked stunned. "Did you make reservations? I've heard you have to get your name in at least a week in advance."

"Gavin knows we're coming. He said to just show up whenever."

Jenna's eyes sparkled.

I put that there. I put that look in her eyes. Sandro wished he could see her look that happy every day. What was wrong with him? He gave himself a mental kick. This was about Paul—nothing else.

"I'm so excited to try Oliva!" Jenna exclaimed. "*And* to have a serious talk with Paul, of course."

She was teasing him and despite his worry, he liked it. "At least ten minutes of serious talking. Promise?" Sandro asked.

"Promised."

Her smile was so warm he just wanted to bask in it, like sunlight. Let the rays of her kindness reach into his dark corners.

"I've got my bike," she told him. "So I'll meet you both there?"

The image of Jenna flying through the streets of San Francisco on a bike went Technicolor in his imagination. He hoped she kept her teaching outfit on. He pictured the fancy dress she was wearing right now pushed over her knees, her high-heeled dancing shoes sparkling on the pedals, her hair streaming like fire behind her. It was a great vision.

"It's on Twenty-First Street. At Valencia," Jenna was saying. "Do you need directions?"

He shook his head. "I've got the map on my phone, thanks. Is half an hour enough time for you to get there?"

Jenna glanced at the clock on the wall. "Sure." She flashed him a smile different from her usual wide, warm one. Almost shy. "See you there." She walked over to the tables by the ballroom entrance and started chatting with parents who were waiting to pick up their kids.

It was just a dinner, he reminded himself. A dinner and a conversation because he needed her help with Paul. But he couldn't fool himself—a heart-to-heart with Paul was not the part of the evening that he was looking forward to. He wanted this time with her.

He watched as she said goodbye to the parents and crossed the dance floor, then disappeared into the staff dressing room. Yanking his unruly eyes away, he went to drag his little brother away from his teenage harem.

WHEN JENNA WALKED into the tiny dressing room, Nicole was there, running a brush through her long brown hair. She was surrounded by the typical detritus of a dance teacher—jazz shoes, a pair of strappy sandals, an enormous makeup bag half open and three different outfits laid out. She must have been deciding what to wear for her private lessons this evening.

"Marlene has me teaching my own salsa class now," Nicole informed her without even saying hello. "Thought you should hear it from me, you know, in case you felt concerned."

"Concerned?" Jenna prompted.

"Well, you know, it must be hard, getting older and everything, with new dancers like me breathing down your neck."

Oh, jeez, really? This was where Nicole was taking it? "Nicole, one of the things that's great about being older is you don't feel quite as competitive as when you're young. You feel more secure in who you are and what you do. It was me who suggested to Marlene that you get your own class."

Nicole's face, stunned into silence, was incredibly satisfying. It was sad that in the competitive atmosphere of the Golden Gate Ballroom, an act of kindness or a gesture of support could leave someone speechless.

"Really? How come?" Nicole blurted, pursing her lips in consternation. She seemed truly unable to comprehend why someone would do a good deed for another.

"Because you want it so much, Nicole. You want success. And that's going to take you a long way."

Still not understanding altruism, Nicole shook her head and changed the subject. "I heard you and Brent are getting ready for your next competition."

"Yeah, we're excited about our routine," Jenna said, reaching into her locker for her bag and street shoes.

"Well, give me a few years and the right partner and I'll give you a run for your money."

Jenna looked up to see if Nicole was joking, but there wasn't a glint of humor on her face. Just pure determination. "I'm sure you will," Jenna responded, suddenly feeling weary.

What Nicole said was true, really. In the world

of dance, or any sport, there was always someone right behind you, desperate to take your spot. Most of the time Jenna was able to ignore the competition and just focus on her own dancing, but lately the competitive spirit in the ballroom was beginning to wear on her. What would it be like, she often wondered, to work with people who were actually *hoping* for your success?

Jenna kicked off her dance shoes. She pulled on her jeans and laced up her black Converse sneakers. She quickly traded her dress for a T-shirt and wished she had brought better civilian clothes to work. Though this dinner with Sandro was most definitely not a date, she wouldn't mind looking a little more sexy—just to make sure he knew what he was missing.

Maybe this grunge look was for the best, though. This outfit radiated "I don't care what you think of me" and that was the message she needed to send tonight. Sandro might be able to melt her with one glance, but he was a player and she didn't want to play. End of story.

Remembering her promise to Marlene, Jenna forced herself to try one more time with Nicole. "If you'd like, I can give you my notes from our beginning salsa classes. And maybe we can get together and go over your plans together."

"Why?" Nicole gave her a searching look, obviously wondering what the catch was.

"Because you're new at this and I want to help," Jenna told her.

"Maybe." Nicole furrowed her perfectly plucked brows and pulled a lipstick from her bag, then flipped open a compact and applied the plum shade. "But I think I can do it on my own."

Jenna swung her tote over her shoulder. "Have a good evening, Nicole."

"See you," Nicole answered vaguely, without looking up.

Jenna pushed her way out the double doors of the ballroom, thankful for a break from dancing for a night. That conversation hadn't gone well, but at least she could tell Marlene she'd honestly tried to help Nicole.

She unlocked her bike, put her helmet on, and forced all her doubts about Nicole and the ballroom to be quiet. She pushed all her strange excitement at the prospect of dinner with Sandro back into the unruly corners of her mind. It was time to focus on one thing only—navigating the hazardous streets of San Francisco during rush hour.

Hefting the canvas messenger bag that served as her purse onto her back, she pushed off the sidewalk and pedaled between the traffic and the line of parked cars that bordered Brannan Street. Biking through San Francisco involved running a daily gauntlet of threats and today was no exception. Jenna swerved out of the way of a taxi that snuck up behind her on its silent hybrid engine. A pedestrian stepped out from between two parked cars and she skidded to a halt to avoid hitting him.

"Sorry," he muttered. She watched him cross the street, dodging cars and curses from irate drivers. At least her ride to and from work was never boring.

Jenna liked the idea of biking, though not always the reality. San Francisco was such a green city. It seemed as if everyone was involved in some sort of environmental activism. But between teaching and rehearsing, there wasn't a lot of time for Jenna to jump on the eco-friendly bandwagon. So biking to work was her small contribution. And it helped to keep her in shape when she taught all day and couldn't fit in a workout.

Sighing, she pushed off and started pedaling again, keeping a wary eye on the sidewalk for more unexpected pedestrians. She was watching so carefully that she didn't see the car change lanes toward her until its door was inches from her leg. "No!" she heard herself scream and she jerked the bike away from the car.

The sedan hit her back wheel instead of her leg and sent her careening sideways into a parked delivery truck. Jenna threw her arm up to protect her face. The impact pushed her arm down, but at least she turned and hit the truck with her shoulder instead. Then her head smacked into the metal with a resounding thump to her helmet, but as she went down, she knew that somehow she was going to be okay. Then it was asphalt grating on hands and knees as she sprawled forward, her bike landing awkwardly on top of her.

Chaos ensued as Jenna lay facedown, trying to calm her racing heart and give thanks to the universe that she was still alive. Her shoulder pulsed and her cuts stung, but that was the extent of her injuries as far as she could tell. Footsteps skidded to a halt by her head and she felt someone lift the bike off her, asking if she was all right.

Another voice interrupted. "Here, let me. I know her."

She looked up and saw people crowding around and Sandro kneeling over, tousled hair haloing his face, his normally olive skin pale, his expression contorted with worry. "Jenna, are you all right? I saw you go down. Help's on the way. Where are you hurt?"

Jenna closed her eyes for a moment. It was ungrateful to curse her luck when she'd just escaped what could have been a horrific accident, but it did seem a little unfair that Sandro was witnessing one of her least graceful moments. But he sounded so traumatized that she looked up again to reassure him.

"I'm okay," she said. "I don't know how, but I am."

"Can you sit up?" he asked. He helped her as she

stiffly pushed herself away from the pavement. She turned over to sit on the asphalt, arched her back to stretch a little, felt her muscles coming back to life. "Who hit me?" she asked.

Sandro's eyes darkened in anger. "The guy took off. We were driving right behind him. Paul jumped out of the truck and ran after him to try to get a license plate number." Sandro's hands came up and gently took hers, turning them over carefully to inspect her torn palms. "Jenna," he said hoarsely, looking from the scrapes to her face. "I'm so glad you're okay."

She was stunned by the raw relief in his expression. This was a very different man than the one she'd met in Benson *and* the one who'd charmed Marlene so easily today.

Sirens that had been background noise grew suddenly louder. Cars pulled away and spectators left as the police pulled up, followed by an ambulance. Sandro moved back so the paramedics could look her over. They asked her question after question and she assured them over and over that she was fine. Finally, they agreed with her and cleaned her cuts and put bandages over them. Then a couple of police officers sat down next to her on the curb and interviewed her about what had happened.

Paul came back without the license plate number, much to Sandro's very vocal frustration, which included a wish that he'd gone after the driver himself and throttled him with his own two hands. Then the police had to explain to Sandro why that would have been a very bad idea. Once they were finished, and everyone left, it was just Jenna, Paul and Sandro, sitting on the sidewalk, leaning against the wall of an old brick warehouse, with Jenna's mangled bike by their side.

Jenna stared at the traffic going by on the street. The evening fog was blowing in and tiny droplets of water misted her face. She ached, but she was so glad to be here to feel the cool air.

Sandro had his head tipped back against the wall, his eyes closed. Jenna nudged him just a little with her elbow. "You know, you and your brother seem to have this thing for coming to my rescue."

Sandro opened his eyes and looked down at her. "I wasn't going to say anything, but now that you mention it, I think maybe *you* should be buying *us* dinner tonight."

Laughing made Jenna's shoulder hurt but she didn't care. She was sitting here, alive, and aches and pains were just more evidence of that.

Sandro put his arm carefully around her and Jenna leaned into him without thinking. She could feel the strength of him underneath his leather jacket, and she nestled just a little closer. She felt surprisingly good—being close to Sandro, with Paul nearby, having just cheated disaster. Then the image of herself facedown and tangled in her bike invaded her peace and reawakened all the fear and adrenaline of the accident. She took a long, shaky breath.

With his free hand, Sandro reached into his coat pocket and handed her a paper bag. "Drink this."

Jenna opened it. There was a fifth of Jack Daniel's inside. "Where'd you get it?" She knew Sandro was supposed to be a bit of a bad boy, but did he really carry whiskey?

"Bob."

"Who?" Jenna tried to remember if she had a student by that name.

"Bob. The homeless guy you give money to every day? He came by when you were with the paramedics. I almost had to hold him back, he was so worried about you. He couldn't stick around—he was on his way to get in line for a shelter—but he told me to give you this."

"Wow." Jenna shook her head, thinking about the ragged man who usually sat on the steps of an empty building a few doors down from the ballroom. "I'm kind of honored, in a weird way. But, no offense to Bob, I'm not sure I want—"

"I checked it." Sandro grinned. "It's unopened. Guess he'd just bought it."

Jenna sighed. "Well, now I know where all my spare change has been going." She cracked the label, unscrewed the cap and took a sip. The fiery taste was just what she hadn't known she needed. She took another. "Not quite how I pictured this evening," she said, motioning to their surroundings, the gray of the pavement blending with the fog as the sky darkened.

Paul laughed. "I think sitting here makes me a real city kid. Though I'm trying not to think about the nasty stuff on this sidewalk."

Sandro laughed. "For a kid who shovels manure every day, I'm not sure what you're worried about."

Jenna knew they really should get up off the grimy sidewalk, but that would mean getting out from under Sandro's arm and she liked it there. But drinking out of a paper bag on a filthy sidewalk wasn't really a good example for Paul.

"Maybe it *is* time to get moving," she gasped as the whiskey burned its way down her throat. She offered the bottle to Sandro. He didn't take a drink, just screwed the top on and tucked it back into his jacket pocket. "San Francisco doesn't usually enforce its loitering laws, but this hasn't exactly been my lucky night."

"That could change," Sandro murmured.

"Dude!" Paul admonished.

Jenna felt her cheeks get hot and glanced up at Sandro in alarm.

"That is *not* what I meant." Sandro was looking down at her now and his skin was flushed. He was embarrassed—something Jenna hadn't thought possible. And it was endearing. "What I meant is that we can still go to Oliva and get amazing food. *If* you're still up for it?"

Jenna tried to get some control over her thoughts, which kept drifting to the other meaning of *lucky night*. "Are you kidding? Dinner at Oliva? Meeting the chef? It would take more than getting up close and personal with the pavement to keep me away."

The smile Sandro gave her should have required a license. Crashing into a delivery truck might have been worth it just to be with him like this. He leaned down and for a moment Jenna thought he was going to kiss her. It worried her how much she wanted him to. Instead he looked at her, eyes serious and still, and brushed her cheek with the knuckles of one hand.

"I'm glad you're okay." He paused, studying her face, and Jenna reminded herself to breathe. His voice went quiet, almost to a whisper. "You're beautiful, you know."

Jenna was locked into place by his words and the feather touch of his hand, gently tucking a piece of her unruly hair behind her ear.

Sandro suddenly looked as stunned as she felt. As if his own words had only just sunk in. He removed his arm, pushed himself off the wall and stood. Then held out a hand to help her clamber to her feet.

"Let's get your bike loaded up. And then we're going to eat at Oliva, bandages and all."

CHAPTER SEVEN

IT WAS FUN to be a VIP. One word from Sandro, and the hostess at Oliva promptly marched them past the waiting crowds, through the packed restaurant and out onto a tiny back patio. Paved in mossy brick, with the jasmine climbing up the walls giving off a sweet smell, the patio at Oliva lived up to its mythical reputation.

"This is magical!" Jenna exclaimed. "How in the world did you get the patio?"

"Connections, baby, connections." A voice she didn't recognize answered for Sandro. Jenna turned toward it in time to see a small stocky man striding out of the building. "Salazar!" He yelled it as if it were a battle cry and launched himself at Sandro. He landed with his arms around the larger man's shoulders, laughing with a wild, high-pitched cackle.

He jumped back down, punched Sandro in the shoulder and turned to Jenna. "You must be Sandro's *gorgeous* date! What the hell is a goddess like you doing with this loser?" He had pale blue eyes so wide-open they almost bulged. They made him look amazed and frantic all at once. Light brown hair stood up on end above his round face. With the heat lamp behind him it looked like a halo, but one look at his lived-in face and it was clear he was no angel. "I'm Gavin. Gavin Lawton. Welcome to my restaurant."

Wild. Jenna couldn't think of any other adjective to describe the energy that radiated off of Sandro's friend and Oliva's famous chef. Gavin shook her hand vigorously, looked her up and down appreciatively and then was on to Paul.

"Baby Sandro!" He pulled Paul into a bear hug and gave him what was apparently his signature sock on the shoulder. Jenna was glad she'd been spared that particular sign of affection. Paul managed to keep his feet and shook Gavin's hand, laughing. How could you not laugh? Gavin was an elf on steroids—tiny, bulky, moving everywhere at once.

He clapped his short fingers together. "Sit down!" He pulled out a chair for Jenna, sat down next to her and then turned to Sandro. "It's amazing to see you again, my old friend. Now, are you ordering? Or trusting me to send you out some of the best of my recent creations?"

"We may regret it, if some of your creations are as creative as they used to be." Sandro grinned at his friend. "What do you think?" he said to Jenna and Paul. "Should we try your luck with whatever Gavin here decides to feed us?"

"You sure I can't just get a burger?" Paul asked, obviously bent on tormenting his older brother.

"Say that word here again, Baby Sandro, and I'll have you back in the kitchen scrubbing pots," Gavin told him with a delighted grin.

"Right. No burgers. Got it." Paul said, shaking his head. "Sheesh. You're just like my brother."

"I will take that as a compliment. Your big brother is one of the finest cooks I've ever come across. It was a pleasure to train with him and even more of a pleasure to steal his ideas."

Sandro laughed at that. "Back atcha."

Gavin ran his fingers through his hair, staring at the wall somewhere beyond Paul's head, obviously deep in thought. "I've got it!" he announced after a few moments. "You, my friends, are in for the meal of a lifetime." He bounced out of his seat and turned to the waiter who was standing nearby. "Raul? Olives and bread, please? And…" his brow wrinkled in concentration "…a rich red, I think, to accompany this feast." He clapped his small plump hand on Sandro's shoulder. "I've got a new one I want you to try. A blend of Monastrell and Syrah." He glanced at Jenna and Paul. "Grapes," he clarified. "You'll love it."

"I'm sure I will," Paul enthused.

"Not you, bro." Sandro glared at him. "A Coke for this guy," he told Raul.

"You can't serve that swill with this dinner." Gavin's hands went to his hips.

"Gavin, you want him to have wine? Even watered down, it could cost you your license. You're in America now."

"Yes. I know." Gavin shook his head in evident regret. "And the liquor laws are idiotic and people's palates appalling. But the money's good." With that he turned on his heel and left the patio in a flurry, hustling Raul inside, demanding that the wine, the hideous Coke, the olives all be brought to the table immediately. He reminded Jenna of a pirate captain rallying his motley crew. All he needed was a peg leg and an eye patch.

There was a silence on the patio after he left, a calm after the storm that was Gavin.

"Wow," Jenna finally said. "He's something else. You worked with him?"

Sandro smiled ruefully. "And studied with him and lived with him for a year in Spain while we were apprenticing. It was never boring."

"I bet. The guy has the energy of about ten people."

"One of the reasons this place is so successful, I'm sure." Sandro looked around at the patio. "I want a patio like this at my place. What do you think, Paul? That lot behind the building... Want to help me build a patio there?"

Paul sighed. "Not really, but you probably don't care."

Sandro laughed. "You're right, bro. I don't. I own you now that I'm helping you get these dance lessons. You should be grateful. Building my patio will teach you some real life skills to fall back on."

"Hey!" Jenna interjected. "Dance is a real life skill!"

Sandro raised an eyebrow. "Really?"

"I have a good job! I get paid decently!" Prickles of irritation surprised her.

"And if the ballroom-dance fad fades?" There was real concern on Sandro's face and Jenna remembered that this was all about Paul's future. It wasn't about her.

"It won't fade that much. And if it does, I'll teach other types of dance, or exercise. It's not much different than cooking. Restaurants come and go."

"But people always need food," Sandro said emphatically. "They don't *need* dance."

"People have always needed dance...."

Raul interrupted their brewing argument with the wine, olives, salad and appetizers. The liver pâté wasn't really Jenna's thing, but there was a white-bean cream that was insanely delicious and between them she and Sandro wiped the dish clean with their bread. The salad greens were so fresh that their delicate flavor held its own with the tangy dressing. And just when she didn't think she could eat more, Raul brought out pork with smoked pumpkin risotto and it smelled too good to pass up.

After a few unforgettable bites, she turned to Paul. It was time to keep her promise to Sandro and earn her supper. "So what did you think of class today?"

Despite his plea for a hamburger, Paul had been putting away large amounts of the gourmet meal with a blissful expression on his face. At the mention of class, his expression darkened. "Honestly? It was a lot harder than I imagined it would be. I can't believe how good everyone else is. They know exactly what you mean practically before you're done saying it."

"Only because most of them have been in dance classes since they were tiny, Paul," she assured him. "Give it a few weeks of hard work and you'll be on your way to catching up."

He sighed and took a sip of his soda. "Do you think it's just too late? Maybe I've already missed my chance."

Jenna had no idea he'd felt so overwhelmed. "Look, with any new skill, there's a language, a vocabulary that you have to master. As long as you still love dancing, everything else will fall into place."

"On the other hand," Sandro interjected, "we could always find you another hobby. Basketball maybe?"

Jenna glowered at him. "Let Paul figure out what he wants, Sandro." One day of working with Paul had shown her more raw talent, more innate timing and grace, than she'd seen in any other student she'd taught. If Paul quit now, it would be an enormous waste of that potential. She wanted to help him become the dancer he was so clearly meant to be.

And maybe she had a little self-interest in this. Training a student like Paul would be a feather in her cap, and she could use all the feathers she could get if she was going to open her own dance studio.

She'd coach Paul a little more during class tomorrow to help him through this overwhelmed stage. And maybe she needed to think of ways to keep his spirits up. Jenna knew all too well how the everyday reality of being a dancer could tarnish your dreams. An idea struck.

"Next Saturday night, Brent and I are competing just south of here, at one of the big hotels by the airport. It's our biggest competition of the year. Maybe you two could come?"

"Really? That would be awesome!" Paul said. "Sandro, can we go?"

"I'll get you the tickets. I could use a cheering section." Jenna knew seeing the professional dancers would help Paul stay excited about dance. Seeing her peers kept *her* inspired.

Sandro glanced at her, sending a clear message that this wasn't the conversation he'd hoped to be having. "We'll see. It will depend on you, Paul. If you keep your focus on your dancing, where it belongs, I'll take you."

Paul paused, a forkful of risotto in midair. "What

do you mean?" He looked at Jenna. "Did I mess up somehow?"

Jenna glared at Sandro. She didn't think the stern, scolding approach would help Paul right now. "No, you didn't do anything wrong!" She smiled at her student. "You did great. I think your brother's just a little worried about the social side of things in dance class."

"Oh, you mean the girls?" Paul flushed and took a sip of his Coke. "Yeah, I figured you'd be upset about that, San."

"You're here to dance. Jenna has been great about letting you take this class. I'm risking our family's wrath to get you here. So stay focused on the dance, not the girls." Sandro's voice was firm and Jenna could suddenly picture him as a dad. He'd be a good one.

Paul rolled his eyes but his expression was good-humored. "Right, bro. Ignore the girls. Got it." Then he sobered and looked at Jenna. "I promise I won't let them distract me. I really appreciate this opportunity and I won't let you down."

"I know you won't," Jenna said, smiling gently at him. He was such a sweetie. Then she looked at Sandro and put a little steel in her expression. "And your brother knows it, too, doesn't he?"

"Yes. He does," Sandro conceded, smiling at her ruefully. "But he'll be watching carefully, just in case."

Paul grinned at him. "Seriously, Sandro, you can relax. The girls are nice, but I'm here for the dancing. I have my goals and nothing's going to mess with that."

"You're a smart kid," Jenna told him. She should borrow some of his wisdom. Here she was, with all *her* goals finally attainable. A possibility of winning another championship and almost enough money saved for her own dance studio. But instead of keeping her eyes on her dreams, she was so distracted by Sandro that her mind kept wandering to the way it had felt to lean on him after the bike crash and the way he'd touched her and told her she was beautiful.

He was bad news. Jack had warned her about him—she needed to listen to that warning. But looking at Sandro right now, so protective of his kid brother, a complicated mix of love and concern on his face... A huge part of her wanted to get to know this dark, difficult and kind man, even if it made no sense, even if it put her heart at risk again.

SHE WAS A LOT tougher than he would have guessed. Sandro watched Jenna take another sip of her wine, set her glass down and sit up straight, stretching her back out just a little. She'd taken a horrible fall on her bike and her hands and elbows were peppered with bandages, but she'd still come to dinner. And she was a great dinner companion. Funny and upbeat, *and* he liked the way she stood up for Paul, even if he didn't always agree with her opinions.

He took a sip of wine, then slid the glass away. The rich berry taste had hints of pepper and clove. It was a delicious combination and he savored it. A few sips was all he allowed himself anymore. A taste, just to get to know the wine, absorb its character and file it away for future reference. He wanted to be knowledgeable of wine—he was determined to serve the best of it in his restaurant— but he drank almost no alcohol anymore. It was amazing what waking up behind a Dumpster in the chill of a New York dawn could do to your partying instincts. In his case, it had pretty much obliterated them.

Jenna was watching him when he looked back over at her. Her eyes were the brightest blue he'd ever seen. The corners creased as she smiled at him a little tentatively. When she laughed, her nose crinkled and a dimple appeared in her cheek. If he were a funnier guy, he'd make her laugh all the time just so he could watch the way it transformed her face.

What was he thinking? He turned to the mundane to hide his confusion. "Are you feeling okay, Jenna? Do you still hurt?" he asked. The weird thing was, he really wanted to know. What was it about her that made him so protective? He'd never felt that way about a woman before. Quite the opposite. In his haze of ego at being one of New York's most sought-after chefs, he'd prided himself on being the guy women had to watch out for—wild, unpredictable, always up for a good time. Women seemed to find it sexy, always seeking out his company—and he'd been happy to oblige. "We can take you to the doctor if you need it."

He knew he shouldn't, especially with his brother watching, but for the second time that night he couldn't resist touching her. He reached over and took her hand in his own. Her eyes widened and he could feel her pulse jump.

"I'm fine," she said weakly. "I don't think I need a doctor."

"Let me know if you start to feel different." He wanted to do something for her, to take her home and tuck her beneath some blankets. Give her tea and painkillers and make every bruise on her body go away. Which was bizarre because normally his fantasies about women didn't involve tea and blankets.

"I will." She pulled her hand gently out of his. He let her go with reluctance, feeling the cool and empty night air on his palm after she'd gone. He picked up his water for something to do and took a gulp.

There was a small tornado of movement behind him and he turned to watch Gavin's approach. Behind him was a waiter—not Raul this time. Poor Raul was probably hiding after his boss's earlier tirade. This unlucky employee was pulling a cart over the rough bricks of the patio, trying not to tip the coffeepot, the pyramid of cups or the array of desserts that looked like individual works of art. Chocolate towers, tiny tarts with glistening fruit in perfect patterns, cups of what looked to be chocolate mousse all teetered precariously.

"Sweets for the sweet lady?" Gavin asked, gleefully rubbing his hands together. "Sandro, I'm going to steal this beautiful woman away from you. After falling in love with my brandied chocolate mousse, she'll never want to leave my side."

Sandro ignored the stab of jealousy caused by his friend's words and instead leaned back and pasted a relaxed smile on his face, making it clear that Gavin's threat didn't mean a thing. "Good luck trying. She's not really mine, so stealing's not necessary. But I happen to know that she's a dancer and doesn't eat a whole lot of dessert. So if you want to win her over, you might have to change your tactics."

"A dancer?" Gavin grinned at Jenna in pure delight. "And I didn't think it was possible for you to be more perfect. Sandro, I'm in love."

It was time to change the subject. Jenna wasn't his, but the more he listened to Gavin's flirting, the more he wished she were, and that he really *did* have the right to tell Gavin to back off. "You've come into your own here, my friend. You should be truly proud of this place." The envy was back but different. Gavin had what he wanted, and he was holding on to it, not screwing it up as Sandro had, with a career-killing cocktail of drugs, alcohol and sex.

The mixture of regret and shame that twisted inside of him was familiar—Sandro had lived with it for almost a year. He reminded himself that Gavin was just ahead of him a little. His restaurant might not be Gavin's Oliva, the hippest place in a big city, but it was going to be a solid, welcoming place in Benson. And Benson was where he belonged. It was a good compromise. It was a safe place to rebuild his career and reputation.

"Thank you." Gavin's words jolted Sandro out of his thoughts. "It is a pain in my ass twenty-four hours a day..."

"But you love it." Sandro finished Gavin's sentence for him. It was easy to. He knew the feeling well.

Gavin sat down at the table in between Jenna and Paul, facing his old friend. "I have put my assistant in charge of the kitchen with the understanding that if he screws up in the next fifteen minutes, while I sit here and have coffee with my friends, he will be out on his ass. Sandro, you have twelve minutes left to tell me how the hell you ended up back in California and how you found the gorgeous Jenna and managed to talk her into eating a meal with your sorry self."

"We met in my hometown, through friends."

Gavin looked genuinely surprised. "That sounds pretty tame for the Sandro I knew before. No late-night bars? No secret rendezvous in the walk-in fridge?"

He never should have brought Jenna and Paul here tonight. He should have known Gavin would want to talk about the past. "People change, Gavin," he countered.

Gavin laughed. "Sure they do." He gave Sandro an exaggerated wink meant for all to see. "Jenna, did Sandro ever tell you about the night we got chased out of a village in Spain?"

"No," Jenna answered. "Sandro hasn't told me much about himself." She glanced at him briefly and Sandro wondered what she already knew. Jack might have said something.

"Well, I'll tell you, then."

"Gavin!" Sandro interrupted. "Let's spare Jenna the sordid misadventures of our youth." He didn't want to revisit any of it ever again.

"Oh, no." Jenna was smiling now. "You heard all kinds of embarrassing things about me at Samantha and Jack's house. Now it's your turn to provide the entertainment."

"Trust me, it's not entertaining." Sandro took a

gulp of the coffee, hoping the warmth would settle the waves of mixed emotions inside him.

"I beg to differ, my friend." Gavin grinned and leaned back in his chair, sipping some coffee and settling into his tale. "Sandro and I were apprenticed at one of the finest restaurants in Spain. It was in the Basque region, because Sandro here has always had this crazy idea of getting back to his roots."

"It's not crazy." Sandro had to defend himself a little. "And they've got some of the best restaurants in the world there, in case you missed that somehow."

"Okay, fine, the food is amazing. Insane. All this nouvelle cuisine, you know. They were some of the first to serve food that looks like some kind of sculpture. Sauces made from fresh ingredients all pureed together. That kind of thing. And every other building has a pintxo bar—"

"A what?" Paul asked.

"It's like tapas." At Paul's blank look Gavin put his head in his hands in mock despair. "Sandro, have you taught this boy nothing? Tapas, Baby Sandro? Delicious food from Spain served in small portions meant to be sampled and savored?" Gavin took another sip of his coffee. "But I digress. So we're living in this city, San Sebastián, working our tails off in this fabulous restaurant, and one day

Sandro goes outside on his break and spots a man coming in to eat with his two beautiful daughters."

Sandro interrupted his friend. "Do you really have to tell this, Gavin? My little brother is here."

Gavin laughed and reached over to deliver his signature punch to Sandro's shoulder. "You bet I do, amigo." He turned to Paul. "Listen and learn, Baby Sandro."

Sandro groaned into his hands. "Gavin!" he admonished one last time. The last thing he needed was for Paul to hear this pathetic tale. Especially when he'd just lectured him about staying away from girls.

The animated chef gave a grin of pure glee. "So anyway, after this family was done eating, Sandro here sneaks out of the kitchen and follows them down the street. And he overhears that they live in this village just a few miles out of town."

"So basically, he's a stalker," Jenna interjected.

She was still smiling but Sandro could see that the sparkle had faded from her eyes. Well, maybe it was best for her to know the truth about him. He'd hoped spending time with her would be the dose of reality he'd need to forget her, but it was clear that the more time he spent with her, the more he wanted her. So maybe this needed to happen. *She'd* get a dose of reality instead and want nothing more to do with him. In the long run, they'd both be better off for it.

Oblivious to the havoc he was creating among his listeners, Gavin went on. "The next day we had some time off, so Sandro drags me to this tiny village and makes me wait around in the one café in the village square until finally these girls walk by. And then Lady-Killer here starts chatting them up in his bad Spanish. Somehow he pulls it off, and they sit down and we order more drinks and the future is looking pretty bright.

"But I guess the girls' father got wind of what was going on. The next thing I know, he's by our table with a couple of his buddies, and they're waving these massive scythes at us and yelling all kinds of words that I won't repeat in front of such a lovely lady. So we jumped up and hightailed it out of the village with these scythe-wielding farmers chasing us!"

"Why did they chase you?" Jenna was grinning and Paul had dissolved into laughter.

"Well, it was a little hard to translate what they were yelling, since we were busy running for our lives, but apparently, Sandro here had already—" he glanced at Paul "—um…how should I put this… 'dated'…most of the girls in our town. He'd built up quite a reputation in the area, and these gentlemen weren't about to let him expand his territory into their village."

"Don't listen to him." Sandro's voice felt strained

with embarrassment. "Gavin, your ability to spin a yarn is as masterful as always."

"And you're worried because I talked to a few girls after class today?" Paul asked indignantly.

"Learn from my mistakes, grasshopper." Sandro put this elbows on the table and rested his forehead in his hands. "My life is your cautionary tale."

"Evidently," Jenna said dryly.

"Well, I can see a few scythe-wielding farmers haven't slowed you down any," Gavin assured him. "You must still have the legendary Sandro mojo if you've managed to woo fair Jenna here."

Jenna was blushing now. "Gavin, I think you've got the wrong idea."

Paul started laughing. "Bro, there's a lot I don't know about you."

"There's no mojo. And no legends," Sandro said. This was going from bad to worse.

"No legends? You are asking me to sit here with a captive audience and refrain from telling any more stories of the infamous Sandro Salazar? Not even the one with the *New York Times* restaurant critic?" He turned to Jenna and Paul with a salacious wink. "Rumor has it she got a chance to *review* a lot more than just his food!"

"Okay, buddy." Sandro put a hand on Gavin's arm, trying to get his friend to be serious. "We've got some underage folks at the table. It's past time to change the topic." He tried to keep his voice light but anger was bubbling in his blood. Not at Gavin but at himself. He should never have brought Paul and Jenna here, where they would be exposed to his sordid past. "So, new subject. Tell me how you managed to get your hands on such a piece of prime real estate for this joint you have here."

Gavin laughed. "Let's just say the landlady is a special friend." Then he sobered. "But seriously, Sandro, I need a wingman here. I had no idea when I opened this place how crazy San Franciscans are for good food. We're swamped every night and I'm tired. Any chance I can talk you into joining me?"

Out of the corner of his eye, Sandro saw Jenna look at him sharply. He wondered what she was thinking. Would she want him here in the city? She'd want Paul here—that much was obvious. But after the stuff she'd heard about him tonight, she'd most likely prefer he keep his distance. Which was fine because cities like this were off-limits to him. He'd already proved once that he couldn't handle it.

Maybe Gavin had done him a favor tonight by bringing out some bits of his wild past and putting them on display. No way was he going to regress to that person he'd been. "Thanks for the ask, Gavin, but I'm done with city life. I'm just here teaching a few classes, building my savings. Then I'm opening a place in my hometown."

"What? Tell me you're not going to go serve up a bunch of bland food to a handful of Basque sheep herders."

Sandro laughed. Gavin had a way of getting right to the heart of things. "I like to think times have changed, even in Benson. I'll keep some of the old Basque ways. Some tables will be family style, and I'll stick with some of the most popular dishes. But I've been coming up with all kinds of recipes where I take traditional Basque dishes and transform them with modern influences."

"Nice." Gavin nodded thoughtfully. "I'm impressed. You think there's a market out there for food like that?"

"I do." He hoped there was.

"I wish you well, my friend. And if your gamble doesn't pay off, there's always a place for you here. As long as you keep your paws off my customers. The angry daddies of the Mission District have a lot more firepower than those guys who chased us in Spain."

JENNA DECIDED SHE was truly glad for Gavin's plain-spoken teasing. She needed this extra reminder about Sandro. She'd been so caught up by what had happened today. He'd helped her with Marlene, cared for her after the bike accident, brought her to this amazing meal and she'd gotten sucked in. So mesmerized that she'd forgotten Jack's warning.

Sandro was wild, he was a womanizer, and he was most definitely not for her.

She stood up, her chair scraping the bricks of the patio. "Gentleman, this has been amazing. I cannot thank you enough. But I think my *disaster via bicycle* is catching up to me."

"What? You are running out on this man?" Gavin turned to Sandro in mock dismay. "Have you lost your touch, my friend? I've never known you to…"

"Gavin!" The annoyance Jenna had noticed in Sandro's face earlier was in his voice now. "Jenna and I are not dating."

Of course they weren't. So why did the strange disappointment Jenna felt thicken her throat, making it impossible to speak? Logically, he was the last man she should be dating. But if he wasn't interested, why so much tenderness after the accident?

She knew the answer, thanks to Gavin. Thanks to Jack. Because this is what Sandro was like when it came to women. She pictured him as he'd been this morning, leaning over the desk at the ballroom, charming Marlene. He was a pro, and she knew it—and she'd fallen for it anyway.

Sandro stood up and took her hand again. "Jenna, let me take you back to your apartment."

The last thing she was going to do was let the "legendary Sandro mojo" anywhere near her apartment. Anything that *mojo* might inspire between them would mean nothing. His kindness meant nothing. The way his hand had felt wrapped around hers right now meant nothing. He'd just said so himself.

"I'll walk." She took back her hand. "The fresh air is just what I need." She thanked Gavin, and said good-night to Paul, with disappointment and recrimination roiling through her veins.

Outside the restaurant she hauled her poor bike out of the back of Sandro's truck. It was bent and wobbly but she could wheel it the four blocks home. The weight of it made the cuts on her hands sting. Her pride stung, too.

When she was out here in the cold air like this, she knew what she wanted—to stop spending her time and energy on men like Sandro Salazar. So why was it so hard to remember that goal every time she was with him?

She started down Valencia Street, regretting her choice of routes immediately. The sidewalks were crowded with people. They spilled out of bars and art galleries and stood in line for restaurants. She steered around the various groups carefully until she finally turned down Twenty-Fifth Street, leaving the chaos behind. It was never very safe to walk through her neighborhood at night, but tonight she didn't care. The damp wind, blowing her hair every which way, settling moisture onto her skin, was soothing. And after such a confusing evening, it was a relief just to be alone.

CHAPTER EIGHT

JENNA TURNED ON the iPod and walked quickly back onto the dance floor, where Brent was waiting. She put her left hand on his upper arm, the right poised with his in the air. They'd danced together so long that the frame they created felt like home. She gathered the muscles of her back and her abdomen and concentrated on feeling every one of Brent's movements, ready to respond in kind with her own.

The familiar notes of the upbeat music surrounded her and soon she and Brent were flowing across the floor, working as one body within the dance, all of her aches and pains from her bike accident forgotten as the hours of practice, the connection and chemistry between them worked their magic.

They came to the point where the first lift would be and stopped. Brent tipped her into a dip that wasn't a part of the choreography. Jenna gasped in surprise, and Brent looked down at her, an impish grin on his face, and kissed the tip of her nose. "Stop!" she told him, and he set her back on her feet.

"That's what you get for being so adorable in that

dress today." His compliment inspired only annoyance. He was wasting their time.

"Brent, you have to stop messing around! We have so much work to do—"

"Your cowboy is here."

So that was what the kiss had been about. He must have spotted Sandro while they danced and decided to mark his territory. Jenna resisted the impulse to kick her partner in the shins.

"He's not *my* cowboy," she growled at him. "Let's try it with the lift now." She couldn't help glancing over to the tables, where Sandro was helping Paul unpack his duffel bag.

"Don't be mad at me," Brent said.

Jenna looked back at him. His pale skin was flushed with exertion. "You do this every time!" she said.

"I do what?" Brent was staring at her, genuine confusion in his pale blue eyes.

This was what made their situation so strange. He didn't realize that he only chased her when he thought someone else was interested. He couldn't see the pattern in his actions. And she didn't have the energy to have the fight she knew they'd have if she tried to explain.

"Can we just focus on the dance, please?" She turned away and walked back to the iPod to start the song again. When she turned toward the dance floor, Brent was right there behind her. He took her hand and led her back to the middle of the floor. He never did that. One more display meant for Sandro's benefit. She glared at him and they got into hold so they could dance the opening of the routine again.

It went even better this time, despite their little spat. When it all came together like this, it was the most exhilarating feeling. Jenna spun across the floor away from Brent, relishing the way the steps fit the music. She paused, held her pose along with the elongated notes of the song, then turned, arms back, chest out, to look at Brent. They made eye contact and she went for the lift.

With running steps she crossed the floor, making sure her timing was just right. One final turn and with her arms raised, she launched herself at Brent, noticing only when she was already airborne that he wasn't looking at her anymore—he was staring at Sandro.

Jenna gasped and Brent turned and tried to catch her. It was too late. He was able to get one arm under her leg so he broke her fall a bit, but most of her slammed into the floor. The shoulder she'd hurt the night before flared with pain as she landed hard.

Brent was kneeling by her side within seconds. "Jenna? Jenna, are you okay? I'm so sorry! That was my fault."

Jenna put her head up warily. As far as she could tell, nothing was permanently damaged, but a lot of things hurt. Again. "What happened?" she asked. "How did you drop me?"

Brent didn't answer, just looked over her head with a worried expression spreading across his features.

Jenna craned her neck to see behind her, trying to figure out what had caught his eye. Sandro was standing right there.

"What the hell do you think you're doing?" Sandro's voice was low but it carried perfectly, the words riding an audible wave of fury. He was towering over them, fists clenched, mouth a grim line. "Why the hell were you looking at me instead of Jenna?"

"Dude…" Brent started.

"Sandro." Jenna turned all the way around, wincing and stiff. She looked directly up at him. "Falls happen. Brent made a mistake. It's okay."

He knelt down next to her. "It's not okay. He's your partner. He's supposed to take care of you, but instead of paying attention to the dance, he kept smirking at me."

"Brent?" Jenna asked. "What's going on?"

Brent sighed. "I'm sorry, Jen. I got distracted for a second. I messed up. I'll do better next time."

"Next time?" Sandro looked at Jenna. "Is there going to be a next time? He could have seriously hurt you!"

"Of course there will be a next time." Jenna tried

to check the rising annoyance. He was making a scene at her place of work. She didn't need to add to her problems with Marlene.

"Look, I don't know what any of this has to do with you," Brent told Sandro. "But Jenna's my partner and my friend, and I won't let it happen again." Brent looked visibly shaken and more remorseful than Jenna had ever seen him.

"Good," Sandro said. "You'd better not."

"Who are you to tell me what I should or shouldn't do?" Brent stood up. Sandro stood, as well. Both of them had hands curled into fists.

"Stop it." From the floor, Jenna glared at both of them. They were such idiots. Such boys. "Stop arguing."

They stopped. But from the way they were glowering at each other, Jenna knew they weren't finished. Sandro held out his hand to Jenna. "Can I help you up?"

Jenna didn't want help, but she also didn't want to fall over again in front of him. She grudgingly took hold of Sandro's hand and used his strength to support her while she stood carefully, feeling how her knees and ankles took her weight, thankful beyond measure that nothing seemed to be broken or strained.

This past twenty-four hours had been completely hazardous to her health. Was the universe trying to tell her something? The only message she could decipher was that gravity seemed to have gained new strength where she was concerned.

"I can't believe you're even doing a jump like that after last night," Sandro admonished.

"What happened last night?" Brent turned to Jenna. "What's he talking about?"

"You didn't tell him about the bike accident?" Sandro glared at both of them now. "Jenna, you should be taking it easy today, and as her partner, *you* should be helping her do it!"

"What bike accident?" Brent stared at her in alarm.

Jenna tried to fathom how she was the one who'd been dropped and hurt, yet both of them were now upset with *her.* "I didn't say anything because our competition is in a week and we're not ready. We need to practice."

"Not if you're hurt," Sandro interjected.

That was enough. Jenna rounded on Sandro. "You don't get to do this. You don't get to come in here and get involved in my life!"

"Not to split hairs, Jenna, but you sure got involved with mine, which is the only reason I'm here in this ballroom right now."

"You made the ultimate choice to bring Paul, not me." She didn't want to fight with him. Not here. She took a deep breath. "Sandro, I'm fine. I know you're trying to help but I don't need your assistance. Can you please let me work this out with Brent?"

"Only if this yahoo promises to be a little more careful!"

"Sandro..." Jenna started.

"Yahoo?" Brent burst into mocking laughter.

"Well, I'm sure I can come up with some other names that would suit you better."

Jenna saw Sandro's fist curl again. "Both of you, stop this now!" she commanded, keeping her voice low. Her students were arriving and a few of them were glancing over. It was time to restore order around here. "Stop telling me what I need! I am fine and neither of you has the right to tell me what to do. Brent, in the future, please focus on our routine, especially when there's a lift involved! Sandro, stop yelling at him! Now, is everybody satisfied?"

Both men looked chagrined. They nodded and if Jenna hadn't been so upset, she might have laughed at their sullen expressions.

"Then I need to go teach." She turned and headed toward the dressing room for a moment of privacy—and maybe an ice pack for her shoulder.

Sandro's voice was soft, but it carried. "Jenna, can I have a moment?"

She turned to face him. "To scold me some more? Or perhaps to threaten my dance partner again?"

He walked toward her slowly. "I'm sorry. I really am. I don't know what's going on with me." He ran a hand through his dark wavy hair. "I don't know why I feel so responsible for you." He looked away for a minute and Jenna waited, stilled by his words.

"I know you don't need me…. Maybe it's that old idea that once you save someone's life, you're always connected to them. Except I didn't save your life—I just helped peel you off the pavement…."

He looked so muddled that Jenna felt kind of sorry for him. Then inspiration struck. This morning was not going well, but maybe something good could come from it for Paul. "Well," she started, "if you're really sorry, then make it up to me. Bring Paul to my dance competition."

"Jenna." Exasperation flared in Sandro's eyes again. "I just don't think Paul needs—"

She cut him off. "Fine. I get it. If you're *not* really sorry—"

"I *am* sorry," Sandro interrupted. He sighed. "Okay, you win. I'll bring him." He glanced over to the DJ booth, where Brent was now chatting with Nicole. "And if that partner of yours drops you again, at least I'll be there to scoop up the pieces."

"Sandro, you are not allowed to make another scene!"

"But—"

"If you do," Jenna threatened, only partly joking, "I'll just find another dance competition and make you escort Paul to that one, too. And then I'll find another, and another…"

Sandro smiled reluctantly at her ridiculous threat. "Fine. No scenes. I promise." He glanced at Brent one last time. "Though it pains me to say it."

Jenna was impressed by her own brilliance. Paul would get to see a real, professional dance competition. She wanted him to stay inspired. He was too good to even entertain the thought of giving up. Jenna closed her ears to the voice in her head that was whispering about another benefit to all this: she'd get to see more of Sandro. She shouldn't want that, but she did.

"So I'll see you at the competition, then?" She had only a few minutes to clean up and get that ice pack before class started.

"Yes. And honestly? I'm looking forward to seeing you dance."

She studied his face, trying to ascertain whether he was sincere or just habitually charming. There was a tenderness in his eyes that startled her. Her stomach fluttered and her thoughts scrambled. "My class. I have to get to my class," she managed to blurt out.

"Right. Your class." There was a pause while he looked at her, and her cells and synapses melted into something about the same consistency as a roast marshmallow. "Well, take care of yourself today," Sandro finally said. He didn't move.

"You, too," she told him. "I mean, cooking and

all. Not that cooking's dangerous…but, I mean, don't get burned or anything." What was she saying?

He was still smiling at her and the look in his eyes had narrowed and darkened into the look she recognized from when they'd sat against the wall after her bike crash. The look that made her think he was about to kiss her. Feeling it on her skin and all the way inside her, Jenna thought she just might fall over. Again.

She started backing away. She was sure it seemed strange but she didn't care. She had to put some space between them.

"No burns," he said softly, and a flicker of worry eclipsed his smile. "I'll see you later, Jenna."

He turned and crossed the dance floor, stopping to give Paul a high five before he walked toward the exit. He paused at the front desk and said something to Marlene. She laughed delightedly and watched him as he pushed through the doors and out into the street. Jenna watched him go, too, her own dose of worry darkening her spirits for a moment. What had just happened? What was this thing between them?

Whatever it was, she had to put it out of her mind. She'd just seen how he'd completely derailed Marlene's concentration with one passing comment. She should take heed of Jack's warning and Gavin's stories, and not pretend Sandro would somehow be different with her.

Sandro was part of an old habit she had to break.

The charming-womanizing-guy habit. She'd promised herself she'd avoid men like this. She'd promised herself she'd keep her focus on work, where it belonged.

There was movement across the room. Her students were strolling onto the dance floor, stretching, chatting and laughing as they warmed up for class. All the worry dissipated. These kids were what mattered. They were her future, and the simple joy they brought was way more important than the confusing and off-limits complication that was Sandro Salazar.

CHAPTER NINE

NO BURNS, HE'D told her. But looking at Jenna as she walked onto the dance floor, Sandro knew he'd lied. She was the most beautiful thing he'd ever seen and he was burning. He'd thought of her all week, and now he was here watching her dance and realizing he was on fire and in trouble. How could he have thought that he'd somehow be immune to her lush frame and ethereal beauty? And now he'd have that costume haunting his dreams, as well.

She was wearing something tiny. It was like a bikini on top, except swaths of light, sparkly fabric wrapped around her arm and one shoulder. Below her lean, muscled torso was another piece of fabric, sort of a skirt but with all kinds of pieces missing in interesting places. Her lips were red and her eyes were dark with makeup, but she'd managed to avoid the clown look of so many of the other dancers.

The dance floor was enormous and crowded with many couples, all waiting for the competition to begin. Jenna's focus was entirely on Brent, and Sandro found himself wondering if they'd ever been a couple. They were gorgeous together, that was for sure. Brent's medium height and blond good looks were a perfect contrast for Jenna's petite feminine frame. Sandro watched as Brent bent down and said something into Jenna's ear and her wide smile illuminated her face. He could see it from across the cavernous room and jealousy crawled over him like some kind of skin disease. He wanted to be the one to put that smile there.

The dancers all seemed to know exactly when the music would start. A hush went over them, and each couple struck a pose, their focus laser-sharp on their partners. Then the music began, and on the first note each dancer swung into motion and followed the driving Latin rhythm perfectly, showcasing their elaborate steps as the judges wandered the perimeter watching them intently.

"This is awesome!" Paul whispered, and Sandro knew he'd just lost his last scrap of hope that maybe Paul would grow disillusioned with the world of ballroom dance. His little brother's face was lit up with excitement, his eyes were bright and he was taking it all in with an eagerness that Sandro couldn't fathom. Where Sandro saw layers of paint and weird spray tans, Paul evidently saw magic.

Suddenly Sandro pictured himself in a high-end cooking store, his hands on the perfect sauté pan. He remembered the way he used to feel when his food was cooked to perfection and plated into a work of art back in New York. Maybe he couldn't understand Paul's love of dance, but no one had understood Sandro's love of cooking, either. He'd had no encouragement to follow his dreams and it had made his journey difficult. Maybe Jenna was right. Maybe the best way to help Paul was to make sure he didn't have to pursue his dream all alone.

Then Jenna and Brent spun into view and that was the last coherent thought Sandro had until the song was over. Her dancing was exquisite. She was so light on her feet she looked as though she barely touched the ground. Her legs lengthened into elaborate lines, her arms shifted smoothly, and the way her hips moved, well, it was just hot. She was completely sexy, completely at home in the dance, completely present. He could tell from the way one of the judges lingered at the edge of the floor close to where they danced that she and Brent were moving on in the competition. For the next sixty seconds he was aware of nothing but Jenna.

Holy hell, no wonder Brent was in love with her. The way she shimmied and shook around him, well, no guy could be expected to resist that. It was lucky for him that Brent clearly didn't have the balls to actually do anything about his feelings.

Lucky for him? Sandro groaned inwardly and looked away from the dance floor for a moment to clear his addled brain. He was here because she was Paul's teacher and she seemed to feel that

Paul would benefit from seeing this insane circus of sequins and spandex. He was here because he'd acted like an idiot at her dance studio the other day and he owed her one. He wasn't here to think about developing any feelings other than unavoidable abstract lust for Jenna Stevens.

When the music stopped, the audience was on its feet and Sandro cheered and clapped with as much enthusiasm as the rest. Paul looked over at him with a knowing smile. "Doesn't look like you had such a miserable time after all."

Sandro elbowed him in the ribs. "Shut up. This was all for you, bro. What did you think?"

"I know you don't understand, but I want to be able to dance like that. I want to be out there competing someday."

"You're right. I don't understand the desire to dress up in tight pants and heels and wiggle your hips in front of a bunch of people." Sandro laughed when Paul got an elbow jab back at him. "But if it floats your boat, bro, more power to you."

"Well, at least I don't want to put on an apron and cook in the kitchen!" Paul shot back.

"Touché." Sandro laughed and mussed his little brother's carefully styled hair. "I knew there was a reason I liked you so much, you little—"

"Shhh!" Paul whispered.

The judges were finished conferring and three

numbers were called. One of them was Jenna's. She and Brent had a chance to dance in the final.

As the last round got under way, Sandro had interest in nothing but Jenna, silently cheering her every step as she danced her heart out on the floor below. And when she and Brent were declared the winners, he was the first back out of his seat, cheering for her in sheer happiness, feeling her triumph as his own.

HE LEFT PAUL watching a performance by some kids about his age and went to find Jenna. He needed to be polite and congratulate her, or at least that was what he was telling himself. Reality was, he didn't have any clue what he needed, but he just wanted to be near her.

She wasn't in the lobby, so he started down a wide hallway that bordered the ballroom and found her about halfway down. It was a lot less crowded down here. She had thrown a long, loose sweatshirt over her costume and he was a little sorry about that. He was surprised to see her alone, with no family or friends around to celebrate her victory. There was no sign of Brent, either.

"Hey," he said, and she looked up from the strap of the shoe she'd been trying to remove.

"Sandro!" She seemed genuinely pleased to see him and stood up. He couldn't resist. He reached down and gave her a hug. She was warm and he liked the feel of her soft sweatshirt over her muscular arms.

"You were amazing out there, Jenna. Congratulations!"

"Thank you," she said, smiling warmly. "I so appreciate you being here." She looked around him and frowned. "Where's Paul?"

For the second time since he'd met Jenna, Sandro felt completely, irrationally jealous of his little brother. He wasn't used to beautiful women looking over his shoulder in search of another guy, especially not a teenage squirt like Paul. "Still watching the dancing," he told her.

"Is he enjoying himself?"

"Yes." Sandro decided to make her day. "I give up. I'll never understand it, but he loves this dancing stuff. I've never seen him as excited as he was watching your competition. You were right, Jenna—he was meant to do this."

Her wide smile got even wider. "Are you serious? You're not going to be all grumpy about it anymore?" She looked like a kid who'd just got the best Christmas present.

Sandro laughed. "I can't promise not to be grumpy. Or not to worry. But I'm glad I brought him to San Francisco."

Jenna surprised him by reaching up and throwing her arms around his neck. She could barely reach, so he instinctively leaned down to reciprocate. His hands went to her waist and the curve there was almost all he could think about. That and the way she was so small under his hands—until her hips flared out in a perfect pinup-girl curve.

She must have caught his train of thought, because she froze and looked up at him, eyes wide and a deep blue under the layers of eye shadow and sprinkles of glitter. And he couldn't help it. He knew it was a mistake, but all caution fled when he leaned close enough to feel her breath on his lips.

He brought his mouth down with no finesse, no skill, just the desperation of a thirsty man too long without water. Her mouth opened for him, and his own low sound of relief muffled her gasp. He'd wanted to do this since they'd sat on the sidewalk after the bike accident...maybe ever since she'd teased him at dinner on Jack's ranch. One hand left her waist and reached for her hair, but her hand caught his and brought it back down.

"Photo opportunity soon," she murmured against his lips.

He tasted her lightly there, where her words had been, and her arms around his neck tightened and pulled him closer, inviting him to explore the velvet skin inside her mouth. He staggered forward, losing balance, and she stepped back with him until she was pressed against the wall next to the bench. They didn't break the kiss, somehow moving as their tongues twined with each other's, as their breath went harsh and ragged, and his body pressed into hers.

He didn't know how long they stayed against the wall like that. Long enough that his mind had narrowed down to sex and nothing else. Long enough that when he heard someone mutter, "Get a room," he felt as if he was emerging from some kind of euphoric and distant place he'd only ever gone to before with the help of narcotics. This was Jenna's workplace, his heated brain remembered. Down the hall was a lobby full of Jenna's colleagues.

"We should stop," he murmured into her mouth, and took one more kiss, long and slow, his thumb trailing her cheekbone, not wanting to leave her silken skin.

"This is crazy," she whispered as he pulled away. She brought her hand to her mouth, immediately self-conscious of the lipstick he'd smeared. She smiled behind her hand then, her eyes lowered from his, and one finger came up, tipped in a scarlet nail, and trailed the outline of *his* lips, wiping lipstick from there, as well. He closed his eyes—it felt that incredible.

"Jenna?" Brent's voice was behind them.

"Oh, no." Jenna's voice was so soft only Sandro could hear it. He tipped her head forward so it touched his chest. He wanted to kick himself. When he left New York, he'd vowed to treat all women with a new level of respect, the respect they deserved. And here he was, with the first woman he'd wanted since then, and he'd put her in this awkward position—lipstick smeared, hair and clothing in disarray, right in front of her dance partner.

"Brent, hey." He turned his head just enough to see Brent out of the corner of his eye but hopefully not so much that the other man could see the lipstick on Sandro's face. He pulled Jenna close to his chest to hide her. "Jenna and I were talking and she got a little emotional. Can you give us a minute?"

"Jenna, are you all right?" Brent started to step closer and Sandro felt irritation creep up.

"I'm good, Brent." Jenna kept her head against Sandro's chest. He could get used to having her like this, nestled in his arms. "Sandro's right—I just got emotional...but I'm okay."

A shriek of "Brenty!" came to their rescue and Sandro felt Jenna smile against him. He heard Brent say "Mom!" and then there were all kinds of high-pitched, squealy congratulations as Brent went toward the cacophony. Jenna took advantage of the distraction to reach for her bag and pull out a packet of makeup wipes. She used one to clean the lipstick off Sandro's face and then he did the same for her, enjoying the intimacy of tracing the line of her mouth and making it perfect again.

"Am I good?" She looked up and Sandro couldn't

help it. He leaned down and kissed her again, gently this time, on the cheek.

"You're beautiful," he assured her. "Perfect." And he meant it.

JENNA HOPED SANDRO had done a good enough job on her makeup that it wouldn't be obvious to Brent, and his entire family, that she'd just been making out against a wall with her student's big brother. What had she done? Gone against everything she'd promised herself, that's what. But breaking promises had never felt so good.

She glanced at Sandro, and he smiled at her ruefully, shaking his head a little as if he couldn't believe what they'd done, either.

"Jenna, get over here, please! We need a picture of the two champions!" Brent's sister, Sarah, was next to her with admiration in her eyes. "You were amazing out there! Congratulations!"

"Wait for me?" she asked Sandro, trying to keep her voice quiet.

"Sure," he murmured, his voice laced with humor and seduction. "As long as you want."

She tried to think of something else, something serious or depressing, to take away the flush Sandro's kisses had left on her cheeks.

Brent was holding out his arm for her. Jenna went to him and posed while Sarah snapped photos. Ballroom dance was a tradition in Brent's family. His mother had been a champion in Poland and Sarah was already a huge success in youth competitions.

After the photos, Jenna stepped back to let Brent celebrate with his family. Hugs, flower bouquets and happy chatter surrounded her as her peers mingled with their loved ones. The loneliness Jenna felt in these moments after competition was familiar, but it still hurt. Her family's indifference meant she celebrated her victories alone.

"Jenna!" She looked up and saw Paul jogging down the hall. "Congratulations! You were awesome!" Paul stopped a few feet away and the admiration and excitement on his face wiped away the traces of Jenna's self-pity.

"Did you like it?" she asked.

"Yeah! I couldn't believe it! I mean, I'd seen you practice a little, and I knew you were good, but I had no idea... How'd you get *so* good?"

Jenna laughed ruefully, thinking of her lifetime of dance classes and rehearsals. "Lots of classes and lots of practice."

"Jenna?" Brent took her hand. "We need to get into the ballroom for our official photos." He pulled her in under his arm. Jenna knew in an instant that he was doing it to show Sandro their connection and she lifted his arm and stepped out from under it. She wouldn't be a pawn in whatever guy game he was playing.

"Sure," she answered. She picked up her bag.

"Give me a few moments to freshen up." She needed to make sure the damage from Sandro's epic kisses wasn't immortalized in their photos.

Brent nodded and wandered toward the main ballroom, his happy family in tow.

Sandro seemed to read her thoughts. "Your family couldn't make it today?"

Jenna sighed. "It's a long story."

"They want her to be a lawyer," Paul added.

"How is it my baby brother knows more about you than I do?" Sandro asked, a wry smile on his face that melted something inside her.

"Maybe he's been paying more attention," she teased, then stopped abruptly, remembering just what kind of attention Sandro had been paying her only minutes earlier.

Sandro's voice was serious. "I've been paying attention, too. Trust me."

She could feel each word as a featherlight touch. She hoped her elaborate makeup hid her blush. "I can't thank you two enough for coming," she said. "But I have to get going."

"Congratulations again, Jenna," Paul said.

"Paul, can you give us a second?" Sandro asked. "Meet me by the front door of the hotel?"

"Sure," Paul said, his eyes full of questions that somehow he had the restraint not to ask. He turned to go and made it a few steps down the hall before turning around. "Don't do anything I wouldn't do!" he called, all little brother again in an instant.

"Goodbye, bro." Sandro's voice was more a command than a farewell.

Paul continued down the hall and Sandro regarded Jenna for a moment, obviously trying to think of what to say. She braced herself. Here was the part where the player in him took over. The part that was going to either proposition her or say that he'd gotten carried away and put some distance between them with an apology. And that was okay, she reminded herself. So she'd kissed him. It was a momentary distraction from her real life and now it was time to refocus.

"Can I see you again?"

It wasn't at all what she'd been expecting and her mind went blank. She stared and no answer came.

"I mean, like a date or something." He paused, ran a hand through his hair, looked down at the carpet then back at her again with resolve in his dark eyes. "I know it makes no sense for either of us. I can't be in San Francisco that often. But I want to spend more time with you."

Jenna tried to find words. Her first instinct was to say yes, to shout it out. But when had her first instinct ever done right by her? Her whole plan was to follow her brain, not her instincts.

But instead her mind latched on to his words. *I can't be in San Francisco that often.* He wouldn't be sticking around, which meant there was no chance of a future for them. She'd been working on accepting things in her life as they were, without trying to change the outcome. Could she accept that whatever was between them would be short-term only? Because if she could accept that, she could have a little more time with him. And she knew without one ounce of doubt that she wanted him to kiss her again.

After all the trouble with Jeff, maybe it was her turn to have a little fun for once. She'd go into this with eyes wide-open, knowing how it would eventually end, not trying to change things she couldn't. His work in San Francisco was short-term. He'd be gone before he could derail her plans—or her heart.

"There's a party next weekend," she told him. "Saturday night. A big one, for the ballroom. Marlene hosts it at her apartment. Would you like to go?"

Sandro paused and looked away for a moment. He seemed to be weighing the idea. Then his eyes were on hers again. "I'd like that," he said.

"Great! I promised I'd help her set up, so can you meet me there? I'll get you the directions when you drop Paul off on Saturday morning. The only catch is that I have to spend an hour at the party reading tarot cards."

"What? Why?" He was staring at her as if she'd just announced she'd be flying to the moon.

"It's a fund-raiser. We're all asked to lead an activity and the money we earn goes to the scholarship fund."

"And you're a fortune-teller?"

"No!" She laughed. "You don't know tarot cards? They can give you guidance about problems. Plus, they're really cool-looking."

"So what do they say about us?" he asked.

"I don't know—I'd have to try it first!" Jenna said. She'd thought about it, though, a few times now.

"You should do it. Maybe it would give us a little guidance."

"Guidance for what?" She was playing dumb and they both knew it.

Sandro crossed the distance between them in two strides and his hands were firm on her shoulders. He looked down at her with an expression of desire so strong it sent her insides into meltdown. Nuclear-style. "Guidance for this thing between us, Jenna. This thing we both know probably shouldn't happen."

And then he kissed her, and she forgot all the problems, complications and reasons why she shouldn't kiss him back. All she could do was cling to his shoulders as the heat seared her, as his mouth raged over hers, as the hotel disappeared and all that was left was Sandro. And then he set her back on her feet, kissed her once on the nose and was gone down the hall to find his brother.

With the memory of him blazing across her lips, Jenna stumbled off to the ladies' room to apply more makeup, and hopefully gain some semblance of calm, before her photo shoot.

CHAPTER TEN

IT WAS BEST NOT to look for him every thirty seconds, Jenna reminded herself, dragging her eyes away from the entrance to the party. The trick was to focus on what Frank was telling her about his recent trip to Singapore. Frank was a student in her salsa class. He worked as a computer programmer and he was actually pretty cute in a nerdy-scientist sort of way. So why was she watching the door for a chef-cowboy-ladies' man who didn't even live close enough to have a real relationship with?

Jenna sighed. The answer was simple. Because when he'd kissed her up against the hotel wall at her dance competition, it had scrambled her brain, her common sense and possibly her entire nervous system. Memories of what it had felt like in his arms had her drifting off when she should be focused. She swore she could still feel the trails his fingers had left behind on her body. It was clear she was doomed to repeat her pattern of falling for unavailable men, and the worst part was, right now she didn't even care. She just wanted to see him again.

When Frank paused for breath, Jenna excused herself and went to look for her friend Tess.

Once she found her, Jenna wished she hadn't. Tess was leaning against the wall by the front door, relaxed, alluring and so very confident. She was looking up at Sandro, who was looking down at her with his head tilted. Probably listening to something witty and provocative that Tess was saying, because that was how Tess was.

Tess—tall, blonde and gorgeous in everyday life—looked completely irresistible dressed up in some kind of black sheath that wrapped and ruched in all the right places. Jenna felt panic rise at the very real possibility that Sandro would end up going home with one of her best friends tonight.

She couldn't be upset with Tess. Her friend had no idea that Jenna was even interested in someone. Jenna hadn't wanted to talk about Sandro— she couldn't even explain him to herself. So she'd said nothing about him to Tess when they'd met up for lunch earlier this week.

If Sandro really was the womanizer Jack and Gavin described, then he just might be the perfect guy for Tess. The thought sent a pang through Jenna's heart, but it made sense. Tess didn't like relationships. In fact, when she bothered with men at all, it seemed to be mainly for one-night stands. Tess would be perfectly happy with Sandro's wild ways. And if Jenna stepped out of the picture and let that happen, she might make them both happy and save herself a lot of heartache.

The thought soured her mood. She didn't want Sandro to be with Tess. She didn't want him to reciprocate her friend's interest. But honestly, who could resist her? Jenna stared at her friend with envy. Tess was willowy and shimmery. Next to her sleek blond hair and perfect figure, Jenna's redhaired, curvy self disappeared from view. Eclipsed. She'd experienced it before when she'd been out with Tess, that feeling that she was fading into the background as the men crowded around her sexy friend. Eventually Jenna had gotten used to it and learned to laugh about it.

But this time she didn't want to disappear. *Just don't cry,* she commanded herself. *When you find them off in a corner somewhere, with Sandro's strong hands wrapped around one of your best friends, remember that you were warned about him, and don't cry.*

Jenna couldn't stand to watch any longer. Turning blindly, she almost crashed into a waiter carrying a tray of mixed drinks. Jenna grabbed a glass for each hand, ignoring the waiter's shocked expression, and headed to the dining room. She stopped at the sideboard and took a gulp from one glass, which proved to be a gin and tonic. Not her favorite, but she took another sip of the bitter concoction and tried to will away the tears that burned behind her eyes.

Why was she upset? She wasn't dating Sandro. If anything was going to happen between them, it would only be a short-term fling. But somehow the thought of him with Tess was affecting her and suddenly she wished her friend wasn't here tonight. Which showed how messed up her thinking was, because she loved Tess dearly and her friend was also one of the biggest contributors to the ballroom's scholarship program. Many of Jenna's students had benefited from her generosity.

She drained her first drink, set the glass down and coughed. The gin tasted just as bad on the last sip as it had on the first. She picked up her second glass and brought it to her lips.

"Easy there, Red." She looked up, shocked to hear Jack's nickname for her, and inhaled her drink. Sandro was beside her and his large hand patted her back as she sputtered. *Great. Very dignified, Jenna.*

"Hi," Jenna gasped, eyes watering as the last hideous drop of gin seared her throat. "You called me Red!" It came out as a croak.

"I borrowed it from Jack. Seems to suit you pretty well." Sandro twisted the top off a bottle of water. "Drink this," he commanded. She brought the bottle to her lips and let the icy water wash away the choking gin.

"Seems like maybe I got here too late, if you're drinking like that. Did Brent give you trouble?" His face was hard suddenly and he looked around as if he was ready to take his revenge for whatever injury Brent could have caused her in his absence.

Jenna's voice was hoarse from coughing, but her heart was warm. He was here, and not with Tess. And it shouldn't matter as much as it did. "So far I've managed to stay in a different room than Brent. It's worked pretty well. I'm glad you came."

"So why the boozing?"

Because I thought you were going to sleep with my friend. "I was having a rough night," she answered.

"Well…" His smile soothed her troubled heart. "Maybe your night will get better."

"Maybe it will," she told him. It just had. She gingerly wiped her eyes, still watering from the gin and the coughing fit. "And I've recently learned that no matter how bad it gets, a gin and tonic is *not* the answer."

Sandro laughed, and his smile eased his normally serious expression. He was wearing dark jeans and a black retro-looking Western shirt. His tousled dark hair curled over his forehead, and Jenna resisted the urge to run her fingers through it.

Then she noticed he'd grown quiet, leaning on the sideboard and looking out over the sea of people in the crowded room. "So I met a woman by the front door. She was really…er…welcoming. Eventually I figured out that she's a good friend of yours."

Jenna's stomach knotted. Knowing her luck, he

was probably going to suggest a three-way. Tess's wild lifestyle hadn't really bothered Jenna before, but they'd also never been interested in the same guy before. She feigned ignorance. "I assume you're talking about Tess?"

Sandro nodded, one corner of his mouth up in a half smile. "She's quite a character."

"She can be very…um…enthusiastic," Jenna replied, hating the way her voice halted and stuttered. "She just enjoys flirting. And I never told her that we were…" She stumbled again. What *were* they anyway? "You know…well, that you were coming here because of me."

"Well, I wasn't planning to take her up on her offer anyways." He was grinning now and he cocked an eyebrow, all trouble. "Though I was impressed—it was quite creative."

"I'm sure it was." Jenna flushed. What had Tess said? She would have to grill her friend later. But whatever Tess had tried, the important thing was, *it hadn't worked*. Sandro was here with her and even if it meant nothing in the long run, it meant something now. It meant that at least for tonight, he'd chosen a date with Jenna over wild sex with her stunning friend.

SANDRO STUDIED JENNA as she sipped the water he'd given her. She hadn't really seemed like a partier, but finding her here, downing a gin and tonic like it was water, had him worried. In fact a lot of things about this party worried him. Jenna's friend Tess, for one. He'd shown up here later than planned, eager to see Jenna. Instead he'd encountered a sexy blonde who had pressed herself against him and whispered suggestions that involved a bed upstairs and her complete lack of underwear.

A year ago he wouldn't have hesitated in taking her up on the offer. But tonight he found little appealing about the idea of sex with a stranger. So he'd mentioned he was here to meet Jenna, and the sex goddess, though obviously surprised, hadn't batted an eyelash when telling him that Jenna was one of her best friends.

He found himself once again feeling protective of Jenna. Her supposed best friend was trying to seduce her date and her dance partner was trying to seduce her. He'd hoped to leave all this type of shallow intrigue behind in New York, but here it was in San Francisco, reminding him of one more reason he'd decided to return to his small town.

But Jenna wasn't in his small town. That thought had made him uneasy. He wanted to be the guy Jenna took to parties. He wanted to see her bright blue eyes look to him for laughter and connection. He wanted to meet people with her, see places with her and take her home at the end of the night.

He looked over at her, wondering if she had similar thoughts. She was watching the people in front of them, who were in an animated discussion about some dance step called *ochos*. Her bright blue dress dipped down to show her muscled back. He fought the urge to wrap his hands around her tiny waist; the feel of it had haunted him since that evening in the hotel.

He grabbed a beer off a passing waiter's tray just for something to do. Something to do other than look at the way Jenna's dress hugged her incredible curves. She looked back at him, and he wondered if she'd noticed him staring. He took a sip of his beer, savoring the bitter taste he rarely allowed himself.

"Show me around this place?" he asked. "It's not every day I get to hang out in a San Francisco penthouse."

They wandered through the crowd. It seemed like an eclectic mix of dancers, students, and Marlene's friends and family. People clad in their designer best mingled with the quirky folks who were drawn to ballroom dance. A few couples were in full dance costumes—maybe there was going to be a performance?

Jenna led the way through French doors and out onto a terrace that overlooked the high-rise skyline of the city. There was a dance floor set up and a DJ was playing a fast salsa number. Several couples were on the dance floor, dancing casually, looking as if they were having fun. Jenna stopped by the railing at the edge of the terrace and Sandro inhaled the sharp, cool air. The lit buildings around them sparkled with a rare clarity in a city that spent so much time shrouded in fog and mist.

"So how is it spending time in a city again?" Jenna asked.

Trust her to find the topic that was the most problematic, the most relevant. If he'd believed in psychics, he'd swear Jenna was one of them. He tried to think of a way to answer that question that wouldn't involve talking about his past. "It's a lot more relaxed here than in New York," he finally told her. "I think it suits me a bit better."

"But you wouldn't want to stay in San Francisco?" she asked him, and then blushed immediately.

He glanced at her sharply. Was she dropping some kind of hint? He had to be honest with her. "I don't want to live in a city again. Ever."

She studied him closely and he realized he'd spoken too vehemently. He knew she was about to ask about his time in New York.

Desperate for distraction, he set his beer down. "I can't believe I'm saying this—" he held out his hand "—but do you want to dance?"

Her look of surprise was so enormous it made him laugh. "Hey!" He took the bottle of water out of her hand and set it on the ledge. "My little brother isn't the only one with moves. Don't forget, I lived in Spain, I lived in New York—I've been around a dance floor or two."

The salsa song was over and now it was Ella Fitzgerald singing slow. Despite his brave words, Sandro was frantically scanning his brain, trying to remember the rhythm for a fox-trot. It came in a flash of relief as he took his first step on the dance floor, pulling Jenna into a close hold that he hoped was at least somewhat correct. Two slow steps and two quick ones. He tried to lead firmly as he stepped forward with his left foot. To his great satisfaction, she followed him easily and they made a silent circuit of the dance floor. Sandro attempted to look nonchalant, or at least lost in important thoughts, rather than like what he really was—a guy who was carefully counting the steps.

"How do you know this?" she asked him in evident surprise as he turned her under his arm on the slow steps and brought her back in smoothly.

He tried not to look as relieved and triumphant as he felt at his success. "I had Paul teach me a few moves before I came here tonight. He got a big kick out of it, let me tell you."

Jenna laughed. "I wouldn't have pegged you as someone who was willing to be schooled by your little brother," she joked.

Sandro spun her again. It was easier this time. "A year or two ago, maybe not. But life makes you humble, you know? And he's a cool kid—if it didn't improve my dancing, at least it made him laugh."

"You're a good brother, Sandro. Thanks for letting him study dance with me."

The familiar stress reared up again. He hesitated, lost the rhythm.

"What is it?" Jenna asked.

Sandro looked down at her. She was all kindness and caring. His words came pouring out, even though he knew they made him sound weak. "No one knows about his dancing right now, so he's happy. But at some point it's going to come out that Paul is taking these classes. I just don't look forward to seeing the look on his face once my family starts in on him. Once he's spent a few months living under the label of *that boy who dances* just like I was *that boy who cooks*."

Trying to stop the worry, he pulled Jenna in and inhaled her scent. Cinnamon and jasmine, he decided—he couldn't remember inhaling anything so intoxicating. He pulled her in tighter to get closer to it, even though a nagging voice inside was reminding him that there was no point getting close to her. But he pushed that voice aside and breathed her in, letting himself get lost. At least for a song.

"I have to believe that society has progressed," Jenna said softly into his ear. "Just in the last ten years so much has changed about how people think and what people accept. I have to hope that it won't be nearly as hard for Paul as it was for you."

He clung to her words as closely as he held on to her body. When the music ended, the last few notes of Ella's voice dripping like honey through the stillness, they slowed to a stop and stood for a moment with their arms around each other. Jenna didn't step away and Sandro didn't want her to, relishing the feel of her petite frame wrapped in his arms. And then she looked up at him and he saw the want in her eyes and the full curve of her lip.... He knew that what little self-control he'd been hanging on to had drifted off with the last few notes of music and been replaced with a need to kiss her again that was not going to be denied.

His fingers moved almost of their own accord and wove through her bright red curls and he brought his mouth down on hers and felt the softness of her lips give beneath him. And then he was ravenous for the taste of her, for the cinnamon and flowers, and when a tiny moan escaped her, he pulled her closer and deepened the kiss further.

The music finally broke the spell as the first bars of a classic disco song filled the dance floor around them with laughing, jostling people. His mouth left hers and she opened her eyes and smiled up at him, a little dazed, a little uncertain. He tucked her under his arm and led her off the floor, only one purpose in mind.

There was a large potted lemon tree on the terrace near the penthouse wall. He made a beeline for it and pulled Jenna with him when he stepped behind it. He moved her to face him and felt her uneven breath skitter across his lips just before he kissed her, pulling her against him, one hand behind her neck and the other hand finally doing what he'd wanted to all evening—roaming freely down the exposed skin of her back, feeling her soft skin and her muscle, the silken strength of her under his hands.

Her response to his caress fueled the insane need he was wrestling with inside. Pressing herself against him, her small hands easily found the skin of his back beneath his untucked shirt and trailed along the waistband of his jeans, and he knew his desire had won the battle with his common sense.

"Damn, Jenna. I want you," he whispered. Her breath was coming in shudders when she looked up at him and he leaned down to take her lower lip in his teeth and tug, just gently, and then to kiss her one more time.

"I want you, too," she murmured against him when he pulled back.

"Jenna?" A voice called from the doors between the apartment and the terrace.

"It's Marlene!" Jenna gasped. "And I'm making out behind a tree at her party!" She started giggling then, leaning against him and shaking with laughter until Sandro couldn't help but laugh, too. The image of the two of them emerging guiltily from behind a tree was so ridiculous, so adolescent.

Apparently their shrubbery disguise was working, because Marlene gave up and went back inside.

"I have to go do the tarot cards," Jenna said, wiping the tears of laughter out from under her eyes.

"What?" For a moment he had no idea what she meant.

"Remember? I promised Marlene I'd read tarot cards."

He'd forgotten. He'd forgotten pretty much everything during that dance and that kiss.

"Why don't you let me read yours?" she asked with a saucy smile. All he wanted was to kiss that smile, to feel the shape of her teasing humor under his tongue.

He should take a break, maybe go for a walk, get some distance between them before he made a fool of himself and started begging her for more than she could give right now. He'd forgotten, when he'd pulled her behind the tree, that she was at a work event and not free to act on the heat between them. "No, thanks, Red. I'm pretty sure I know my future. It involves a restaurant in Benson and a ranch with a whole lotta sheep."

"Try it—" Jenna gave him a gentle nudge with her elbow "—before you write it off. Sometimes it can be strangely accurate. And it's not really about the future. It's about accessing our higher self and gaining information about who we really are and what we really want. Who knows? You might learn something, cowboy."

"Nah, I don't think my higher self really needs any more information. I'm pretty sure it's on overload."

"Are you scared?" Jenna leaned on tiptoe and kissed his cheek. "I promise it won't hurt," she whispered into his ear, and his resolve evaporated with the feel of her warm breath.

"No, I'm not scared," he spluttered. "It's just…"

She took his hand. "Come on. You can be my first victim." She led him back through the kitchen and dining room and down a hallway to a bedroom. The view out the window had been covered with a colorful tie-dyed banner with a single human eye, wide-open and staring, painted on it in black. The lights were off and scattered candles flickered. A rainbow of scarves had been draped over the furniture so that the entire place looked like some sort of hallucinogenic cave. Sandro looked at Jenna incredulously and she laughed.

"I set this up earlier. A little ambiance never hurt!"

"It's original," he conceded. "Gypsy caravan meets the hippie shops on Haight Street."

"Well, yes, I took advantage of San Francisco's grooviest neighborhood for a fair amount of my decor." She grinned. "But it was cheap and it lends a certain mystical air, I think!" She sat behind a card table and gestured to the seat opposite. "Now, sit down and let me read your future. If it's really nothing but sheep, we'll soon find out."

He sat, and she lit the candle next to her and he watched her dainty hands, with the red polished nails, hold the flame to the wick. How had he ended up in this psychedelic room, at this chaotic party, with this wild dancer, who, he was pretty sure, actually believed in the power of the tarot? Part of him wanted to just laugh and part of him wanted to run back to Benson as fast as he could. How had his life taken this crazy turn just when he'd been trying so hard to stay on the straight and narrow?

"Relax," Jenna told him, completely serious now. "Close your eyes. Take a deep breath, slowly, in and out. Take another. As you breathe in, allow the peace of this room—"

Sandro opened one eye. "Peace? Really? I feel like I'm being indoctrinated into some kind of rainbow cult."

She giggled. "Shh! Fine. Close your eyes, don't think about rainbows, and find *inner* peace. That's an order! Think of a place where you feel really peaceful. Riding the range, maybe?"

Sandro grinned at that but decided to humor her, as it was obvious she wasn't going to let him escape without a reading. He shut his eyes and tried to imagine one of his favorite places, a big boulder that jutted over his parents' ranch. It ran alongside a small stream and you could sit up there and hear the water running and look down over the ranch as it spread out from the foothills to the valley floor.

He took a deep breath, realizing all of a sudden just how tense he'd been lately and how nice it actually was to sit in this scarf-draped room with Jenna.

Sandro let the breath out and took another, picturing the way the sunrise looked from the boulder, lighting up the floor of the valley in an incandescent march of gold and pink. He imagined Jenna sitting next to him, his arm over her shoulders, her nestled underneath, where, he'd already discovered, she fit so perfectly.

Jenna's voice quietly disrupted his thoughts. "Now I'm going to give you the cards. You need to be the one to shuffle them. While you do, think of a question. Not a yes-or-no question. Just something in your life that's been troubling you or something you've been wondering a lot about lately."

Sandro couldn't help it. He thought of her. He should have been wondering about the restaurant—would he be able to make a success of it? Or about Paul—would he be okay now that he was dancing? But no, the question that dominated his thoughts was about Jenna. What should he do about how much he wanted her?

Sandro took the cards and shuffled them awkwardly. They were bigger than your average deck of cards, and a little thicker. The images on them caught his eye. Swords, people in medieval garb, goblets—everything looked mystical and archaic.

Jenna took the cards from under his hand, where he'd left them after he shuffled, and he could hear her start to deal. "When you are done with your question, when you are ready to receive the wisdom of the tarot, open your eyes."

"The wisdom of the tarot, huh?" He couldn't help teasing her as he opened his eyes, the peace he'd felt picturing the ranch, and her there with him, leaving him calm and happy.

"I'm very proud of that phrase." Jenna grinned at him over the cards. "I've been working this party, and a few others, for several years now. I think it sounds kind of deep."

He laughed at that and loved the way she smiled up at him, shyly but a little defiantly, too, defending her outlandish hobby. Her eyes held such a sweetness that he wanted to spend his tarot time just basking in their light.

"But seriously, if you're open to it, the cards can teach things or offer information about how you might really feel about something you're going through. They're not meant to give an exact answer, just to guide." She quickly dealt the cards in a pattern, four on the corners of a diamond shape, one in the center. "There are a lot of ways to lay out the cards, but for these readings I use a five-card spread. One of the simplest."

She was looking down, concentrating on the cards she'd dealt, her lower lip caught between her teeth, her pale skin glowing in the candlelight. With her long auburn curls trailing around her, she reminded him of a gypsy woman from long ago. Then she looked up at him, eyes wide. "You've got a lot going on here, Sandro."

Of course she'd say that. She knew he was opening a restaurant, helping out on the family ranch, teaching cooking and ferrying his brother to her ballroom every weekend. Yeah, safe to say he was busy.

"Do you see the center card?"

"You mean the upside-down naked lady? Yup, I see her."

Jenna laughed. "She isn't completely naked. Her lower bits are covered! Anyway, that card is called the World and since it's upside-down, we say it's reversed. Cards take on sort of an inverse meaning when they're upside-down. And placed in the center like this, it's the overall theme of the reading. It symbolizes your present state."

"So…my present state is an upside-down half-naked woman?"

"Elevate your mind, Sandro," she teased. "It symbolizes frustration or a fear of change. It can mean that things are in the process of change."

"So I'm in transition."

"Well, yes. And possibly stuck there."

Well, he had to give it to the cards—they were right about that.

"And over here on the left is the card that represents past influences that are still having an effect. You have the Tower here."

Sandro stood up and walked around to stand behind Jenna so he could see the cards the same way she did. The Tower looked pretty formidable. There were people falling off it headfirst and flames shooting out the top. "That doesn't look good," he said, shoving down a twinge of anxiety. She was good at this. She was even sucking him in.

"Don't worry." Jenna glanced up at him, and he was actually glad to see that she was smiling. It didn't matter if he knew this was all nonsense— that tower was creepy. "It looks worse than it is. It means you've been through some kind of enormous change, like getting a new job or moving, and you've done both of those, right?"

"Yup." This was weird. How could these cards be hitting so close to home? Jenna was most likely reading into them what she already knew about him.

She pointed to the lowest card. Another upside-down naked woman—this one poured a jug of water into a pool. "This card also relates to your past, to the reasons behind the changes you made. It usually symbolizes self-doubt, stubbornness and an inability to express yourself."

"This is a pretty grim reading, Red. Wasn't this supposed to be fun?" A shiver went over his skin and he abruptly left her side and went back to the seat across the desk.

"Cheer up! You have to understand, these cards are just information about your past, about things that might be getting in your way. The next two cards deal with the future."

Sandro looked at the last two cards. One had two more naked people—that looked promising. But the other had a man dressed in black, riding a horse with the word *Death* written underneath. *Fabulous*.

Jenna pointed to the Death card. "Don't freak out. It doesn't really mean death. In fact, upright like this it means the opposite. It means rebirth. The end of an old phase of life that's served its purpose and the beginning of a new one. It's the symbol of a major change."

He hated that he felt relieved. That she'd somehow enticed him so far into her hocus-pocus that the Death card had truly worried him for a moment there. "And the last one?" he asked.

Even in the candlelight he could tell that she was blushing. Her voice came out soft. "This card is called the Lovers. Its position in the overall pattern of the spread signifies the potential inside whatever situation you are in."

His heart sped up. "So you're saying…?"

"It doesn't necessarily mean that you'll fall in love," Jenna said hurriedly. "It depends on what you asked, really. Mainly, it means you need to trust your intuition during all of this change. Don't just listen to your intellect. It means you've got difficult decisions ahead and you'll have a struggle choosing between two different paths."

Sandro felt a little sick. He'd agreed to this reading to humor her and to have more time with her. He'd had no idea it would all feel so real. That last card was the worst. He'd already chosen his path. He'd chosen Benson, talked Jack into a business partnership, and started fixing up his aunt and uncle's old restaurant. He'd made his choice. The last thing he wanted was more choices down the road, but these cards were all forecasting exactly that.

Why was he even taking this seriously? They were just cards. It was just a party game.

Jenna was still staring at the cards, her brow furrowed in either concentration or concern. He didn't want her concern. "Well, you said it was a guide, right? So I guess I'm supposed to be ready to make some decisions. It all sounds pretty normal to me."

"Sure," she said quietly, and when she looked up, he saw all kinds of questions in her eyes. Questions he had no interest in hearing or answering.

Thankfully, a couple was waiting out in the hall.

Sandro stood up and motioned toward them with his hand. "These folks have been waiting awhile. Let's give them a turn. You can peer at me through your crystal ball anytime."

She laughed at that and he was glad he could tease away whatever had been bothering her. "I'll catch up with you when you're done here."

She nodded and he left the room, wondering if he could risk another beer. Just the thought sent a pang of anxiety through his gut. He'd wondered after New York if he needed to go to rehab or AA meetings or something. But it hadn't been too hard to quit drinking and drugs. He was just glad to be rid of them. And in Benson he'd never craved them or needed them. So he'd opted to skip rehab and just focus on building a new life. But here at his first big-city party since then, he was already thinking of drowning his discomfort in alcohol.

The living room was packed and the buzz of conversation was deafening. Sandro made a point of walking right by the bar as he went back out to the terrace. He leaned on the railing, taking in the lights and the skyline, unease trickling through him. He didn't belong here. Yet he couldn't stay away from Jenna. He'd said yes to everything she'd asked— Paul's dance lessons, the competition, this party, the tarot reading—and yet he knew deep down that it was all a bad idea.

When this cooking gig came to an end in a few

weeks, one or both of them were going to get hurt. Maybe that was the meaning of that Lovers card. They were on separate roads. Their paths were crossing right now because he was working in San Francisco, but in a few weeks, when his classes here were done, they'd go their own ways.

He glanced over and saw Tess, Jenna's propositioning friend, across the dance floor, listening intently to what some tall, clean-cut guy had to say. A year ago he would have taken her up on her offer and not thought twice about it, even if it had hurt Jenna's feelings. Now he hated that guy from a year ago. He'd kick his ass if he met him. He'd had a tiny glimpse of him tonight when that part of him, the part that could rarely say no back in New York, had flickered to life for just an instant when Tess had whispered her proposition. Self-loathing burned like acid in his gut.

"Dude." Sandro turned toward the voice at his side. A tall, thin young man moved in front of him, blocking his view of the dance floor. He had a goatee and dyed black hair and a long coat, as if he'd just come out of the Australian outback or something. "Wanna smoke some pot?"

Without any discernible thought, Sandro hit him. Not too hard, just enough to see the surprise in the guy's eyes as Sandro's fist connected with his jaw, and the dismay that followed as he toppled backward almost in slow motion and sat down heavily.

Anger fired through Sandro's veins and heated his lungs until if felt as if he couldn't breathe. Not anger at this poor pothead but at himself for the hurt he'd caused. For the way he'd already blown apart his own career once because he couldn't keep his hands off drugs or women. For the fact that here at this party, he was being given way too many opportunities to blow it all again.

Faces passed by him in a blur as he stormed through the penthouse, his eyes fixed on the door, the way out of this place of temptations. This party was proof of why he needed to get all thoughts of Jenna out of his head, regardless of how much that pissed him off.

He got outside the apartment and into the hallway. No way was he standing around waiting for the elevator. No way was he putting himself in temptation's reach for one moment longer. He saw the door for the stairs and pushed through it, scuttling down the endless flights like a man pursued. It wasn't until he was outside in the clear, cold air and the bustle of the city street that he could slow down, breathe again and realize that the only things pursuing him were the demons in his own soul.

He walked home, back to the hotel, back to his little brother whom he'd vowed to keep safe and whom, he realized now, he'd completely failed.

CHAPTER ELEVEN

"PAUL'S IN THE CAR. We're going home and he won't be coming back to class."

Jenna turned from the practice barre where she'd been warming up. It took a moment to register that Sandro was there, towering in front of her, unexpected at seven o'clock on a Sunday morning. When his presence finally sunk in, it brought with it a roiling stomach of hurt feelings and pure confusion.

"Wouldn't *I'm sorry* be a better choice of words?"

"What?"

How could he be so dense? "You left last night. Without saying goodbye."

"Yeah, I did."

Instead of looking apologetic, Sandro just scowled. It was as if the man she'd been getting to know had disappeared, replaced by the Sandro she'd dealt with in Samantha's kitchen. Why did *he* seem so angry? She was the one who'd been ditched at the party. She was the one who'd wandered through the crowd looking for him, only to be pulled aside by her boss, who informed her that he'd thrown a punch and stormed out of the penthouse.

At least Marlene hadn't seemed that upset. In fact, she'd said that no one had known the guy who was hit—he was some kind of party crasher and he left right afterward. If anything, Marlene was now even more enamored of Sandro. Who knew that Marlene had such a thing for manly cowboys who punched people at parties?

But Jenna wasn't enamored. She was done. His desertion last night had hurt, and it showed her that she was already in too deep. She'd been telling herself that she could do this, kiss a guy just for fun, knowing she had no future with him, but she couldn't. Not when it meant feeling the combination of disappointment and embarrassment that she'd felt last night. "Aren't you going to enlighten me as to why you left without saying goodbye? Or why you hit some guy on the way out?"

"Yeah." Sandro looked away and shifted uncomfortably. He ran a hand through his already mussed hair. "No, actually."

Jenna waited but he obviously wasn't going to elaborate. Great. She'd asked a guy to go out with her and it had been so traumatic he could barely speak the next day. She'd thought spending time with Sandro might rebuild her confidence after Jeff, but it clearly wasn't working out that way—quite the opposite. "Fine, don't, then."

"I'm sorry," he said. "It's hard to explain. I just can't do this…be here, in the city, with you."

Well, at least he was honest. Jenna tried to ignore the rejection, regret and other bitter feeling that clustered around her heart. "You don't want to go out with me again. I can accept that. But what does any of this have to do with Paul studying dance?"

"It's just not a good idea, Jenna. It's like sending my little brother into a cage with lions."

"Lions? Sandro, what are you talking about? It's dance class, not zookeeping. There's no danger here."

His brown eyes had purple shadows under them. There was stubble on his jaw, and part of her, the tiny part that wasn't angry that he'd walked out on her last night, was suddenly worried.

"You just don't get it." He waved his hand around, taking in the ballroom and her in one weary gesture. "None of this is good for him."

Jenna suddenly felt tired of trying to understand this enigmatic man. She walked away from him, over to the window. The street was quiet at this hour of the morning. Fog trailed low to the ground. Sandro's truck was parked outside and she could see Paul sitting in the passenger's seat, facing straight ahead, looking miserable. She was crazy about that kid, and he'd worked so hard in her classes and done so well. She owed him one last attempt to reason with his insane brother, and that was it. One last try and it was out of her hands. She turned back to Sandro. "So explain it to me."

"It's a long story, Jenna. You don't want to hear it."

"Don't you think I deserve to hear it? Don't you think your brother deserves a chance for me to hear it? So that maybe we can come up with a solution for him?"

Sandro was silent, studying the ground.

"I've got rehearsal now and class all day, so how about this? I believe you have cooking classes to teach, right? So at least let Paul have one last day of dance instruction. And tonight we can meet up and you can explain why it's so dangerous for Paul to pursue his dreams."

Sandro's hand went through his hair again. The dark locks were getting pretty wild.

"You're exhausted, Sandro. Go back to your hotel, get some rest, teach the classes you've already committed to teaching and meet me for a drink later."

He still didn't answer, so she went to her purse and rummaged around for the little notebook she kept there. She wrote down the name and address of her current favorite bar. When she looked up, he'd gone to the window where she'd been before and was staring out at his truck and Paul. She handed him the paper. "Mack's Place. On Geary. Eight o'clock tonight, and if you can convince me that all this is really bad for Paul, I promise never to bother you again. Not even when I visit Samantha and see your little brother all miserable out in Benson. Deal?"

He didn't give her the smile she was hoping for. "You should have been a salesperson, Jenna. Or a lawyer."

"Yeah. My family thinks so, too. So can we let Paul out of the truck?"

"I'll take him to breakfast first. I think I owe him an apology."

Jenna almost smiled. "I think feeding him is a good idea. And you look like you could use a good meal, too. See you at eight?"

He nodded and walked away, leaving Jenna to wonder if he'd show up tonight. If he didn't, it would be sad *only* because Paul would miss out on his last couple of classes with her. Jenna was pretty sure that last night's date-disappearing act had taken care of any romantic interest she'd had in Sandro.

She was making one more effort on Paul's behalf and that was it. If it didn't work out, then Paul would have to find his own way to dance, despite his complicated family situation and his high-strung, mixed-up brother.

"WHERE YA BEEN keeping yourself, Wee Jenna?" Mack's voice boomed across the room as she shut the door behind her and headed for the bar.

Jenna smiled at the elderly gentleman in a kilt polishing glasses behind the bar. "It's quiet tonight," she said as she hopped onto a barstool and put her purse on the varnished wood.

"Aye, the way I like it now," he told her, setting a glass in front of her. Except when he said the word *now,* it sounded like *noo.* Mack had been behind the bar here for about twenty years but as far as Jenna could tell, he hadn't lost a bit of his Scottish accent. "On most of the other nights nowadays, this place is filled with such young folk. All jabbering away and pretending they know something about scotch. I'm thinking I'll retire soon if they don't give me some peace and quiet."

But there was a twinkle in his faded blue eyes and Jenna knew he loved it. Loved being behind the bar and the center of all that energy, educating the young folk, as he called them, about his beloved single-malt scotch.

"Where's the lovely Tess tonight?" he asked as he swiped the counter with a cloth.

"Working, of course." Jenna grinned. "Sorry to disappoint you, Mack."

Mack's broad smile lit up his creased face. "Ach, Tess knows that one of these days she's gonna get sick of all those young fellas she runs about with and settle down with me."

Jenna giggled. Tess and Mack carried on an outrageous flirtation despite the fact that Mack was a happily married grandfather on the cusp of retirement.

"I'm sure Mrs. Mack will be very happy about that."

Mack lifted a bottle of The Balvenie off the shelf. "Ach, the missus knows I'm all hot air." He grinned. "Thirty years of marriage, and ya think she'd have learnt to take me more seriously." He pulled the cork out, then paused. "You want your favorite tonight, Wee Jenna? Or are you feeling adventurous?"

"No, I've got enough adventure on the way. The Balvenie will be perfect." She loved the sweet, smoky taste, and she and Mack both knew she rarely chose differently.

"Adventure, is it? You'll be meeting a young man, then?"

"Mack, does bartending make you psychic?"

He laughed at that, long and hearty. "If you've been doing it as long as I have, I think so." A couple blew in through the door looking dazed. They were probably tourists, given that they were wearing shorts and evidently regretting their clothing choices in the thick fog of the typical San Francisco summer evening. "I'll leave you to it, then," Mack told her, and headed over to pour the newcomers a drink.

Jenna took a sip of her scotch, savoring the mouthful of flavor, and looked around the room. The jukebox in the back was loaded only with Scottish songs. It was playing the tune Samantha always used to put on, "Mull of Kintyre." She and Tess had teased their friend over the plodding, sentimental song, but Samantha loved Paul McCartney's voice and said it reminded her of time spent in Scotland as a child.

A pang of wistful memory washed over Jenna. She missed her friend. Of course, she was thrilled Samantha had found such love and was getting married soon. But Benson was too far to visit very often and she was used to having Samantha by her side for every life event, big or small. She missed their lunch dates and after-work drink dates and trips to the gym on the weekend for workouts that turned out to be more gossip and giggling than actual exercise.

She still had Tess, the third member of their trio, but Tess was a different sort of friend. She was always there to listen, always there to comfort and protect, but she rarely talked about her own life. Sometimes Jenna felt it made their friendship a bit stilted, especially compared to the stories and secrets she and Samantha shared.

"You started without me." Sandro was there, looking slightly less tired but still as guarded and wary as he had this morning. Despite herself, Jenna wanted to smooth the lines of worry off his face, wishing she could be the one to calm whatever storm brewed inside him. His mouth was set in a tense line and it seemed strange to Jenna that just last night they'd been dancing and his lips had been so hot and demanding on hers.

"Just a slight head start." Jenna forced any memory of his kisses from her mind. He'd made it clear he wasn't interested in any more of them.

"Hope I'm not too late. I had kind of a hard time finding this place. I kept thinking I was in the wrong neighborhood. That you weren't really meeting me in a bar in the Tenderloin."

Jenna was determined to keep their conversation as light as possible. "Hey, the 'Loin is an underrated part of San Francisco! In between the porn shops and liquor stores, you have gems like this—one of the best bars in the city, in my opinion."

Sandro shook his head. "I'm not sure you're going to convince me. I'm not sure my truck will even be where I left it when we're done tonight."

"It will! Well…" Jenna couldn't honestly guarantee much if he'd brought his truck. "It *probably* will be okay. But trust me, if you spent time here, you'd grow to appreciate it! The Great American Music Hall is just a few blocks away. Ever been? It was a brothel when it first opened—all French-looking with gold scrolls and mirrors and fancy columns. They've left it pretty much the same."

"Except, I assume, it's not a brothel anymore?" It was the first smile she'd seen on his face since she'd read his tarot cards last night.

Jenna laughed. "No, just bands play there. Really good bands."

"It's Wee Jenna's young man!"

"Mack!" A flush warmed Jenna's cheeks. "He's not *my* young man. Sandro, meet Mack. Bartender and local scoundrel."

Mack winked at her and turned back to Sandro. "What are you drinking, mate?"

"Just a pint of lager, please."

"You're not gonna join the young lady in a wee nip?"

"No." Jenna noticed how quickly the humor drained from Sandro's face. "I try to stay off the hard stuff."

"Thanks, Mack," Jenna said when he handed Sandro his pint. "Let's sit over here." She hopped off her bar stool and led Sandro to what Tess called the Conference Table. It was against the window, by the door and far enough away from the bar that she and her friends could usually have a pretty good session of girl talk.

They sat down, and Jenna took a sip of her scotch, wondering how to start this conversation.

"I was a total jerk." Sandro started it for her.

"Go on." Despite the tension, Jenna smiled a little at his bluntness.

"I should never have walked out on you last night. If I'd been acting like a grown man, I'd have at least taken a minute to find you before I took off."

"It would have been nice," Jenna agreed. "Might have saved me a few minutes of anxiety." Or a few hours of lying awake last night wondering why she was man repellant.

Sandro took a deep breath and then a swallow of beer and then another breath. Obviously he was psyching himself up for something. "I don't know you that well, Jenna. I don't know what you're going to think of me when I tell you what I need to say. But having subjected you to my various moods and outbursts for a few weeks now, I think I owe you some kind of explanation."

Jenna was glad she'd gotten here early and fortified herself with a bit of scotch.

"There's a reason I moved back to Benson from New York. A lot of reasons, really. But the main one was that I was out of control in New York."

"Out of control?" Jenna echoed. She didn't know what she'd been expecting him to say, but this wasn't it.

"It's hard to explain...but I kind of lost it." Sandro stopped for a moment, traced a scar on the old wooden table. "See, I became this hotshot chef really young. I was given a lot of responsibility and power and a lot of attention from others, including the media. It went to my head. I thought I could have everything and do anything."

Jenna nodded encouragement, trying to take in what he was saying.

"There's something about my profession that brings out wildness in people. Or maybe those of us who are drawn to such insanely stressful work come to it with our own brand of wild. I don't know—maybe it's the long hours, but people can get pretty crazy in those kitchens. And it didn't take long before I started acting crazy, too. I didn't even realize how crazy."

"What do you mean?" Jenna asked. "What kinds of things do you consider crazy?"

"Well, you heard the stories Gavin told the other night. I wish I could say he was exaggerating, but to be honest, that's pretty much what happened. I did stuff like that all the time. Maybe in part because I was so young when I just up and left my family."

"You ran away." Jenna remembered the first night she'd met him, when he'd told her.

"When I was sixteen."

"Just a year older than Paul is now." Jenna pictured herself at that age. She'd been so sheltered, there was no way she'd have been able to do what Sandro had done.

"Yup. My family thought I was crazy for wanting to cook. I've got three brothers, but I'm the oldest and everyone wanted me to learn the ropes and run the ranch for Pops. So they took who I was, and what I loved more than anything, and ridiculed it. Constantly. And told me I couldn't do it and made it clear I was an idiot for wanting to.

"One day I couldn't stand it anymore. I took all the money I could find and left. Hitchhiked here, to San Francisco, and worked in kitchens until I'd saved enough for a ticket to Europe. Talked my way into apprenticeships in some of the best restaurants in France and Spain. Learned it all from the ground up. Then I went to New York and did the same."

"You were such a kid." Jenna tried to imagine it. It was so young to be out in the world, across the planet from all he'd known, burdened with his family's disappointment.

"For a while I was a kid, but it's no excuse, Jenna. I got older, but I never grew up. I'm over thirty now, but until about a year ago, my behavior didn't change. I was still acting like that teenager. I guess a part of that was because of my family—I felt all bruised, you know? I think I just had low self-esteem.

"But I don't want to make excuses. I drank and even took drugs sometimes. Just a little at first, to get me through a long day. But soon the partying became kind of an all-day, every-day thing. I guess I didn't really notice because everyone around me was doing it, too."

He paused and took a sip of his beer, then pushed it away across the table. When he met her eyes, Jenna was shocked to see unshed tears there. "When I was in New York and pretty well-known, there were women. All the time." He was back to tracing patterns on the table with his fingers. "I stopped respecting them, Jenna. I treated them like interchangeable, expendable bimbos and none of them deserved it. Between the drugs and the women and working all the time and never getting much sleep, I became someone I didn't recognize."

The pain in his voice hurt her heart. "I can't imagine. I'm sorry."

"I woke up one morning really early. It was barely light. And I was half under a Dumpster behind some dive bar. There were rats running all around me, blood on my hands from a broken bottle beneath them. I still don't know how I got there."

"Sandro..." She couldn't finish her sentence. It was a horrifying image.

"I packed up my apartment that day. I called work and quit. And I went back to Benson to try to get my head on straight. I've been home almost a year now."

Jenna thought of her mom, drinking to hide from the pain in her life. "Did you go to rehab? Did you get help?" She glanced at his beer and noticed that the glass was still almost completely full.

"I didn't. Maybe I should. But you know, ever since then, I lost my interest in drinking and drugs. I have almost no cravings for any of it. But I promise you, if I start heading down that road again, my butt will be in a chair at an AA meeting immediately."

"So at the party last night..." she prompted.

"A guy offered me pot. Not that it's an excuse."

"You're kidding."

"Before I could even think rationally, I hit him. And then I ran out of there. I just wanted to get outside, to get away from everything."

"Everything?" She wondered if that word included her.

He seemed to pick up on her meaning. "I had a great time with you. I really did. But the party stressed me out. I think Tess threw me off my game first. I know she's your friend, and I don't want to say anything that might offend you, but when she came on to me like that, it reminded me of a lot of the women I knew in New York.

"And then there was the tarot, and I know it sounds dumb but when the cards were forecasting change, I just panicked. I've had so much change lately and I don't really want more, you know? I just want everything quiet and settled."

"I can understand that—when your life felt so hectic for so long."

"I'm sorry for running out on you, Jenna."

"It's okay." She thought about the way she'd felt when she realized he was gone. "I mean, it's not really okay, but at least I understand it better now. I appreciate you telling me all this. And I think you should cut yourself some slack. You haven't exactly had it easy."

"If you're telling me to forgive myself, I don't

want to. I don't want to live in a world where it's somehow okay for me to treat people the way I used to, or the way I treated you last night. These days I try to show a lot of respect for others. But I don't always succeed. I screw up, as you've seen firsthand."

"Just promise me that next time you go on a date, you'll tell the girl if you're going to leave."

"Does that mean you'd consider going out with me again?" His jaw was still tense, but his mouth curled in a half smile.

"You made it pretty clear this morning that you weren't interested."

"I was lying."

"Lying is bad. Number-one dating rule you need to learn."

"I'll learn it. Give me another chance, Jenna. At the very least, I owe you a great evening."

"I don't know." It was flattering that he wanted more time with her. But he'd shown her a glimpse of how much he could hurt her.

"I kind of wish I could have seen you hitting that guy last night!" she teased, changing the subject.

"Isn't that kind of bloodthirsty, Red?"

His smile was getting bigger, just as she'd hoped. "Maybe. Or maybe I just would have enjoyed seeing you get all manly. Kind of like you did with Brent at the studio the other day."

"You enjoyed that? But you were mad at me! You made me go to that dance competition as penance."

She smiled at the memory. "I don't think you had such a terrible time. Did you?"

"Can't say as I did." He was finally relaxed, and his answering grin was slow and lazy. "In fact, it was an awesome day. But you were still pretty upset when I wanted to hit Brent."

Something inside of her that had gone into hiding last night came awake and fluttered. She could do this with him—talk things out and come to an understanding. And smile afterward. It felt hopeful and way more grown-up than anything she'd ever had with Jeff or anyone else. "Just because it was wrong of you to bully my dance partner doesn't mean I didn't enjoy it a tiny bit."

"There's history there with him, isn't there?"

Jenna sighed. Well, if he could be honest, so could she. "We dated for a couple years when we first started dancing together. And it was fun at first. Really romantic. I thought I'd found my partner, The One, artistically, romantically—you know. But eventually I realized he's the kind of guy who's never satisfied—always looking over your shoulder wondering if someone better might come along. And soon someone did, and he broke up with me."

"And now he wants you back."

"Well, he *thinks* he does. He does this every couple years. Gets lonely, thinks his life is empty and decides that if we get back together, he'll feel satisfied."

"And will he?"

Jenna's laugh tasted bitter. "No! I did it once, you know. The first time he wanted me back, I went. The same thing happened. He got restless and started flirting with other people. We'd fight about it.... At least that time I left before he dumped me. But I think I only beat him to it by a couple of days!" It felt good to be able to laugh about it—even with dark humor.

"So what's going to happen with you and him?"

"I guess I'll talk to him—tell him to back off. He sulks, though. That's why I couldn't talk to him about it before the competition. I needed his head in the right place. At least if he gets upset now, it will only affect our classes."

"Do you think you'll keep being partners?"

He'd asked the one question that worried her the most. "I want us to. When he's not being jealous, and we're just dancing, he's a great partner. And we do well together."

"Three-time national champions, right?" He raised his glass in a toast.

It sounded so funny coming out of his mouth. "Yup. But I think we might want different things. He seems content in the ballroom, but I'm going kind of crazy there. I've been there for years, San-dro—since I was a student. Sometimes I love it and sometimes I feel like those pink-striped walls are just getting closer and closer. I want my own place. My own studio."

"Where Marlene can't give your classes away to her niece?"

Jenna laughed. "Something like that, yes. But I don't know if Brent will come with me when I make the move. And I don't want to ask until I've got my own place. He's not great at keeping a secret."

"You've really thought this through."

"Yeah, I guess so." She thought about it all the time. Well, most of the time. Lately she'd spent way too much time thinking about Sandro.

"What makes you so ambitious?" He was studying her face now, making it hard to think.

"I don't know. Part of it is all these problems with Marlene and Nicole. I'm tired of working where everyone is trying to claw their way ahead." She picked up her drink and took a sip, not sure if she wanted to admit the other reason. But it seemed like the theme of the night was full disclosure. "And you're not the only one with something to prove to your family, Sandro. My family has made it loud and clear for years that they think I'm doing the wrong thing with my life."

"And you want to show them what you're made of."

"Something like that. I've recently given up on making them proud or even thinking they'll come around and be supportive. I guess I want to succeed in spite of all their disapproval."

"Sounds familiar."

Jenna looked up and saw the understanding in his eyes.

"What are they like?" he asked.

How could she describe them without talking his ear off? She stuck to the basic facts. "My mom's from a high society–type family. My dad's done really well with a few different businesses. My sister and brother are incredibly successful in their fields. Basically, they think I'm the family idiot."

"Well, then they don't see you the way I do." Sandro stood up and came around the table, settling on the bench next to her. Jenna instantly felt the heat from his leg so close to hers. "I know what it's like not to have anyone fighting for you," Sandro said, taking her hand. "It sucks."

"That's putting it mildly. They think my career is a joke—a hobby gone wild."

"Yeah. My family still gives me girly aprons for Christmas. They think it's hilarious. My brothers threatened to change my name to Sandra growing up."

Jenna giggled. "You'd think they'd just appreciate the good food."

"They're steak-and-potatoes folks. The stuff I cook makes no sense to them."

"It must be weird for them, you know. Out on

a ranch in this world of sheep, trucks and cowboy hats, and here's you with your cooking and Paul with his dancing. It's like you two are a couple of changelings or something."

"Changelings?"

"You know, the old legends? Where fairies replaced human babies with their own children? I guess that's how they used to explain people like you and Paul, and even me. People who just don't fit the mold."

"Well, I guess I should be glad we were born in modern times." Sandro grinned down at her. "Didn't they leave those poor kids out in the woods so the fairies would take them back?"

"Ugh. Yes. Here's to modern times." She raised her glass to his.

They sat for a minute, and Jenna watched the activity at the bar. There was a couple looking kind of awkward, probably on a first date. Next to them was a man Jenna had seen there before. He looked to be in his sixties, tall and thin. He always came alone.

Then Sandro turned to look down at her. "There was another reason I think I left that party, Jenna."

"You needed another reason? Seemed like you had plenty."

"This, Jenna. Us. When I moved back to Benson, I promised myself that if I ever dated again, it would be someone from there. Someone simple and kind of traditional. Someone who made my life easy and safe. You're not any of those things, Red. And it makes no sense. We don't even live near each other. I shouldn't want to be with you."

Her emotions rose and there were tears behind her eyes. "It doesn't make any sense for me, either. Before I met you, I was dating someone who cheated on me. When I met you in Benson, Jack warned me to steer clear."

"He did the right thing." His voice was harsh and low. She could hear the self-mockery in it. The self-hatred.

"Hey," she said quietly. "Remember the cards last night. They were all about change. You came home because you wanted to change."

Sandro's eyes were black in the dim light and she could see the thick, dark lashes that framed them. His high cheekbones and olive skin made him look like some kind of Spanish prince, not a chef and a rancher's son who'd just told her his rather sordid life story.

But strangely enough, right now she didn't care about his past that much. She didn't know the Sandro he'd been in New York—she knew this man in front of her now. He was complicated and difficult and passionate, but she liked him. She liked that he was trying to do something different, to be someone better than he had been. And most of all she liked the way she felt around him. Alive and present—totally in the moment. There was a new-found freedom in the certain knowledge that there could be nothing for them after his teaching job in San Francisco was over.

Jenna put her fingers up and ran them lightly down the line of his jaw, enjoying the feel of his stubble, the bone beneath. His mouth was wide and she traced the edge of his lower lip. A small, almost shy smile pulled the corners up.

Sandro took a lock of her hair in his long fingers and wound it around. "It's the most incredible color. Like I'm holding on to a piece of the sunset." He leaned in and her eyes closed. She felt his smile when his mouth covered hers, when he tugged and pulled at her lower lip, and when his tongue entered her mouth. She slid her hand farther up his jaw and into his hair and pulled him closer, letting herself forget how last night had ended. She wanted to just feel him there, underneath her hands, over her mouth. The bar noise around them faded and vanished so there was only this moment, with the dark taste of him filling her senses.

"Is that any way to behave, Wee Jenna?" Mack's words from across the bar had the other customers laughing and Jenna felt her face heat and her smile end the kiss.

Sandro pulled his mouth away, but kept his gaze on her. Jenna could see the laughter that crinkled the corners of his eyes, putting a warmth there that she wanted to see again. "How about we go for a walk?" he asked.

"Sure," Jenna whispered, barely able to take her eyes off of him as she reached behind her for her coat and purse. Sandro stood and held out his hand, pulling her to her feet, his focus on her so intense that it felt like a weight, anchoring her to the ground when otherwise she might have just floated, she was so lost in wanting him.

"Let me help." He took her coat and held it out and she somehow got herself into it. He pushed open the door to the street and cold fog poured in, prickling her skin awake and alive. A strange excitement hummed in her veins.

She waved goodbye to Mack, who gave her the thumbs-up. Then they were on the sidewalk and Sandro's arm wrapped around her. She snuggled in and walked with her face pressed against the tough hide of his jacket. He smelled like some combination of leather, spices and fresh air. She closed her eyes for a moment and breathed it all in.

There were few people around even though it was only nine o'clock. "Where do you want to go, Red?"

She could feel his breath warming her scalp through her hair. And she knew where she wanted to take him. "My future dance studio. The building I want to rent. It's only a few blocks away."

"You want a dance studio in *this* neighborhood?"

"It's in Lower Nob Hill. Well, the lower part of

Lower Nob Hill. Still, it *is* a bit more upscale over that way." She guided him downhill from busy Van Ness Avenue. Sandro was right—this *was* an especially troubled part of the city and they had to pick their way around a few people huddled under blankets on the sidewalk. Jenna would never get used to seeing them lying there like that.

After a left turn on Hyde Street and a right on Sutter, there was a slightly less grim feel to the neighborhood. And there was her dream. Darkened and abandoned, the old Italian cultural center housed the ballroom that she hoped no one else would discover.

She pointed up to the second floor. "See those windows? They run floor to ceiling. The light that comes in is incredible. The dance floor needs refinishing, the whole thing needs a good cleaning and a coat of paint on the walls, but that's all. There are crystal chandeliers, ceilings painted like a sky full of tubby cherubs and dressing rooms—it's perfect."

Sandro peered through the metal gate to the old glass doors and the dark lobby beyond. "Have you had it all checked out by an engineer? Is it sound?"

Jenna sighed. "Don't ruin my dreams! No, of course not. I managed to find a Realtor who let me in, but it's not even clear yet if the owners will lease it to me. But I mean to talk them into it."

He laughed. "Red, if anyone can talk them into it, it will be you—of that I have no doubt. I know firsthand how persuasive you are. When I woke up this morning, I was sure that Paul and I would be back in Benson tonight."

Jenna stopped. Paul. She'd forgotten him, she'd been so wrapped up in Sandro's story, in the new-found intimacy between them. "What's going to happen, Sandro? Can he keep taking classes?"

Sandro turned to face her, leaning against the gate that blocked the entrance to the building. "I'm worried, Jenna. He's only fifteen, so that's three years of taking crap from people about his dancing before he's free. What if he ends up making the kind of choices I did?"

Jenna wanted to pull him close, offer comfort, but everything between them was so new. She *could* offer words. Ideas. "Sandro, you had no one to support you when you were young, to guide you and help you discount your family's ridicule. Paul has *you* to stand up for him and to give him perspective. He has me and the kids in his dance class."

"But the stakes are higher now. It seems like there are so many drugs available even to kids. You read about it in the paper every day. And he's going into a profession where the women so obviously outnumber the men. How is he going to learn to respect women if they're a dime a dozen? Especially if he already feels as rejected and pissed off as I did?" The angst and worry in his voice were palpable.

"I think you should slow down. Take one worry

at a time. First of all, dancers might do dumb stuff, just like anyone does, but drugs isn't generally one of them. It's impossible to dance that way and we're all about the dancing." She saw a faint smile tilt up the corners of his mouth. "I get that you're scared. You're an amazing big brother to look out for Paul the way you do. But what about also having faith in him? He's a good kid. He looks up to you, Sandro, and he listens to you. I don't think he's going to lose perspective or start disrespecting people."

"Like I did." His bitterness was heavy in the night air between them.

"You were so alone," Jenna said. She went to him, stepped into his arms and sighed when he pulled her close. With her head on his chest, she relished his strength around her.

He buried his face in her hair and his voice was muffled. "You are so wise, Jenna. How did that happen? You seem like you've been on your own, too, without your family, but instead of rebelling and acting the fool like I did, you just became grounded and smart."

It was a serious moment for him, but she couldn't help but laugh. "You're being way too kind! My last boyfriend was cheating on me the entire relationship and I only just figured it out the day I met you. How's that for wise?"

"But you believe in good, Jenna. You see the good. You have hope and optimism and I lost all that."

"I guess I do." She thought of her family and the terrible fiasco of a dinner they'd had so recently. "Well, most days I do."

"You make me want to hope, too."

"What would you hope for?" She closed her eyes, keeping her arms tight around his waist. "If you were hopeful?"

Sandro sighed and she felt his chest move. "I'm not sure. All I wanted before I met you was peace and quiet and a restaurant in Benson. Now it's more complicated. I know I want to keep Paul safe and make him happy."

"Does that mean he can keep dancing?"

She felt his smile against the top of her head. Then he straightened and put his hands on her shoulders, setting her a step back from him. "See? You don't give up." Sandro put two fingers under her chin and tilted it so she was looking up into his face. In the orange glow of the streetlight his eyes were soft. "You're teaching me not to give up, either. And, yes, he can dance."

His mouth came down on hers and his lips were gentle, exploring, sliding over hers so quietly. Jenna felt the thrill of this new intimacy, of knowing him so much better than she did before, of being wrapped up with him so closely. His mouth opened hers, and she savored his taste, kissing him back, tracing her tongue over his teeth. The gentleness between them shifted, heated, and he quickly became more demanding, pushing down, taking control. Jenna closed her eyes to better taste the salt of him, to savor the way his hair felt silky tangled in her fingers, to know the way it felt to be trapped by the steel of his muscled arms.

Sutter Street was gone and there was just Sandro. He turned her carefully until she was the one leaning on the gate. He pressed against her, his lean length covering her until her awareness narrowed to the iron bars on her back and the muscle and strength of him along her front. Her breasts ached where they brushed his chest, and heat that was almost pain pooled in her abdomen.

His hands wrapped around the sides of her neck, her ribs, her waist, and she sensed him everywhere, along and around her. She pushed away from the gate to press closer to him and a low sound escaped his throat when she did. One hand unbuttoned her coat at the same time that she was trying to calm her shaking hands enough to unzip his. He deftly won the race and his fingers slid under her thin sweater, bringing the damp night air with them. His wide palm found her rib cage. His fingers found her bra and dipped inside it seeking her breast. She moaned when he found it and he kissed her more deeply.

The sound of nearby voices distracted her. A car door slammed behind Sandro, then another, and Jenna heard a woman's high-pitched giggling. And in response, a gruff voice so familiar she'd know it anywhere. She gasped and pushed Sandro off her, yanking her sweater down, thankful they were in the shadow of the dark building.

She straightened and watched her father pay the driver through the yellow cab's window. Her stomach flipped in a sickening thud when he took the arm of a woman about half his age—a platinum blonde in a fur coat who leaned on him as he guided her up the steps of the hotel across the street.

"Oh, no," she whispered, and started buttoning her coat as fast as she could. "Oh, no." Tears were starting and she brushed them away with her sleeve.

"Jenna, what's going on?" Sandro asked. "Do you need me to back off?"

"It's not you." She pointed to the hotel, where she could see her father and his companion through the windows speaking with the receptionist. "That's my father," she said quietly. "In the lobby there." She pointed. "He's supposed to be home with my mother."

Sandro craned his neck and she saw his face tighten in anger when he caught sight of her dad.

"I am so sick of him and his lies." The shock was fading as anger took over. White-hot self-righteous anger as recent memories flooded in. His disdain for her at dinner the other night. His callous treatment of her mother and the way he'd brushed off Jenna's concern about her mom's drinking. He was probably hoping his wife would just drink herself to death, and he could have all the women he wanted without the stigma of a divorce.

She waited for traffic to clear and started across the street. Sandro followed and when they got to the foot of the hotel steps, he stopped her with a gentle hand on her arm. "Hang on, Jenna. What's your plan?"

"I'm going to yell at him—what do you think?" Jenna broke free and climbed the steps quickly, afraid she'd lose sight of them. She rummaged through her purse with one hand as she climbed, trying to find her cell phone. She pulled it out and turned it on. "And I want pictures."

She pushed her way through the revolving door, scanning through the glass for her dad and his… girlfriend? Hookup? They were still at the front desk. The receptionist was handing her father a key. Her heart was pounding so hard she could feel it reverberating through her body. She paused on shaking knees. "Say cheese, Dad!" she called, almost spitting the sarcastic words out. And when he whirled, the color draining out of his face, she snapped a couple of photos. "There. Now you have your night out recorded for posterity!"

Her father let go of his companion's hand and stepped forward nervously. "Jenna! What are you doing here?" he hissed. "Were you following me?"

"You think you're so important in my life that I'd follow you around? I was walking by and I saw you go in. When are you planning on telling Mom about this?"

"Your mother? There's nothing to tell. I was just walking Marie here to her hotel. She's in town for business." Marie was standing behind her father, and Jenna saw her frown when he lied.

"Oh, really?" Jenna stepped around her father so she could be face-to-face with Marie. "Marie, hi, I'm Jenna. You're here on business, huh? You weren't about to sleep with my father?"

Marie went pale under her makeup. "Well, I..."

"Jenna, how can you be so rude?"

"That's what you care about right now, Dad? That we're polite to each other? That we don't make a scene?" She took a step closer to him and stopped, hands on her hips. "Personally, I think what matters is that you're cheating on Mom. Though, come to think of it, that's not really news, since you've done it so many times before. So maybe what we should be talking about is how you keep lying to her about it. Deep down she knows you're lying and it's making her crazy. It's making her drink!"

"Jenna, you're overreacting—"

"Stop! Stop pretending that you're better than me simply because you lack any emotions! You might know some things about business, but you don't know crap about being a good person. Stop lying to Mom and the rest of your family. It is *not* okay!" Her voice was ringing out loud and clear, and the few guests who'd been relaxing in the lobby arm-chairs were on their feet, hesitant, probably ready to dive under the tables if Jenna truly lost it and pulled out a weapon or something.

But she stopped short of completely losing it. She might have, but a large, warm hand gently gripped her shoulder and she glanced back. Sandro was there, and there was comfort in his presence. She took a deep, shaky breath and the fiery anger slowed to a sizzle. Relief surfaced. At least her dad's infidelity was out in the open now, and maybe her mom could finally heal.

Her father was staring at Sandro with a stricken expression. He turned to Jenna. "You brought one of your *boyfriends* in here to witness this?"

She laughed at his attempted insult. "Dad, this is Sandro. We were just out for a drink tonight. He followed me in because he's nice, and he wanted to be supportive of me. Two things you couldn't possibly understand."

"Evening." Sandro nodded at her dad. He kept his hand on Jenna's shoulder, making it clear that he had her back.

"So, Dad, are you going to tell Mom about this? Or should I?"

"What happens between me and your mother is our business, Jenna," her father said loftily.

"So I take it that means you'll tell her? Remember—" she held up her camera "—I have photos."

Marie looked so shocked that Jenna wondered if the woman had even known her father was married. His gold wedding band was missing from his hand.

"I think I'll just call it a night," Marie said, taking the keys out of her father's hand. "Good night, Charles."

She turned on her stilettos and marched over to the elevators. Her back was to them as she waited for the car to arrive. She didn't turn around again.

Jenna's father sighed, watching her with regret etched on his face.

Regret, not guilt, Jenna noted. "Go home and talk to Mom. She deserves to know the truth." A numb exhaustion crept over her—she didn't want to be here anymore.

Sandro must have seen it, or sensed it. He steered her firmly to the lobby door, pushing it open for her with one hand, supporting her across the shoulders with the other, away from her mess of a father and out into the welcoming fresh air.

CHAPTER TWELVE

JENNA WAS SHAKING, grateful for Sandro's arm supporting her as they silently descended the steps back down onto Sutter Street. She walked quickly once they hit the sidewalk, and to her relief, Sandro merely followed, giving her some space. He didn't speak until she led them back to Hyde Street. She needed to walk, to burn off the anger and hurt, and there were steep hills there.

"Jenna, wait." She paused in front of a laundry. It was open late and the homey scents of soap and dryer sheets wafted onto the sidewalk. "Can I do anything for you?"

She didn't want to talk, couldn't talk. She just wanted to keep moving until the lump in her throat dissolved. "If you need to get home, I understand," she told him. "But I think I'll take a walk."

"I can go with you, if you'd like company."

"Sure." She *did* want his company, which was kind of odd. Sandro the recently reformed womanizer seemed a strange person to seek comfort from tonight.

Sandro took her hand and they started up Hyde.

Jenna tried to process what she'd seen—her dad about to sleep with someone. She tried to let it go. *Grant me the serenity to accept the things I cannot change.* But the Serenity Prayer was offering little serenity at the moment. At least there was exercise. After conquering a few steep hills, Jenna felt some of the emotion subsiding. "I'm so sorry you had to witness that," she said.

"I'm sorry you had to go through that."

"I don't usually scream and yell in random hotel lobbies."

He smiled down at her. "I didn't imagine that was your usual style."

She felt the need to explain herself. "Just a couple weeks ago I was at my parents' house for dinner. I tried to bring up that my mom is drinking too much. My dad treated me as if I was some kind of crazy person. A pariah. He practically threw me out of the house. So tonight, to see him doing something so wrong, after that night and after all the years he's spent judging me and looking down on me simply because I wanted to dance—it just made me crazy."

"I get it." Sandro smiled. "I admire you, honestly. I sometimes wish I could just have it out with my dad like that. Tell him to stop trying to get me to take over the ranch for him."

"He still thinks you might?"

"While I was growing up, and ever since I got back home. I offer to help. Of course I want to help out—I love the ranch. But I feel like he's always hoping it will turn into more. It won't, because my first priority is my restaurant and it always will be. Plus, it's not fair to my brothers. Joe and Gabe *really* love the ranch. They're the ones who want it. I'm sure it hurts them that he can't acknowledge all they've done and instead spends so much time trying to convince me to take their place."

They'd crossed Jackson Street, and a rumbling and clanking behind them had them both glancing back. A cable car was rounding the corner to turn onto Hyde. "Have you ever ridden one?" Jenna asked.

"Nope," Sandro answered, and a wistful look brushed across his face. "That whole first year after I left home, when I lived here, I just worked nonstop. I never did any of the tourist stuff." He smiled suddenly and reached for her hand. "Want to hop on?"

"Sure," Jenna answered. Why not? She needed an adventure right now. A distraction. Anything. Sandro led her across the street at a jog and when the car pulled up, they jumped onto the outside step. It was nearly empty. Sandro handed the driver their fare and Jenna sat on the wooden bench that always felt like a piece of history. Sandro stood on the step along the outside of the car.

"You can sit." She had to raise her voice over the

clanking sound of the cable. "It's a rare thing to get a seat—it's hardly ever this empty!"

"I've always wanted to ride on the outside!" Sandro was hanging on to the brass pole and leaning out just a little, watching the pavement disappear beneath them. "Just like you see in all the tourist photos. Come on. It's awesome—do it with me!"

Jenna got up and went to stand in front of him, hanging on to the pole as the street slipped dizzyingly by under her feet. It was exhilarating, especially as they jangled down the steep hills, past the old Victorian houses tumbling toward the bay. They were descending into thick fog, the world getting more hazy and mysterious with every block.

"This is way better than I thought!" Sandro called to her. The grin on his face made him look younger, more like Paul.

"It's amazing!" she agreed. The lights on the Golden Gate Bridge and Alcatraz Island were blurry patches of lighter-colored fog, but Jenna pointed them out anyway. It never got old, the vivid landmarks that defined her city.

The car stopped in Aquatic Park at the foot of Hyde Street. The enormous sign that usually spelled out Ghirardelli Square was just a smear of illuminated fog. Jenna led Sandro around the side of the old brick building and up the steps to the fountain, with its bronze lily pads and mermaids. The seafood restaurant was still open. "Do you want to go in for a drink or anything?" Sandro asked.

Jenna was cold but not ready to go inside just yet. She wanted to drink the damp fresh air in enormous gulps. It quieted her mind and lifted her spirits. She pulled her skirt down over her knees, wishing she'd brought more layers. Her vintage wool jacket wasn't meant for outdoor adventures. "Can we keep walking just a little more?"

When Sandro nodded, Jenna led him down the flights of stairs to Beach Street. She crossed, heading for the bay. Waves sloshed at the tiny beach and they walked slowly along the sand. Jenna put her fingers in the water, inhaling the briny smell, and then reached up and touched Sandro's forehead. "There. First a cable car ride, now baptized by bay water. You're officially a true San Franciscan."

"No, *you're* a true San Franciscan, you groovy little pagan."

Jenna burst into laughter at his unexpected teasing. "I'm not a pagan!"

"Just groovy, then."

"Born and raised—what do you expect?" She dipped her hand in for a little more water and sent it spattering over his head. "Is that better?"

Laughing, he grabbed her around the waist and swung her up, dangling her over the foamy shore, threatening to drop her in. She wriggled in his arms and brought her knees up so he couldn't get her feet wet. When he set her down, she took off running, glad she'd worn her comfy combat boots with her dress. Wide cement steps rose above the beach almost like an amphitheater and she darted up to the top, Sandro following, both of them laughing.

It was even darker up here. Mist-shrouded cypress trees shaded them from streetlights. A wall blocked them from the rest of the park and Beach Street beyond. They flopped down next to each other on the top step. The muffled darkness of the foggy night worked its magic and they both quieted. Sandro put his arm around Jenna and she moved close, seeking his warmth.

It was comforting sitting in the anonymous darkness, listening to the water hit the sand. A foghorn cut through the quiet. Growing up in Seacliff, so near the entrance to the Golden Gate, Jenna had heard the sound most nights. Many people found it a mournful noise, but Jenna loved its somber tone.

"Are you okay?" Sandro finally asked. "About what happened with your dad?"

That was a challenging question right now. "I think so," Jenna answered. "I just feel empty. It's so out of my control, you know? I guess I just have to decide whether or not to tell my mother. I'm pretty sure my dad won't."

Staring out into the dark mist, she tried to absorb what had happened. What was wrong with her family? Her dad was cheating, and when she'd discovered it, she'd been wrapped up in the arms of a man so notorious for cheating that she'd been warned away from him by one friend and told his war stories by another. Why the need to play with such fire? Why was she putting herself at risk again? She must have sighed, because Sandro pulled away a bit, forcing her to sit up straight. He looked down. "Jenna?"

"I'm sorry. I'm just upset."

"It can't be easy knowing what you know about your dad."

"It's not him, really. It's me. I'm pathetic. I'm like a case study in a self-help book for people who make terrible relationship choices. My father cheats. So what do I do? I find Brent, who cheated. I find Jeff, who cheated. And now I find you, who cheated on people up until about a year ago and, as far as I know, hasn't actually put his new morals to the test." She regretted her harsh words as soon as she saw him wince.

"I left the party last weekend *because* of my new morals. I turned down your friend Tess because of my new morals. Doesn't that mean anything?" He looked out over the bay, and she could feel his frustration like an aura around him.

"It does…. I mean, it should…. But it's scary for me, you know? To think I'm just repeating the same bad choices over and over."

"So I'm a bad choice." Sandro still wasn't looking at her but at something far out in the darkness.

"*You're* not. But *this* probably is. You and me. A relationship that has no future."

Sandro turned and caught her hands in his. His face was shadowed but she could feel the intensity radiating off him. "Maybe this thing between us has no future…or maybe it does. Either way, I promise you, Jenna, I am not like your dad. I am not like Brent or Jeff. I am *not* one of those guys anymore."

"But can people change that quickly?" Jenna remembered the night by Dolores Park. She'd promised herself she'd stop expecting others to change. But here she was, hoping Sandro would be the exception to the inertia that kept people like her father stuck in their ways.

"What was all that at the party last night, then? The tarot cards. You said it again earlier tonight— that they symbolized change. I don't know if I really believe in all that, but I think I *have* changed, Jenna. I feel it inside. I am living it in my actions and my choices. I know you were hurt by boyfriends and by your father. But I am not like them anymore. And even if I was, I couldn't be that way with you."

"What do you mean?" She tried to scrutinize his face but it was no use. His eyes were just darker shadows.

"I mean that I like you. I admire you. You're

gorgeous and funny and tough and crazy talented. I can't imagine why anyone would cheat on you."

Maybe he was lying, just saying words that she wanted to hear. But she didn't think so. Sandro had done nothing but speak his mind since they met. He'd been nothing but brutally honest. And knowing that drove home the meaning behind his words. He liked her. A lot. She voiced her last doubt.

"Do you think that seeing my dad like that, while we were out together, was some kind of sign? I mean, isn't it crazy that in this big city, we were outside the hotel he chose to visit tonight?"

"Jenna, not everything that happens is some kind of mystical sign! Or if it is, then how about the fact that I came along right after your bike accident— maybe that's a sign that whatever is happening between us is okay? What about the fact that you're a dancer and you met my little brother in our pasture and *he* wants to dance? Isn't that a sign, too?"

"I don't know." She put her head in her hands. She liked to believe that everything happened for a reason. But right now, with everything so complicated, that theory wasn't making much sense. "Maybe."

"Jenna, I came out tonight to explain to you why all of this—Paul's dancing, this thing between you and me—was a bad idea. I was planning to say goodbye and go home. But you convinced me, again, that Paul will be okay. And here I am, trying to convince you that *we* will be okay. What's happening between us feels important. If there *is* a sign we should pay attention to, how about the fact that, aside from running into your dad, this is one of the best evenings I've ever had?"

He had her attention. And whether he was right about all this or not, she was tired of worrying. What she really wanted, she realized, was not to worry or think or analyze. What she really wanted was to feel Sandro's arms around her one more time.

So she reached up through the dark and found his cheek with her hand. It was rough with stubble and damp with mist, and she brought her thumb up to his cheekbone, running it over the ridge there, then down to his lips. He opened his mouth and she very lightly touched his teeth, felt the tip of his tongue with her fingers. And then she got her wish. The worries fled, taking all rational thought with them, leaving behind only desire.

She stood abruptly, stepped in between Sandro's legs, leaned over and replaced her fingers with her mouth. Her hands went to his shoulders and her hair fell around them in a damp curtain as she kissed him, letting her raw hunger show as she explored the depths of his mouth.

At first he was still, likely as surprised as she was by her boldness. Then his hands spanned her waist and he brought her down to straddle his lap.

He matched her need with his own, one hand on her back and one in her hair, bringing her so close that the weight of his mouth on hers was bruising, but with a pain she sought, a pressure she needed.

He kissed his way to her ear, making her nerve endings ripple under his touch, and then his mouth was on her neck, the sensation there causing her whole body to surge into his, to press down on his lap, making him groan low in his throat. She felt the vibration of the sound in the air between them.

Sandro's hands came down around her hips and from there slid easily under her skirt to follow the line of her legs. Her thigh-high socks left the skin above them bare and she could tell the moment he realized it by the sharp, shaky intake of his breath and the way his teeth bit down on her shoulder.

She brought his chin up with her fingers and kissed him again, deeply, gasping into his throat when his fingers slid down the lace edge of her panties. She was wet for him, and when he realized it, his eyes opened and he looked into hers and that slow, lazy smile she loved tilted up one corner of his mouth.

"You are so insanely beautiful," he whispered against her cheek, and then he watched her eyes as he trailed his fingers through the slickness. She forced herself to keep his gaze, to not look away or let shyness dull the moment but to live with no fear, in the present. She couldn't control the future, but she could choose how to live in this moment, and she was choosing to let this gorgeous man touch her like this.

She leaned forward and took his lower lip between her teeth and bit gently, then sucked there and he rocked into her in response. His fingers entered her, bringing heat and insane longing with them, but she didn't want to be in this hot, vulnerable place without him. Slowly, she lifted herself off of his hand, feeling the cold air when the warmth of him slid away. "I need you—inside me," she gasped.

He let out a harsh breath and tipped his head down, resting it on her chest. "I need you, so much, but I don't have..." His voice trailed off.

She could hear the frustration and how much he wanted them to be together.

She kissed the top of his head, and he looked up and returned her kiss softly, a slight scrape of teeth on her lips that sent a shiver down her spine. "My bag," she gasped, suddenly remembering. "I think I might have a condom...." Left over from Jeff, but she didn't mention that.

"I love a modern woman," he murmured, and kissed her reverently.

Jenna leaned over to grab her purse off the cement below them while he held her waist to keep her from falling. She brought the bag up between them and fished around until she found the small cloth sack that held emergency supplies—a few tampons, a travel toothbrush and, glory be, a condom.

"How are we going to do this?" he whispered when she showed it to him.

"Isn't that supposed to be your specialty?" she whispered back, and kissed him again. She ground her hips against him and that one movement caused so much desire that she was unbuckling his jeans before she was even conscious of it. She freed him and wrapped her hand around his erection and followed it with the condom. Kissing her deeply, Sandro lifted her up, pulled her full skirt around them so it veiled their bared skin and gasped when she lowered herself over him.

His arms around her back supported her when she might have collapsed from the feel of him inside. Heat filled her, fueled her, so that she was oblivious of the way the cement stairs dug into her knees or the way his hands on her waist gripped her so tight that they bruised as he guided her. The only thing she was aware of was that it was Sandro, so deep within her, and how perfect it felt to be this way with him. She buried her face in his hair, the faint spice and salt of him mixed with the fresh cloud scent of the fog.

The pressure inside her built every time he pushed into her, and she tilted her pelvis forward to take him even deeper. He held her then, a hand behind her head, his mouth trapping hers in a searing kiss. She felt him pulse deep inside her body, a rhythm her muscles absorbed and mimicked. Then the pressure turned into pure energy, pure feeling that peaked and burst into sparks and shards that seemed to scatter and shimmer through her muscles. All she could do was cling to him while her body shook with his. And when she finally stopped shaking, he kissed her softly, over the skin of her face, her eyes, her lips, and then pulled her closer still. He was sheathed inside her, arms strong around her, his head buried against her chest. Jenna looked around hazily, surprised to see that the bay was still there, and the chill fog still swirled around them— they hadn't actually been transported to some other, even more dreamlike place.

Jenna stayed there, resting her cheek in his hair, listening to the foghorn, the rhythmic slosh of the waves, the occasional car on the street beyond their sheltering wall. She felt limp and languid and didn't want to lct go, but her legs were cold and getting so stiff she didn't know if she could straighten them again. "Sandro," she whispered, though she didn't know why she was suddenly worried that someone might hear them.

"Mmm?" He looked up from her chest.

"I have to move."

He carefully helped her off him. She was grateful for her skirt around her as she rearranged her underwear and pulled up her socks. When she turned back, he was dressed, as well, and gathering up her bag for her. He pulled her close and kissed her and there was a new intimacy there, along with the same desire as before but amplified somehow. Maybe because now they knew how incredible they truly were together.

Sandro pulled back slightly and Jenna bit her lip, pressing down on the place where his mouth had been. Regretting its absence. "We have to get you warm," he said. "Let's go find something hot to drink."

He kept a sheltering arm around her all the way back to Beach Street, so careful with her, as if she was fragile and precious. He walked her into a pub that boasted a late-night menu and the best Irish coffee in the city. They headed for a back booth. Sandro insisted they sit side by side so he could keep holding her, and he ordered the coffee—Irish for Jenna and plain for him. Jenna curled up against the strength of him, trying to absorb what had occurred. How somehow an evening that had started because she'd wanted to help Paul had become all about Sandro and herself.

The waitress brought their drinks. The heat and the alcohol were a perfect remedy for Jenna's frozen limbs and she sipped the scalding liquid eagerly.

Sandro took his arm back to drink his coffee. Setting the cup on the table, he turned in the booth so he faced her. "Now I can see you," he said. He pushed a curl off her shoulder. "That was amazing. Completely unexpected and incredible. Thank you."

Jenna flushed. "You're welcome." She knew she should say more but her brain seemed to have gone to sleep from the whiskey in her coffee, or maybe from the amazing sex.

"It was good, right?"

Sandro the infamous womanizer needed reassurance? She put a hand on his thigh, leaned over and kissed his cheek. "Unbelievable," she assured him. An accurate description. When she woke up tomorrow, would she believe she'd been so daring?

He studied her closely. "You're okay with it?"

"Of course. Why, what's wrong?" Jenna wasn't sure she really wanted to know. She didn't want her perfect memories spoiled. "You didn't like it?"

He took her hand. "It was the best. Seriously. But I feel kind of guilty, like it shouldn't have been that way, at least not our first time."

Jenna stared at him, trying to figure out what he meant. Then it hit her. "It reminds you of the stuff you used to do in New York." They'd just had sex and he was comparing her to the women he'd slept with before. Things he'd done with them. Suddenly she felt sick. She jerked her hand out of his.

"No!" Sandro sat bolt upright.

He reached for her hand again but she was reluctant to give it. His eyes were dark and pleading but all she could think was that she'd taken such a risk tonight, done something she'd never done before, and to him it was old news. Maybe even boring.

"Look, I wasn't thinking of any of that. I promise you, Jenna."

"Then what did you mean?" Her voice sounded tired even to her.

"Well, I guess I'm wondering if I should have made us wait until we could make it perfect, you know? It seems like I should have made sure it was nice, respectful…" He broke off, seemingly stuck for words.

"Not just some recreational sex on a bench in the city? I'm sorry if it wasn't *perfect* enough." She threw his words back at him.

"I didn't mean it that way. I already told you it was incredible and I meant it."

Jenna was trying to understand, but the rational part of her brain seemed to be having trouble returning after she'd kicked it out earlier—kicked it out so she could enjoy the moment and not analyze it all. Unfortunately for her, Sandro hadn't done the same, and his postgame analysis didn't seem to be in her favor.

Sandro reached out and ran his knuckles along her cheek. She couldn't help but lean into the sensation.

"I feel like you're trying to misunderstand me," he said quietly. "Are you regretting it?"

"No!" The memory of how magical it had all

seemed came back and taunted. The bay, the hum of the foghorns wafting through. She didn't regret it— did he? "Yes. I don't know. Look, I think I should just get going. It's been a long night." She took one last fortifying gulp of coffee.

"Wait," he said. "I'll see you home."

"No, that's okay, really." Her head was spinning with exhaustion and a healthy dose of embarrassment. He'd wanted it to be respectful and nice, and she'd straddled him on a bench in a San Francisco park. He must think she was just like all the women he'd known back in New York. "I can grab a cab outside and be home in no time."

She turned to go, then turned back. She couldn't leave it like this. "I just want you to know that before tonight I'd never done *anything* like that. And up until now I felt like it was incredibly exciting and way better than *nice*."

Sandro reached out, and for a moment it looked as if he might stop her, but then his hand dropped to his side. "I meant it when I said it was one of the best nights of my life. And somehow it got even better. I've gotten in the habit of overthinking things. I wish I'd just kept my mouth shut."

She knew he was trying to make her feel better, but she was way too exhausted to process anything else. "Maybe it's better you didn't," she said numbly. "I'd always rather know the truth."

She walked quickly out of the pub, grateful to see

a cab right outside. A getaway car. But there was no crime scene to flee, just a lot of confusing desire. And the baggage that both of them were carrying from their past mistakes.

She got into the cab and directed the driver to the Mission District. Her whirling thoughts slowly calmed as she looked out at the neon signs of Van Ness Avenue. The strange thing was, there were only two things she regretted right now: that Sandro had regrets and that he might think less of her.

She was strangely proud of herself. She'd managed to do what she'd promised on that bike ride after her terrible family dinner a few weeks ago. She'd let go of any expectations. She'd had sex with Sandro without hope of it turning into something more, without needing more from him than his immediate desire for her. And to live in just that one moment had been fabulous and unforgettable. It had felt a lot like dancing.

Worry crept in after that thought. She'd never been able to dance with any moderation. No matter how many hours she spent in the ballroom, she always looked forward to more. If sex with Sandro felt like dancing, she'd just have to hope it didn't have the same addictive qualities.

Jenna rested her head against the cold glass and let her thoughts drift back to what it had felt like to be with him—to see the desire in his eyes and feel the desperation and passion in his touch.

Sandro had seemed disappointed tonight. Tomorrow there might be disappointment for her, as well. But tonight she just wanted to remember how it had felt, how incredibly phenomenal it had been, to be wrapped up in Sandro Salazar's arms.

CHAPTER THIRTEEN

"CHAMPAGNE!" JENNA INSISTED. "We're shopping for a wedding dress. Champagne is mandatory!"

Tess placed their order with the harried waiter and then pulled out her phone, all business. "We've made it to only two of the shops on our list. We need to step up the pace if Samantha's going to find the perfect dress by the end of the day!"

"We'll eat fast," Samantha said as she picked up her water glass and turned her green eyes on Jenna. "But there's something I want to talk about today besides my wedding. Jack mentioned something about you seeing Sandro here in the city. Why have you not mentioned this to your loyal girlfriends?"

"Jenna!" Tess exclaimed, outrage lifting her perfectly sculpted brows. "You've been holding out on me! Who is Sandro?"

That was a good question. There seemed to be a lot of Sandros. The polished chef who made incredible food in Samantha's kitchen, the tortured man with the troubled past, the sweet friend who'd supported her when she'd seen her father. And, of course, the incredibly hot guy she'd had sex with on a bench at Aquatic Park a mere thirty-six hours ago. The memory made her blush.

"You are beet-red! What is going on?" Samantha asked.

The champagne arrived and Jenna took a large gulp of hers. Tess suddenly leaned forward. "Wait a minute. Is Sandro the studly guy who was looking for you at Marlene's party?"

"Marlene's party?" Samantha stared at Jenna in shock. "You saw him at the party? Why haven't you told me about any of this?"

"I don't know," Jenna said. "It's complicated."

"You know I made a pass at him, right?" Tess asked. "I'm sorry. If I'd known he was your date, I never would have done it."

"It's okay, Tess. You didn't know."

Samantha was looking from one of them to the other in disbelief. "Get this country girl up to speed here. Jenna, you invited him to Marlene's but didn't tell Tess? And, Tess, you didn't know who he was and made a pass at him?"

"You can't blame me!" Tess smiled appreciatively. "He's a handsome guy."

"Jenna, why are you keeping this so secret?" Samantha asked.

"There wasn't much to tell. There still isn't. He lives in Benson and I live here. His brother's only studying with me for another week or so. It was just a temporary thing, while he teaches a cooking class in the city."

"Jenna, do not get into this pattern again." Tess's expression was stern. She always looked out for those she loved. "You are so nice, and you let men take advantage of you. He'd better be paying for those lessons!"

Jenna smiled at her friend's fierce protectiveness. "He's paying the full rate, don't worry."

"What's this guy like?" Tess turned toward Samantha. "Is he good enough for our Jenna?"

Samantha took a sip of her champagne and stared into it, as if the answers might be found in the bubbles. "That's a tough question. He seemed nice when he cooked for us at the ranch. That's where he and Jenna first met. He's gorgeous and obviously talented. Jack has enough faith in him to invest a bunch of money into the restaurant he's planning."

"But?" Tess prompted.

"He used to be really horrible about women," Jenna blurted out with a knot in her stomach. "You know, egotistical, unfaithful, that kind of thing."

"Great." Tess sat back, looking defeated. "Jenna, that is *not* what you need."

"It's pretty much the last thing I need."

"But the problem is," Samantha chimed in, "there's this crazy chemistry between the two of them that just about lit our house on fire when they were together."

"Oh." Tess was silent for a moment, staring down, tapping her fork on her napkin. Jenna could tell she was worried—Tess never fidgeted. "Jack left New York a long time ago. Maybe his information is old."

Jenna was relieved that her friend had introduced the idea. It made her feel a little less desperate. "He says he's totally changed—left all his bad habits behind in New York. But I don't know…. Can people change that much?" She remembered her dad, heading into a hotel with yet another random woman.

"Yeah, I wouldn't count on it," Tess said. "But hey, if he's been around, maybe he's totally amazing in bed or something. It might be worth it."

Jenna suddenly remembered the way he'd felt, so deep inside her on that bench. The blush returned.

"Jenna, have you slept with him?" The grin on Tess's face would have been at home on an alley cat.

"Shush!" Samantha scolded her. Then she brought her voice down to a stage whisper. "Jen, did you? Isn't that playing with fire?"

"Probably." Jenna leaned an elbow on the table and rested her head in her hand. "It was really, really amazing," she confessed.

"Sometimes it's fun to be a pyro," Tess murmured.

Jenna laughed. It was good to have a friend who was never shocked. "I guess I took a page from your book for once, Tess. I just wanted to be with him.

I know there's no future for us in the long term. But we really like each other, so I just went for it."

"But, Jenna, what about everything we talked about in Benson? About you staying focused on your career right now?" Samantha signaled to the waiter. "We're going to need some more champagne, please."

"Well, I've been thinking about that a lot since Sunday night...."

"Which is when, I take it, you had wild sex?" Tess interrupted.

"Yes, and..."

"And where exactly did this wild sex take place?" Tess was like a terrier with a bone when it came to details.

"Aquatic Park."

"What?" The squeal that emerged from her two friends had people at neighboring tables looking over.

"You heard me!" Jenna said, unable to keep the grin off her face. It was kind of fun to be the wild one in her little group for a change.

"As in outside? Where anyone could have seen?" Tess asked, her voice much quieter now, thank goodness.

"Well, it was foggy and dark," Jenna answered. "But, yeah, I guess someone could have seen something." And then her composure was gone and she buried her face in her hands for a moment. "Can you believe I did that?" Her voice came out as a squeak.

"No," Samantha answered.

"Yes," Tess said. "And it's about time, too. After all those years of waiting around for Jeff to get home from a gig, it's good you had yourself some fun." She raised her champagne and Jenna brought hers up to clink glasses with the wildest woman she knew.

"I guess you're right." Jenna sighed. The cool bubbles calmed as they slid down her throat. "It seemed like the perfect opportunity to have a fling. He lives in Benson and his class here in San Francisco ends next week. So there's no interference with my work and no risk I'll get emotionally involved." Ha. She already was. Jenna might be avoiding his calls but she hadn't stopped thinking about him for more than five minutes.

"Well," Samantha conceded, "maybe it's good in that way. Your goals won't get derailed."

"Exactly." Relief that her friend understood was quickly usurped by the general confusion she'd felt all week. "But in the short term, I'm like a fish out of water. What do I do next?"

"Don't look at me!" Tess chided. "I generally just avoid the guys I sleep with. Then I don't have to worry about any awkward questions like that."

"What have you *been* doing?" Samantha asked.

"Honestly? I've been doing exactly what Tess

said. Avoiding him." Jenna felt guilty every time she looked at her phone and saw a new message from Sandro.

"Really?" Her friends said it in unison, but Samantha looked shocked while Tess looked delighted.

"I'm just not up for any more heartache. I guess it's like a preemptive goodbye." Jenna tried to muffle her doubts about her own behavior. It wasn't like her to ignore someone's calls. And it wasn't like her to be such a coward. But her revelation in the cab the other night had been spot on. She was addicted.

Ever since Sunday she'd been craving what she and Sandro had had together at Aquatic Park as if it were water or food, necessary for survival. So, as with any addict, she needed to quit. Cold turkey.

As an attempt to justify her actions, she added, "I just thought it might be nice to be the one who leaves first for a change."

"You think?" Tess said blandly, encompassing all Jenna's bad luck with men in those two simple words. Laughter momentarily pushed away her nagging conscience as the truth in Tess's words sunk in.

"Okay, enough!" Jenna said when their laughter subsided. "This was supposed to be Samantha's day and we're talking about me." She tried manufacturing enthusiasm, even as the fact that she still had to call Sandro back and tell him goodbye felt like misery waiting to happen. "We need to plan our assault on the next shop. Samantha, your dress ideas, please."

Samantha pulled out a folder full of photos she'd ripped from bridal magazines. As Jenna scanned the pictures, memorizing her friend's dress preferences, she tried to quell the jealousy that crept in. Jealousy that Samantha got to walk down the aisle and join her life with the man she loved, while Jenna was going to say goodbye to Sandro, and move forward alone.

"WHAT THE HELL?" Sandro looked at Paul, then set down the hammer he was holding.

"I want to enter the talent competition." Paul's jaw was set at a stubborn angle.

"You want to get up and dance in front of the entire town?" Sandro had visions of eggs being thrown.

"There's scholarship money at stake. I could use it for lessons. Next time you have a cooking class, I could go back to San Francisco with you and work with Jenna some more."

Jenna. She hadn't returned his calls. After a couple lame voice mails, he'd had to just stop trying. He was willing to be slightly pathetic, but a guy had his limits. The trouble was, the memories of the time they'd spent together wouldn't fade. Right in the middle of his day, out on the ranch or here in the restaurant, he'd get some image so sharp and clear it was as if he were transported back to that moment with her. He'd lose all sense of where he was and get lost in the scent of her, the feel of her, how she looked at her dance competition, hanging off the side of a cable car, or shuddering over him at Aquatic Park.

"Sandro? Are you listening?"

Case in point. He dragged his mind back to Paul. "But it can't be that much money—is it worth it? People are gonna give you a lot of crap, Paul. Just Joe and Gabe alone are going to heap it on. Dad's going to walk around with a cloud of disappointment hanging over him, and for the next three years, until you can get out of here, you'll have to watch him do it. Trust me, it isn't fun."

"I'm ready to do this. I want the money and more than that, I'm tired of lying to Mom and Dad. I want my family and friends to know who I am and what I do."

Sandro took a gulp from his water bottle and set it down a little more heavily on his half-built bar than he should have. Water sloshed out on the raw wood. With a curse, he grabbed a rag and mopped it up, glad for something to do, even if he'd have to sand the watermark out later.

"Look, Paul, I've supported you in taking these classes. But you don't know what you're in for if word gets out you're a dancer. What about school? No offense to Benson, but I'd bet a lot of the guys in your class are budding little hicks. They're gonna be thrilled to have a dancer to pick on."

"I can handle it, Sandro. There're a few kids like that, but I have a lot of good friends."

"They'll call you names. Tell everyone you're prissy. All kinds of things like that. You read it in the news all the time. Bullying is so bad these days kids are killing themselves over it."

"Sandro, jeez, have you been reading Mom's magazines? You're paranoid! I'm okay. I'm not ever going to kill myself. I don't care what people say about me. I just want to perform in this show and win the money."

He knew he had to let his little brother make his own choices. But it was hard. "I just don't want to see you hurt." *Or get all screwed up inside, like me.*

Paul must have known Sandro's initial tirade was over, because he looked relieved. "I think things are different than when you were in high school. Kids do more stuff like this. They go line dancing. The school has a drill team now and guys are on it. There's a coed chorus and they dance a little, too."

"Seriously?"

"Yeah. I'm thinking of trying out for the drill team when school starts."

"I guess you're right, then. Times have changed since I went to Benson High." Sandro felt some relief at the thought. Maybe all this time, he had been overreacting.

Paul started sanding the bar again. "Sandro, I don't really know what you were like when you were my age. But I think maybe I'm different. Stuff doesn't bug me as much as it bugged you. I don't really care what other people say."

Sandro hoped that was true. He really did. But he knew he had to trust Paul. That was the underlying message, loud and clear. It hit him then that a bit of Jenna had rubbed off on him, if he was suddenly thinking about things like underlying messages. He wished she were here right now. If she were, she'd agree that he and Paul were different. She'd mentioned it before. Somehow his baby brother was a hell of a lot more resilient than he'd been.

He sighed. "All right. I support your decision, Twinkle Toes."

Paul's wide smile was filled with relief. "Thanks, Sandro. And you'll help me tell Mom and Dad, right?"

He was about to say no, but then he remembered what he'd been like just a few short weeks ago. Telling Paul to give up his dreams based on things that had nothing to do with his brother and everything to do with his own fears and his own mistakes. He owed him one.

"Sure, Paul, I'll help you tell them. But not just yet. I've finally got some time to work on my restaurant this week and I'm not giving that up. And then we've got our last weekend in San Francisco.

How about we hold off for a bit before we drop this bomb?"

"Sure." Paul's eyes were shining—he was that happy. "And thanks. You're the best. I know it will all work out."

Sandro hoped he was right, for both of their sakes.

SAN FRANCISCO WAS nice right before dawn on a weekend morning. In the last half hour, while he'd been leaning against his truck on the sidewalk near Jenna's dance studio, Sandro had heard a few cars and seen a couple joggers, but mainly the street was empty. Teaching in San Francisco had reminded him how much he truly enjoyed city life. He liked it calm and still, as it was now, *and* crowded and bustling, as it would be in just a couple hours. Cities had their own moods, as if all the people in them came together to become one giant creature.

He definitely missed being a part of it. When he let himself think about it, he could see a life for himself here. San Francisco was a much smaller city than New York. Way more comfortable. He could picture a restaurant here kind of like Oliva but a little less upscale, a little more rustic. He could imagine a cool living space, maybe a loft in an old converted warehouse.

But that was a pipe dream. He didn't do well in places like this. He hadn't even been able to handle

one party without running out and making Jenna
feel horrible. He'd returned to Benson for a reason and he had a good life waiting for him there.
A safe life.

The fog was thick and Sandro was getting cold.
But he didn't want to wait in his car, because then
he might miss her. He'd learned that Jenna was very
skilled at avoidance, which was why he was up at
the crack of dawn, trying to catch her on her way
into the ballroom.

He felt like a stalker. He couldn't believe that he'd
been reduced this. Part of him was pissed that she
wouldn't answer his calls, and part of him thought
it was kind of ironic. Legendary ladies' man Sandro Salazar finally meets the woman of his dreams,
and she won't even talk to him.

All weekend he'd been trying to speak with her in
person, since she wouldn't return his calls. But when
he'd dropped Paul off at the ballroom on Saturday
morning, his heart racing a little at the thought of
seeing her again, she hadn't been there. Instead he'd
found Brent, who'd informed him, with barely dis-
guised glee, that Jenna had an early-morning appointment and would be arriving late to class.

So Sandro had made a new plan to catch her at
the end of the day. He'd even bought flowers. But
when he'd arrived to pick up Paul, bouquet clutched
in his hand, Jenna had been nowhere to be found.

When he'd asked Paul, his brother had said she'd rushed out straight after class, car keys in hand.

It was the first time he'd ever had nonstop thoughts about someone that didn't just involve sex. He wanted to know how her week was going. He wanted to hear her thoughts and feelings. He wanted to just hear *her*. Trust his luck that the only woman he'd ever had all these cravings for wanted nothing to do with him.

He figured he knew why. Here he'd been telling her he'd changed, that he was a different guy since leaving New York. Yet the first chance he got, they were having sex in some dark corner. Outdoors. She'd said she was fine with it, but once she got home and thought it through, she'd probably felt completely disrespected, and he didn't blame her.

But maybe if he could apologize, explain things, ask for a do-over, she'd be willing to give them another chance. Because there was something between them that he wanted, and needed, more of.

He heard her car before it came into view, the staccato of the Mini engine echoing off the silent buildings. His mouth went dry and he sipped the coffee he was clutching for warmth more than the caffeine buzz. She pulled up to a parking spot across the street, hopped out and stepped lightly over to the sidewalk to pull her large bag out of the passenger seat. "Jenna," he called softly.

She hesitated for a moment, then turned to look

at him. She looked as adorable as usual in skintight pegged jeans, pink Converse low-tops and a bulky navy blue sweater wrapped around her against the chill. Slowly, she crossed the street to where he was waiting.

"Can we talk?" he asked.

"That *should* be music to my ears." She gave him a wry smile.

"Yeah, I figured with most women that's better than a pickup line." He regretted it as soon as it was out of his mouth.

She bit her bottom lip. He could almost hear the thinking. *Well, you should know.*

"Jenna," he said softly. "Talk to me. Why are you avoiding me? Did I do something wrong?"

She instantly softened. Of course she would. She was way too kindhearted to ignore the pathetic desperation in his voice. "No, you've been great." She looked around, as if hoping for some kind of rescue from this conversation. When none came, she spoke again. "You haven't done anything wrong. I think I did. You obviously regretted what happened between us last weekend."

She was worried that *he* regretted it? "I could never regret that, Jenna. I just wished I'd given you the romantic experience that you deserved. Champagne. Roses. A bed. Somewhere warm and private and beautiful."

She stared at him for a long moment. He saw pink

wash over her cheeks like the sunrise. "I thought it was perfect just the way it was. I loved being with you and I don't regret it. But I think that's all we get. We don't really have time for any more than that."

"But we could have more. We could have had this weekend if you weren't in hiding."

"Well, yes." She looked troubled. "But what's the point? Isn't today your last cooking class? You're not going to be back here after this. We'd only get more connected, more attached, and then you'd be gone."

"Well, we could meet up. You could even come out to visit Benson."

She looked back at him, her blue eyes wide and dark, considering his words.

"Look, Jenna. I know I seem like a bad bet. I *was* a bad bet. But I'm changing. And I want to spend time with you. Hell, you're the first woman I've *ever* wanted to spend time with like this! Can we try it?"

She sighed. "I want to. Of course I do. But long-distance relationships don't work out. And I can't spend my weekends driving to Benson. I need to teach as much as possible if I'm ever going to open my own ballroom."

"So we won't have a relationship. Come to Benson just for the weekend. We'll hang out, as friends." Wow. He was really desperate. He'd just offered celibacy to a woman who had taken over all his fantasies. "I'd like more time with you."

"I can't come to Benson," she said.

"Why not?" Maybe if she spent a few days in Benson, she'd fall in love with the place, as her best friend had. Maybe she'd fall in love with him. His own thought startled him. Did he really want that?

He did. So he played his last card. "What if I told you that Paul needs you?"

"Why? What's wrong?" Alarm sharpened her voice.

He shouldn't be so envious of how much she cared for his baby brother. "He's fine. But he's got it in his head that he wants to enter this local talent competition. He's decided to show everyone his dancing and just put it out there. But he needs my parents' permission."

"He's going to tell them? About dancing?"

"Yup. And I was kind of hoping that we could both be there to support him."

"But won't it be a little awkward if I'm there, too? I don't know them."

"Maybe. But, Red, I've got firsthand experience with your powers of persuasion. If anyone can talk them into it, you can."

"*We* can. There's no way I'm doing this without you by my side every step of the way!"

Which was exactly what he'd been hoping to hear. He could feel his grin spreading from ear to ear. "Of course I'll be there. I'll even do most of the talking, I promise. So you'll come? Next weekend?"

She pulled out her phone and brought up her calendar. Frowned at it. "I'll have to get someone to cover my classes."

"How about Brent? He was pretty happy to cover for you yesterday morning when you had your *appointment*."

"Oh, yes." She flushed. "Sorry about that." She looked away for a moment, studying the concrete wall of the ballroom. Then she looked back, and he saw determination in her eyes. "I know I've been rude. I'm sorry. It sounds cliché but I'm just trying to avoid getting hurt again. I guess I just need a break from heartache."

"I can see that," he said. "But who's to say this will end in heartache?"

She rolled her eyes at him like the teenagers she spent her Saturdays with. "And can you think of any other way it might end?"

"I'll put my mind to it," he teased. But he had a feeling in the pit of his stomach, as he watched her open the ballroom doors and go inside, that for the first time in his life, the heartache at the end was going to be almost 100 percent his.

CHAPTER FOURTEEN

As soon as she saw Sandro in a cowboy hat, Jenna knew she was in big trouble. It hadn't occurred to her that the Sandro on his family ranch might look a lot different than the Sandro she'd seen in the city. As he strode toward her car, she had to put her hand to her jaw to make sure it wasn't hanging open.

"Red!" he called from a few yards away.

She got out of the Mini and leaned on the door, but she still couldn't answer him. She was way too busy taking in the faded and ripped jeans, the battered brown boots, the straw cowboy hat tipped down to block the late-afternoon sun. Jenna was a city girl through and through. She'd never thought much about cowboys. But she knew the image of Sandro in his ranching clothes was now etched permanently in her mind.

"Howdy, pardner," she said, hiding her confusion in a silly joke.

"Hey," Sandro stopped a little awkwardly in front of her. Neither of them spoke for a moment. Finally he broke the uncomfortable silence. "Um, I'm glad you're here."

Jenna didn't know how to act, either. She'd practically accosted him that night they'd had sex. And
she figured that would be it. It was so odd that Sandro, the notorious womanizer, had been the one
reaching out, wanting more contact. She'd been
thinking about it, and she'd realized that she had
no idea if his pursuit was genuine. Maybe he was
just a guy used to getting everything he wanted
from women, and for the first time he was experi-
encing disappointment.

"This is gorgeous," she finally said, waving her
arm vaguely at the craggy peaks that rose behind
the old gabled ranch house. Scrubby pastures rolled
out on either side of them, speckled with sheep.
More pasture stretched down the hill behind her
to the flat valley floor below.

"Thanks. So are you."

"Smooth, Sandro, very smooth."

He laughed aloud at that. "Well, I must have some
skills left if I talked you into six hours of driving."

"It's nice to see that your ego is recovering nicely
after all your mishaps in New York," Jenna teased.
"But you know I'm only here because I'm crazy
about your little brother."

He clutched his chest in mock pain. "You wound
me, Red."

Their initial clumsiness with each other was
gone. It was incredible to see him so relaxed and
happy. But it also killed any fragment of wishful

thinking that might have been wafting around her brain. Faint wishes she'd barely acknowledged, that maybe he'd decide he preferred San Francisco to his life of rural exile.

"Want a tour?" he asked. "We have an hour or two before dinner."

"Which, by the way, I'm not looking forward to. What kind of masochist signs up to get involved in another family's problems? As if I don't have enough of my own." She was only half joking. She wanted to support Paul and his dreams, but she wasn't looking forward to dealing with his parents.

"Well, Paul and I are incredibly grateful. Maybe I can drive out for *your* next family dinner. I'm going to owe you one."

"My dad would be thrilled to see you again, I'm sure."

"Hey, I thought he and I developed a nice rapport in the lobby that night."

Jenna could feel the laughter easing the tension she'd felt about coming out here. Maybe they really could end up friends.

Sandro walked her around the side of the house and down a gravel drive that led to a huge barn, its wood siding gray with age. "Have you talked to your dad since the hotel?" Sandro asked quietly, much more serious now.

"No. But it's not like we were in the habit of talking much anyway."

"And your mom?"

"Drunk dialing me every night, pretty much. I went over there once this week to try to talk to her about all the calls and the drinking, but she kept pretending none of it had happened. It was so surreal! Every time I brought it up, she'd say she was fine, that she was sorry if she'd called too late in the evening. Then she'd ask me some question about my life. If I didn't know she was just trying to change the subject, I'd be flattered that she suddenly finds me so interesting!"

He laughed. "I dunno, Jenna. Drunk dialing was never my thing, as far as I remember. But it seems like she's trying, in her own twisted way, to reach out to you. I'm not saying you should put up with it or try to talk to her when she's drunk, but maybe *it's a sign* that she senses something is wrong?"

"It could be.... I never thought of that." Jenna tried to muster some sense of hope. It didn't come. "Or maybe she just wants to cuss someone out and I'm the lucky winner."

He put his arm around her shoulders and she allowed herself to lean on him for a moment. "I believe it'll work out, Red. If I could change, so can she. Maybe she just needs her equivalent of a Dumpster, and rats."

"You really know how to give a girl a pep talk, Sandro!"

"Ha! Come on, I'll show you some sheep. Small fluffy ones. They're bound to cheer you up."

JOHN SALAZAR LEANED back from the dinner table, his weather-worn face creased in a scowl. The lamplight caught his peppery-gray hair and surprised Sandro. His father was getting older, something easy to forget during the day when John was stomping around the ranch barking orders.

His father wove his broad, work-worn fingers together and contemplated them for a few long moments and Sandro resisted the urge to make a sarcastic comment that involved the words *any day now.* He took a taste of wine instead, a rustic red his uncle made with grapes from the western foothills. Good, but not good enough for his restaurant. He put the glass aside and looked over at Paul, giving him a reassuring wink.

His father finally spoke. "Absolutely not. Dancing is for girls." Somewhere down the table one of his brothers snickered and Sandro glared in the direction of the sound.

"It's not, Pops. You know that. Ballroom dance is men and women dancing together." There was a quaver in his voice but Paul was standing his ground.

Jenna chimed in. "We have several young men training at the ballroom, Mr. Salazar. And honestly, Paul is more talented than all of them. I haven't ever seen anyone with such an innate ability."

"And you've been teaching him? Without my permission?"

Sandro saw Jenna's face flush. "Pops! Please don't be rude to my guest. Jenna had no idea. *I* signed the papers so he could take the classes. So if you're mad at anyone, be mad at me."

"My apologies, Jenna. Of course I'm mad at you, Sandro." His father's brow furrowed. "You lied to me. You told me that Paul was helping you with your cooking program. Why would you be so dishonest?

"You need to ask? After the way you just told him no? After the way you *all* treated me when I told you I wanted to cook?"

Sandro's mom was wearing a sorrowful expression that Sandro recognized all too well from the endless talks they'd had before he'd run away. "Paulo." She always used the traditional versions of their names when she was upset. "Can't you find a way to listen to your father? He needs you on the ranch on the weekends."

"I've been doing extra chores during the week," Paul said.

Sandro watched his dad, who had his head down, staring at his hands. "Pops," he said quietly. "I know you don't see it right now, but if Paul dances, things with the ranch will still work out. We don't *all* have to be ranchers to be a family."

"But we have a family business. *Ranching* is our family business. Not cooking. Not dancing." The words were so familiar. The memory of all the old fights—the fights that had led him to pack his bags—had Sandro's fists curling under the old pine table.

"Dad, you have two other sons who love ranching. Two sons who are happy to take up the family business. You don't need all four of us."

"With all of you working together, you could take this ranch further than I ever could. Expand."

"Joe and Gabe will do that just fine on their own. You should be glad you've got *any* sons who want to ranch. Let alone two who are so good at it."

His father sighed and looked at Sandro with years of regret heavy in his face. "I don't need reminding that my sons are not the same."

Luckily, Paul spoke before Sandro could bite out the angry words simmering inside. "Sandro's right, Dad. Joe and Gabe will do an amazing job. You don't need me."

And in what Sandro deemed a brilliant move, Paul turned to their mother. He was the youngest, her baby, and she couldn't resist much that he asked. "Ma, remember when Sandro ran away?"

His mother looked at Sandro, then away quickly. "Yes, of course. How could I forget?"

"He ran off because cooking is his calling. He *needed* to do it. That's how I feel about dance. Can you understand that?" Implied in his words was the veiled threat that if he didn't get to dance, he might leave, too.

"I can understand that I don't want another of my sons to do what Sandro did. To go through what he went through." Sandro's mom glared at her husband. Sandro saw old bitterness there and for the first time wondered how his decision to run away had affected their marriage.

Sandro's father stood up abruptly, shoving his chair back in the process. "I've got a few things to check on outside," he muttered. He walked quickly to the back door, grabbed a coat off the nearby peg and was gone, the screen door slamming behind him.

"Boogie fever…" Gabe's voice, twisted in an off-key falsetto, started the familiar disco tune.

"I've got to boogie down!" Joe finished for him and the two dissolved in laughter.

"Knock it off," Sandro barked at them. "Give the kid a break." The laughter subsided and Sandro pushed his chair from the table, needing a break. "I'll clear, Ma," he told her, and grabbed some dishes to head into the kitchen.

"Don't forget your apron," Gabe called after him.

Sandro set the dishes back on the worn tabletop and made his way slowly and casually to Gabe's chair. He put his hands on the back and before his brother realized what was happening, Sandro pulled the chair so far backward that Gabe's legs were waving in the air, his torso almost parallel to the ground. "Actually, I think it's your turn for dishes, bro," he told him. "So you can wear the apron tonight."

He let Gabe go and the chair crashed forward, almost toppling the younger man out as it fell. Sandro knew it was an incredibly immature move, but it gave him great satisfaction.

Paul stood up. "I'll clear the rest, Sandro. That way I don't have to listen to these idiots." Sandro looked at his little brother closely, trying to tell if the needling had gotten to him. But Paul was beaming, apparently relieved to have finally told his family about his dancing.

"Okay," he said reluctantly. He felt as though he should stay with Paul, but it seemed as if his little brother wanted to fight this battle on his own.

"Go on," Paul said. "Go show Jenna the happening Benson nightlife or something."

Sandro held out his hand to Jenna. "I'm not sure I can promise *happening,* but want to go out?"

Jenna thanked Sandro's mother, who responded cordially if not exactly warmly. Guilt seeped into Sandro's conscience. Maybe he shouldn't have gotten Jenna involved in his family drama. He led her to the front door and they bundled up in coats against the mountain night. "How about a drive?" he asked.

Even in the darkened hall, he could see her eyebrow raise.

"Not like that! I want to show you something."

The eyebrows went even higher, if possible. Then she burst out laughing at her own joke. "Fine. What are you going to show me, cowboy?" It was a suggestive murmur and he had to remind himself that she was just playing around. She'd made it pretty clear that she wasn't going to allow a repeat of their night at Aquatic Park.

"Come on, Red. Trust me."

"They all say that," she countered, but she followed him out the door and down the creaky porch steps. In the driveway, by his truck, she looked up at the sky. "This is incredible!" she exclaimed. "There's no way you'd ever see stars like this in San Francisco."

A flicker of hope lit inside him and Sandro quickly squashed it. Admiring the night sky was a far cry from chucking her entire career to move to Benson.

Sandro took an appreciative breath of crisp air and looked up, too. He'd come home for exactly this. For the air and the peaks and the big vistas in all directions. He'd come so he'd be dwarfed by the landscape, so he'd relearn his place in the order of things. His ego had raged out of control in New York. He'd been willing to endure a few insults from his family in exchange for the perspective that living out here provided.

Despite Jenna's protests that she was perfectly capable of opening her own door, he helped her into the truck. When he climbed into the cab beside her, he was way too aware of her warm presence in the cold dark. If they were dating, he'd reach over and take her hand, wrapping it up in his own. He took her hand anyway, happy when she didn't protest.

He spoke what was nagging at him. "You know, it's kind of embarrassing to have someone witness the inner workings of my dysfunctional family."

He could barely see her in the shadows of the cab, but somehow he sensed her smile.

"Well, then we're even. And the conversation is actually startlingly similar to the ones we have at my family dinners. 'Why do you want to dance? When are you going to get a real job?'"

He laughed softly, wondering how she always seemed to say just the right thing to soothe him. "You probably don't tip your brother back in his chair, though."

She giggled. "No, that's a new one to me. But the next time my sister offers to help me get a *real* job, she might find herself stuck back in her chair, contemplating the ceiling. Though my mom would flip. All the chairs are antique, of course."

"Of course." Sandro chuckled.

Jenna looked out the window a moment before speaking again. "I'm not sure I'm helping much. So far your parents just seem to be mad at me. I feel like I'm intruding."

"Give them time." He'd seen the questioning way

his mother had watched Jenna. "I have a feeling my mom is so desperate for a break from all the Salazar testosterone that she just might listen to you."

The road from the ranch wound toward the tiny group of lights that was the town of Benson.

"It looks so small," Jenna said. "Don't you ever feel lonely, knowing this is all there is?"

Sandro wanted to reassure her, to paint his town in a better light without actually lying. "Well, it's not like we're on the moon. Drive north and you've got towns like Gardnerville and cities like Carson and Reno."

"But they're all hours away. It's not practical for every day."

"Well, south of here you've got Bishop."

"That's not much bigger than Benson! It doesn't exactly count as city living."

"Nope," he conceded. "Benson has enough civilization for me these days. You ever thought of living in a place like this?" He tried to keep his voice light, as if it weren't a totally loaded question. Which it was.

"When Samantha moved out here to be with Jack, that sure made me think about it. I mean, after all, the allure of this place took my best friend away from me."

"Well, I reckon it wasn't just this place that pulled her away." Sandro grinned in the dark, thinking about how hard his friend Jack had fallen.

"Yeah. Love. It messes everything up," Jenna said, and he wasn't sure she was joking. Then she changed the subject. "So what's up first on my tour?"

"My restaurant." He wanted her to see his dream in action. He pulled alongside the sidewalk in front of the old Basque Country Inn, owned and operated by his great aunt and uncle until about ten years ago, when they'd gotten tired of the routine and offered it to the highest bidder.

When no one had wanted it, they'd just boarded it up and retired to a property outside of town. Uncle Carlo spent his days fly-fishing and his aunt kept busy with her hiking group, her horse, her sewing circle and general town gossip. They were two of the most content people he'd ever met, even more content now that Sandro was reviving their dream. They'd leased him the restaurant and everything around it—a dilapidated farmhouse, a couple acres of land and a big old barn—for barely any money at all. Once the restaurant was on its feet, he'd offer to buy the entire property from them.

He cut the engine and looked over at Jenna. "You showed me the doorway of your soon-to-be dance studio. Ready to see what I've been working on?"

"As long as there aren't any cheating family members hanging around."

He put his hand on her arm at that. "Hey, you never know."

She smiled sadly and he went around to open her door for her, only to find her already on the sidewalk. "You city girls don't believe in chivalry much, do you?" he teased, hoping to cheer her up. It worked.

"I guess we just don't need it." She smiled at him. "Plus, what would I do sitting there in the truck while you walk around it? It seems so weird!"

"The woman who reads tarot, believes in signs from the universe and baptizes people with bay water is calling a guy opening a car door weird?" Sandro shook his head in mock dismay and had her giggling again. He'd spend every day thinking of dumb jokes if he could make her laugh like that more often.

He took her hand, leading her to the door of the old wood-sided building. "It *is* weird. But it's tradition. Like this place. It dates back to the 1800s. It's even got the old false front on it." He opened the door and flicked on the lights. "Of course, it's a mess right now. Definitely a work in progress. Kind of like me."

JENNA'S FIRST IMPRESSION was sawdust. The smell of cut wood filled the air and though she could see that Sandro kept a neat workplace, a fine dust coated everything and a huge power saw sat in the middle of the huge dining room.

"What a beautiful space." It really was. Old

carved molding with a floral motif surrounded the windows and ran between the walls and ceiling. An ornate chandelier hung from a plaster medallion in the center of the room. Matching sconces were on the walls. Jenna could see where Sandro had replaced some window trim and a few floorboards. "Are you leaving it mostly the same?"

"Just making repairs," Sandro replied. "I'm gonna take out the old wallboard and replace it with colored plaster. I want to keep the vintage feel but I think the plaster is a bit more classy—a European touch."

"It'll be really lovely." Jenna could picture exactly how it would look. Warm, rustic and inviting. "I think you've got a great vision."

"It's good to hear you say that. Only Jack has seen this place, and my family." Sandro motioned to the left and Jenna saw a second dining room.

"This is a big place!" she exclaimed.

"I think this is going to be more of a cocktail area, for people to wait and maybe order some bar food. It's cold here in the winter. I can't exactly ask folks to wait outside."

There were tools out on the bar and Jenna went over to admire what he'd been working on. He'd managed to match the shape of the trim to the window moldings.

"When do you plan to open?" Jenna asked, pick-

ing up a catalog of chef's equipment from the bar
and thumbing through it idly.

"Six months, I hope. Maybe a little later than
that if I'm being realistic. I could hire a bunch of
workers, make it go faster, but honestly, I'm having
a good time doing it all myself."

"Therapeutic?" Jenna asked.

"Kind of." Sandro looked away, out at the dark
night beyond the windows. "Sometimes I think I'm
just procrastinating, you know? Making sure I'm
on the right track before I step back into the world
of the kitchen. I don't want to mess this up."

"You won't, Sandro. I'm sure of it. Besides—"
she smiled at him reassuringly, trying to lighten his
mood "—just how much trouble can you get into
in this mini town?"

He laughed. "Thanks for your faith in me, Red."

She wished she could see his smile every day.
"You're welcome. But are you sure you'll be satisfied here? I saw how much you enjoyed Gavin's restaurant, and you said yourself that there's no market
for food like that in Benson. Do you worry you'll
be bored?"

"Being bored would be a good thing. I've had
enough excitement to last a lifetime."

Jenna heard the strain in his voice and wished she
could take back her question. It had been selfish.
She'd been unconsciously trying to get him to con-

sider relocating to San Francisco when she should have been accepting their situation as it was. She'd vowed not to try to change people, and here she was, doing it again. It was time to get back to their comfortable light humor. "Now, do you have any other hot spots of Benson you'd like to show me? The town hall maybe? The corner store?"

"You obviously have no appreciation for small towns!"

"I'm born and raised in the city, cowboy. You're going to have to convince me of their charms."

"Challenge accepted." Sandro opened the door and they stepped out into the night. "But there's so much charm it's going to be a busy weekend. We'd better get started."

He held out his hand and Jenna took it as he opened the car door for her. She loved the way it felt to have him touching her, even in this simple way. She felt as if she'd follow him anywhere as long as their hands were molded together.

But when he pulled up in front of the local high school and led the way to a drainpipe, she wasn't so sure.

"C'mon, Red! It's the best view in town!"

"The gym roof? Are you serious, Sandro?"

"You can't say you know Benson until you've seen it from this angle. Just climb this fence." He pointed to a rusty panel of chain-link next to them.

"When you get to the top, put your foot on the bracket that holds the drainpipe to the wall. Grab the pipe, and you can pull yourself onto the roof. I promise I'll catch you if it doesn't work out."

"That's comforting," Jenna quipped.

"You're a dancer. An athlete. You'll be fine."

"I'm a dancer who seems to fall every time you're nearby."

Sandro pointed to the fence. "Up you go."

The night air was crisp and so clean it almost hurt her lungs. Jenna looked up at the roof. Responsibilities, common sense, adulthood all seemed to fall away in layers. She wanted to be a teenager, up on that gym roof with Sandro. She gripped the freezing metal links with her hands and climbed. Once at the top, she leaned over and put her foot on the bracket. She pushed off from the chain-link and grabbed the pipe with both hands, clinging there with a squeal, her heart pounding.

"Good job!" Sandro jumped up onto the fence and in seconds was right next to her. He put a hand on her back to steady her. "See that pipe sticking out of the roof? It's really strong. Grab it and use it to pull yourself up."

She reached over the roofline and grasped the pipe and pulled first one knee, then the other onto the roof. "Oof!" she exclaimed as her shin scraped the rain gutter. And then, "Oh, my gosh!"

All around her were the stars, no longer just over the town but crowded and clustered across the enormous bowl of the sky to the horizon, running even denser in the crystalline river of the Milky Way. On one side of her, they blazed over the flat of the valley as far as she could see. On the other, the huge crags of the Sierra Nevada blocked them out with the deeper blackness of mountain silhouette. It was one of the most beautiful and awe-inspiring sights Jenna had ever seen. She lay down on the roof to try to take it all in.

"See, there are things you miss out on when you spend your whole life in the city." Sandro sat down next to her.

"I guess so." Her voice sounded quiet in all that empty air.

"Do you like it?"

"Well, *like* doesn't seem like the right word for something so raw."

"I missed this living in New York. It's like your senses go into kind of a daze in the city. There's just so much stuff going on. Here I always feel connected to the sky, the land, the weather, the seasons. It's all right here, in your face."

"And now that you're living here, do you ever miss New York? I mean, not the bad stuff that happened but the city?" She wanted to kick herself as soon as she said the words. What pathetic part of her kept trying to get him to rethink his plans so he'd fit into hers?

He paused then answered. "Sure. But Benson is a good place to live my life. I know I can make good choices here."

"Well, with this sky to watch every night, I can see how it might inspire you. Or at least remind you of where you really belong, in the big scheme of things."

Jenna's phone buzzed in her pocket. Who could be calling her this late? She sat up and pulled it out. It was a number she didn't recognize. Unease pitted her stomach. Weekends were Mom's worst time. Could this be the call she'd been dreading? The DUI with jail time or the alcohol poisoning? She answered. It was her mother and her fears expanded. Suddenly it was hard to breathe. "Mom! What is this number? Are you okay?"

"I am, actually." Her mother's voice was calm and polite and Jenna almost dropped the phone in surprise. Her mom was sober? No string of profanity? No slurred accusations?

"Jenna, are you still there?"

"Yeah, I'm here." She was confused, but at least she could breathe again.

"Oh, good, I thought I'd lost you. The phone's a little unreliable here."

"Unreliable *where?*"

"I'm north of the city, in Marin. At a rehab facility. I checked myself in today."

Jenna did drop her phone then, but luckily, Sandro had quick reflexes. He handed it back to her. She took a breath shaky with gratitude. "That's incredible, Mom! How did this happen?" She paused, realizing she was terrified to say the wrong thing. To make a mistake that would send her mom out the door of rehab and back to the bottle.

"I don't really know. I woke up this morning so sick of myself. Sick of sitting at home angry and drinking, getting flabby and bloated while your father's out with half the women in this city."

"You know about the other women?" Jenna had spent the past week worrying about the photos she'd taken, wondering if she should show them to her mom. It would be liberating to delete the toxic images from her phone.

"I think I've known for a long time. I just didn't *want* to know. But when he didn't come home at all the past couple nights, I guess it just finally became real. Something clicked. I called my friend Adriane. Remember her? She went to rehab a few years ago. She showed up on my doorstep within the hour and drove me here."

Jenna felt relief so profound it seemed to bend her limbs, relax the muscles she had no idea she'd been tensing for years. She glanced over and saw Sandro watching her anxiously. She gave him a thumbs-up and he smiled, looking relieved, as well.

"Honey, I can't talk much now. There's only one phone and other people are waiting. And there's a meeting in a few minutes. I'll call you later with more details."

Jenna wondered if she'd ever be able to accept a call from her mother without wondering which version of her mom, drunk or sober, would be on the other end.

Her mother said goodbye and hung up. Jenna sat staring at her phone. It was strange that such a tiny machine could impart such a life-changing message. Her hands shook and she could barely get the phone back into her coat pocket.

"Are you okay?" Sandro asked quietly.

She wasn't sure she could talk without completely losing it. "Um…my mom is in rehab."

"That's incredible!" His arm came around her shoulders, pulling her into his warmth. "I can't imagine how good that must feel."

And then the tears came—as if leaning on him was the permission they'd needed to finally spill over and release the heartache, fear and constant anxiety that her mom's drinking caused. Jenna cried for all the late-night phone calls, all the mornings she'd gone to the house to make sure her mom was still alive, all the stomach-wrenching times she'd pictured what it would be like if she wasn't. And

Sandro just held her, murmuring soft words of comfort into her hair, enveloping her in his tenderness and cradling her in the strength of his arms.

CHAPTER FIFTEEN

SUNLIGHT POURED IN through the tall window. Jenna got up, dragging a quilt with her against the morning chill, and looked out at the view, struck again by the grandeur. Mountains piled up and tumbling behind each other as far as she could see, lit from the east by the morning sun.

But she would have had an equally nice view if she'd stayed at Samantha's, and she wondered if she should have. It was awkward being here, a guest that Sandro's parents didn't want, bringing news about Paul that they didn't want to hear.

And then there was Sandro. She'd barely made it through the evening without kissing him. After she cried all over him on the gym roof, there was an intimacy between them that made a kiss seem inevitable. From the gym, they'd gone to a local bar, where she'd tried a Basque punch that sent her head spinning. But by drawing on every ounce of willpower she possessed, she'd managed to keep her hands off him.

It hadn't been easy. All evening, every time she looked at Sandro, that familiar thrill had moved over her skin—the quickening of her breath, the rippling memory of what it was like to kiss him, to feel his hands on her body. Somehow he was more irresistible than ever. She loved this cocky, cheerful, cowboy version of him. Paul's decision to tell his parents seemed to have freed Sandro from some of his angst. Or maybe it was because he was in Benson, and this was where he was meant to be.

One more day and one more night, she reminded herself. Thirty-six more hours of willpower, and then she'd be on her way back to San Francisco, knowing she'd done all she could to help Paul dance.

With a sigh, she went to find her jeans. Apparently they were going riding today. Jenna just hoped she remembered how. Sandro had already rescued her from a collision on her bike and a crash in the ballroom. She didn't relish adding a fall from a horse to that list.

SALAZAR FAMILY TRADITION required that once a year at the end of summer, they all rode up to the alpine meadow that overlooked the ranch and had a family picnic. Jenna was wrapping sandwiches in plastic wrap and helping Sandro's mom place them in leather saddlebags for transport. Sandro and Paul were saddling the horses.

If it weren't for her uncomfortable purpose here, Jenna thought she might enjoy the day. There was something so homey about the farmhouse kitchen with its scarred pine table and wood-burning stove in the corner. But the silence coming from Mrs. Salazar was glacier thick. It was time to crack the ice between them and it was clearly going to be up to Jenna to do so.

She put her last sandwich in a bag and turned to face her hostess. "Mrs. Salazar, I feel very odd being here. Sandro and Paul invited me thinking my presence might be reassuring to you. They thought that if you and your husband met me, you'd feel better about Paul's dancing. That obviously isn't the case and I'm sorry if I am intruding this weekend."

"Men," Mrs. Salazar said disdainfully, surprising Jenna. "They think they know what's best and they rarely do. And you can call me Barbara."

"Thank you," Jenna said, wondering what to say next.

Barbara solved her problem by speaking. "I've always known Paul was artistic. Sandro, too. They take after my side of the family. I'm a quilter, you know, and my mother paints. My aunt and uncle owned the restaurant before Sandro, and they were great cooks. So I understand my boys a little more than John does, I think."

Jenna was stunned. This was not what she'd expected.

"But it's hard for John," Barbara went on. "His family is practical. Traditional. Settled in their ways. It's difficult for him to see his boys wanting

something different than what he's offered them—
what he's worked so hard to provide them."

"I can understand how that might be. I'm not a
parent, so I don't know what it's like to have your
kids grow up and become their own people. I imagine it's a challenge." Jenna thought about her own
parents from that angle all of a sudden. What was
it like for two such conservative people to have a
daughter who only wanted to dance?

"It's the best and the hardest thing you'll ever do."
Barbara smiled faintly. "I don't think a minute goes
by when I'm not worrying about one of my boys or
another. And when Sandro left so young…" Jenna
could see the emotion in the older woman's face
before she turned away.

"I bet it was frightening," she said softly, hoping
she wasn't being too intrusive.

"I don't think I've ever really gotten over it."
Barbara opened up the refrigerator and rummaged
inside, then emerged with a head of lettuce. "Now,
enough of this. Whatever the reason you're here,
you are our guest and a friend to my sons. So enjoy
yourself, Jenna. You are welcome here."

JENNA MIGHT HAVE been laden with saddlebags, but
she felt lighter after talking with Sandro's mother.
She staggered down the steps from the porch and
along the gravel drive to the barn, hoping she

wouldn't drop something or tip over from the weight she was carrying.

"Jenna, hang on!" Sandro ran up beside her. "You're crazy, carrying all that. Let me help!" He tried to take the bags, but when his hand groped for the bottom of the pile, he grabbed her hand instead. She jerked her arm back, not wanting to feel his strength. It would only make her want things she couldn't have. The bags fell to the ground and they both dove after them, hitting heads.

"Oof!" Jenna rolled off the saddlebags and landed roughly on her side in the dirt. "Ouch! Sandro!"

"My head!" The muffled complaint came from somewhere under the pile of saddlebags. And then the laughter started. "What is it with you, Jenna Stevens? Why are you so graceful with everyone but me?"

And then she was laughing, too, still lying on her side with her cheek in the gravel. "You're my curse, Sandro Salazar. You've cursed me with clumsiness from the moment we met. Terrible things happen to me when you are nearby!"

She sat up slowly, gingerly, taking inventory. Looking up, she saw he was pushing off saddlebags and doing the same. Dry grass clung to his T-shirt and there was a smear of mud, or something worse, down his face. His mouth was open in laughter and his eyes were surrounded in smile lines and then they both said, "It's a sign!" at the exact same moment and Jenna laughed so hard she cried.

Eventually laughter subsided to giggles, though every time she looked at Sandro and saw his filthy face and wide grin, the laughter started again. Finally they were done and quiet, lying side by side in the gravel next to the tangled heap of saddlebags with the most brilliant blue sky glowing overhead. Jenna realized that despite her pounding forehead and filthy clothes, she was happy just lying in the sun next to Sandro. His hand found hers and held on and this time she didn't pull away. It felt too good.

"Maybe we can agree that not everything is a sign?" he asked softly.

"Maybe." Jenna smiled.

"Or maybe we can agree that we get to pick and choose which life events count as signs. For example, can the way your hand feels in mine right now be counted as a sign? Because if it is, I'm pretty sure I'm exactly where I'm supposed to be."

"I guess we could consider that a sign," Jenna conceded. She tried to keep her voice casual but his words felt warmer inside of her than the sunshine did on her skin.

Sandro leaned on his elbow so he was looking down at her, his handsome features framed against the bright sky. He lowered his mouth to hers and kissed her softly, so gently it was a feather's touch, but enough to have Jenna's breath catch. "That feeling between us. Is that a sign?"

"I'm not sure," she whispered. That feeling was making her tremble.

"Let's try to make you sure." He brought an arm over so he was lying half across her, his hands on either side of her head supporting him while his mouth came down on hers—the gentleness gone.

There was power behind his kiss. His lips opened hers and his tongue lanced into her mouth, exploring, taking, and he wound his fingers in her hair, kissing her even more deeply. All discomfort was gone, from the bump on her head to the gravel poking into her back. Instead there was only Sandro and that feeling he'd voiced before—that she was exactly where she was supposed to be.

"That's definitely a sign," she whispered against his lips, and knocked his hat off as she reached up behind his neck to bring him down for another bone-melting kiss.

"Is this some kind of San Francisco thing?" Sandro froze and Jenna ended the kiss abruptly, looking up to find Joe looming over them, a huge grin on his face. "Because if it is, I'm gonna have to visit there more often."

"It's gonna take more than just visiting to talk a beautiful woman into kissing you like this, Joe," Sandro shot back.

"Gentlemen, keep me out of your virility contest," Jenna admonished, ducking from under Sandro's arms and pushing herself to her feet, dusting herself off. "Come on, cowboy," she said to Sandro. "I think Joe's presence here is a sign that this isn't really the right time or place to study up on any more signs."

Sandro laughed. "Later," he promised, and the look he gave her held so much desire that Jenna felt it all over her body. She should *not* be doing this with him. But she was right back where she'd been that night in San Francisco, telling herself lies about how she was fine just living in the moment.

"Saddle up, lovebirds. And promise me you didn't destroy all of Ma's sandwiches."

"That I can't guarantee." Sandro picked up the saddlebags and held out his other hand to Jenna. With his straw cowboy hat tipped back on his head, saddlebags flung over his shoulder, brown eyes laughing, he was in his element and he was beautiful.

For a moment Jenna had a hard time connecting him with the haunted man who had confessed to such a troubled history in a San Francisco bar—the dark and dangerous man who had held her against an iron gate on a shadowy city street while he ran his hands over her body. And she realized that Sandro had two sides, two ways of being, that he was trying so hard to reconcile into one whole man.

IT WAS INCREDIBLE to ride again, though Jenna wasn't used to a Western saddle. She'd been trained in the English style—jumping, dressage and posting to the trot—during the hundreds of hours she'd spent at the stable as a girl. The loose reins and long stirrups took some getting used to, but Sandro had put her on a dainty, responsive quarter horse mare with the unfortunate name of Peanut who was patient with her mistakes. And soon she had the hang of it because Peanut made it easy, responding to the slight pressure of Jenna's calves against her side or the weight of a rein laid gently against her neck.

"Jack Baron trained her," Sandro told her when she commented on Peanut's easy handling.

"He's got talent. No wonder Samantha fell for him."

"I'm not sure that was the *exact* talent that got her attention," Sandro scoffed, and Jenna grinned.

"Did you just make a dirty joke, Sandro Salazar? Does this mean we're truly friends?"

"That joke was not dirty." His smile was wide, confident and sizzling. "And I think we both know we're a lot more than friends." Just then Paul beckoned to him to ride ahead. Sandro raised his hand in acknowledgment and turned back to Jenna. "Oh, and when I talk dirty to you? You won't have to ask about it. You will know exactly what's happening." And with that he nudged the big gray gelding he was riding into a gallop and was gone, leaving

Jenna about a hundred degrees warmer and lost in contemplating the meaning behind his words.

She was deep in a very pleasant reverie when Sandro's father rode up next to her. "You know what you're doing, don't you?

At first she thought he was giving her some kind of warning about his son and her heart thudded. But following his glance at the way she held the reins, she realized he was actually talking about her horsemanship.

"Oh, well, yes. I think so. I rode a lot when I was younger. I mean, not Western, though," she sputtered on, flustered. *Way to make a good impression.* But when she looked up at him, she saw the grudging respect in his eyes and realized that her horsemanship could be the thing that softened him.

"I've missed riding—I love it," she told him. "And I love being out here. You have such a lovely ranch."

"Thanks," he said gruffly. "It's been in our family since this area was first settled."

"Have you always raised sheep?"

"We're Basque. Our ancestors raised sheep in their country, on the border of Spain and France, and they brought their traditions here."

"It must be amazing to be a part of something with that kind of history." Jenna didn't know if she was about to make a mistake but she decided to say what was on her mind. "I can understand how hard it would be to see a couple of your kids move away from that heritage."

Mr. Salazar looked up the trail to where his four sons were riding together, laughing uproariously at something Gabe had said.

"Last night I sat outside after dinner. And I was thinking that maybe that's why my ancestors came to America in the first place. So that their great-great-grandchildren would have the freedom to do something different if they wanted. So they'd have the choice."

"Maybe one choice doesn't always exclude another," Jenna reminded him. "Sandro might want a restaurant, but he's told me how much he likes working with you on the ranch again."

Mr. Salazar looked surprised. "You're a smart lady, Jenna. I can see why both my sons are so taken with you."

Was he possibly relaxing his stance about Paul's dancing? "Thank you, Mr. Salazar. I appreciate you saying that."

"So are your parents happy that you're a dancer?"

Jenna hesitated, then decided on honesty. "No, not at all. They'd much rather I was a doctor or a lawyer."

He nodded. "I guess I understand their concern." He was silent for a few moments, clearly deep in thought, considering his words carefully, and Jenna had a moment of panic that she'd said the wrong thing, blown this conversation, and Paul would never forgive her.

She tried to remain centered and not worry about what Mr. Salazar thought of her. But it was hard because she was falling in love with his eldest son and she wanted his family to like her.

Falling in love? The three words made her dizzy and she clutched at the saddle horn. She was *not* in love. That was impossible. Yes, she had a huge crush on Sandro. A perfectly safe crush since there was no way they could be together. So she couldn't be falling for him....

"Are you happy with your choice, Jenna? Really happy?"

It was hard to focus on Mr. Salazar's questions when those three words, *falling in love,* were pingponging around her brain. "Yes, I've been very happy. It's exciting, I do what I love and I am always learning new things."

"And if you get hurt and can't dance anymore?"

"I'll do something else. So many people switch careers nowadays, Mr. Salazar. They predict that most of us will have at least two or three careers in our lifetimes. And I also love teaching dance. If I get hurt, I could just do more of it."

"And you honestly think Paul's got talent?" Mr. Salazar watched her carefully.

"It's what brought me out here this weekend. He

has more natural talent than anyone I've ever met. I think he'll be incredibly successful."

The older man just nodded and stared at the trail ahead. Jenna left him alone with his thoughts, hoping he would come to the right decision.

They were heading uphill now and the trail followed a creek that washed over stones and tumbled over boulders and logs. Nature's garden, Jenna thought, amazed by the accidental beauty of it all. The whole day was taking on an unreal quality. The conversations she'd had with Barbara in the kitchen and Mr. Salazar just now. Sandro's sweet and seductive words and kisses. He genuinely seemed to care for her....

"So are you going to take us all dancing tonight?"

If a meteor had shot out of the clear sky and landed on her head, Jenna would not have been more startled than she was by Sandro's father's question. "If...if you like. Is there a place to go around here?"

"We've got a great dance hall in Benson. And they get a good crowd on Saturdays. It's been years since I've taken my wife out dancing. Maybe it's about time."

Glee shot through Jenna and she grinned at the older man. "I guess it is! And I would love to be a part of it."

They'd reached the meadow. Mr. Salazar rode over to where Joe, Gabe and Paul were dismounting. Sandro rode back to meet her, looking like a Western hero on the big gray horse he sat on so easily. "Everything going okay?" he asked.

"Sure," she said casually. "Your dad just asked me if we could go dancing tonight." Sandro went pale and wide-eyed, his mouth partially open. Then his eyes creased, the color returned to his face and his smile grew into pure joy. He took his hat and threw it into the air with a whoop that startled both their horses.

"Jeez, Red. I leave you alone for five minutes and you're running around working miracles! Hell, I knew there was a reason I fell in love with you!"

They both froze at his words. Sandro looked stricken, then horrified as embarrassment crept in. He dismounted and walked his horse over to get his hat. He clapped it back on his head and walked back to Jenna with reluctant steps. "I can't believe I just said that," he told her, looking up.

"Maybe you were just a little awed by my persuasive powers," she joked awkwardly, trying to get them both off the hook. She swung her leg over and dismounted, taking Peanut's reins in her hand. "Or maybe you've got sunstroke."

She handed him the reins. He was staring at her as if he were seeing her for the first time. "I'll leave you to deal with the horses," she told him.

"Sure." He was still staring.

"And I'll go get us something to drink." She

stumbled off to where Barbara was unpacking the picnic, trying to figure out what had just happened and if there'd been any truth lurking in Sandro's words. She wouldn't acknowledge that her heart was dancing in celebration. It also seemed wise to ignore the part of her traitorous brain that had given voice to her own deep feelings, even before Sandro had blurted out his.

CHAPTER SIXTEEN

"ARE YOU SURE you're ready for this, Red?" Sandro helped her down from the cab of his truck. "You look amazing, by the way."

"Thanks!" For the occasion she'd put on a pair of vintage blue cowboy boots she'd picked up at a thrift store at some point and a cute retro top with a matching full skirt.

"You look like Dale Evans."

Jenna grinned. "I am going to assume that's a big compliment in these parts."

He pulled her close and kissed her firmly on the mouth. "It sure is."

It was the first time he'd kissed her since the dust and the saddlebags earlier that day, since he'd said something about love.... Jenna tried to decide if the kiss felt any different and realized that everything felt different. She'd thought that by avoiding Sandro after their night at Aquatic Park she'd rid herself of any feelings for him. But clearly it was too late for that. She was falling in love with him—maybe she had been for a while.

On their incredible night in San Francisco, as he

hung laughing off the side of the cable car, she'd felt the stirrings of it. As they'd walked by the bay, as he'd touched her, the feelings were there, just eclipsed by the insane desire. But his kindness on the gym roof as she cried last night, and his goofy laughter and teasing when they'd fallen into the dust today, had solidified those feelings.

She should have been scared. If she had an ounce of sense, she'd get in her car tonight, drive back home and end this dead-end thing between them. But the oddest thing was, when she was with Sandro, she *wasn't* scared. She was happy and excited. Joyful, even. It was only when she was alone that she remembered she was going to lose him. And that hurt.

It was kind of like life, she thought. You could live your life in total fear because you know it will end one day. You could hide in your house, paralyzed, afraid to walk out your door because you might get hit by a bus or something. But Jenna didn't want to waste her life hiding from the inevitable and that applied to love, as well. Maybe it was better just to enjoy this time with Sandro, so when it ended, when it was over, she could say that she really, truly had loved.

Joe, Gabe and Paul pulled up in Joe's truck and jumped out. "Family night out!" Joe said, running a hand through his curly hair in a gesture so like

Sandro's. "Can you believe Mom and Pops are coming, too? And Paul's gonna show us his moves."

"Yeah, right," Paul said, all classic teenager around his big brothers.

Sandro pulled the door open and they walked into a wall of sound. The loud buzz of people talking and laughing, balls on the pool tables racketing into each other, and country music blasting over it all. Sandro's parents were already there and Mrs. Salazar waved them over to where they had saved a table near the dance floor. She looked flushed and pretty, with a silk flower clipped into her hair and a floral blouse tucked into her jeans.

Gabe mumbled something about beer and headed toward the bar, Joe following. Sandro, Paul and Jenna sat at the table and Jenna's eyes immediately went to the dance floor. People were moving in perfect unison, following identical steps but all putting their own personal style into their movements.

"This is amazing!" She knew a few standard line dances, but to see a whole room of people in jeans and cowboy boots moving in sync to the music was a novelty. She felt as if she were on a movie set. Sandro's father was giving her a questioning look.

"We don't really have much of this in San Francisco," she explained. "Can you do it? Will you teach me?"

"Why, Jenna!" Mr. Salazar teased. "We figured you'd be out there teaching us!"

"I know when I'm in the presence of greatness, Mr. Salazar," she quipped back. "And I don't mess with perfection." She tugged at Sandro's sleeve. "So get up and get me dancing, cowboy! I *need* to know how to do this."

The song ended and some people left the floor, while others lingered, waiting for the next song. "I guess it's as good a time as any," Sandro said. "Mom? Pop? Paul? You'd better get out there with me. I'm pretty rusty."

Paul led them to a spot on the dance floor. Mr. Salazar lined up next to him with Barbara at his side. "Stand behind us, kids. We'll show you how the real folks dance." Mr. Salazar gave Jenna an exaggerated wink.

Jenna laughed. "John Salazar, I like you. I'm getting schooled and that's a good thing."

The music started and Jenna noticed how everyone on the floor began to mark the beat with their bodies, all awaiting the first step. And then the first step came and everyone in the entire room took it except Jenna, who realized that she really was a fish out of water. Eyes glued to Paul's feet, she began to break his moves down into steps she knew, trying not to crash into anyone in the process. A grapevine step, a toe touch, shuffle step sideways for four beats, then back the other way. A half turn with a leg hitch to the outside and back to that grapevine step. The teacher learning from her student.

Pretty soon she was going the same direction as everyone else, much to her relief, and a few moments later she had it. She relaxed into the repetitive motions of the dance and only then glanced over at Sandro, who was dancing beside her. He grinned at her with a quick wink and an expression that was all appreciation.

Jenna couldn't look anywhere else. Sandro imbued each simple step with his own lanky brand of cowboy sexy. Jenna stumbled watching him and he laughed and she figured there was a reason everybody faced the same direction during a line dance. Because the sight of men like Sandro, so at ease in their bodies, cowboy hats tilted just so, long denim-clad legs moving to the music, well, it wasn't really a sight a girl could take in and still manage to remember the choreography.

The next dance was also unfamiliar, but Jenna insisted that Paul and Sandro stay on the floor to teach her. Next it was the song from *Footloose* and the dance floor erupted in the most fun, lively steps straight from the movie and Jenna truly felt as if she were in heaven.

The music ended and Sandro claimed he needed a break after such a girly song. They walked back to where his family was sitting. His parents went back out on the dance floor and Jenna watched them. Barbara was laughing at something her husband said as he took her hand, spinning her around.

"Look at your parents out there!" Jenna exclaimed.

Sandro looked over. "I don't know when I've seen them this happy. Jenna, I wasn't wrong when I said we needed you out here. You've got some kind of magic."

"Maybe it's all that San Francisco groovy pagan magic?"

He burst out laughing. "Yeah, that's it."

People headed back out onto the dance floor. "I could do this every night!" Jenna said, watching them. "Choreography to follow, tons of people dancing—why don't we do this in San Francisco?"

"It's just one more charming thing we have here in Benson." Sandro took a sip from his water bottle and smiled. "Are you sold on small towns yet?"

"I like them better than I did," Jenna admitted. A new song came on and the people on the floor grabbed a partner and swung into something that looked a lot like a two-step. She jumped out of her chair and held out her hand to Sandro. "I can do this! Take me out there, please?"

Sandro stood up and his answering grin went straight to her knees, which didn't bode well for successful dancing. Jenna wondered if that was why she was so clumsy around him—his knee-weakening smile.

Then one of his strong hands wrapped around hers and the other supported her back so it didn't matter if her knees wobbled, and he launched into the two-step with an easy grace. And Jenna relaxed in his arms, determined to enjoy these precious moments with him.

JENNA HAD THE most angelic smile when she danced. You could tell she was born to do it, that the music hummed in her blood and sparkled in her soul. Sandro wished they could just stay like this, with none of her worries clouding her face, none of her fears darkening her eyes.

And none of his fears, either, because he was having plenty. Ever since he'd announced out of the blue that he was in love with her, his own worries had kicked in. He'd never felt anything like this before. He had no idea how to be in love, especially with someone who lived so far away. Yet here he was, leading them both down this road that didn't have any kind of clear ending. Actually, the ending was very clear. Unless he could talk her into staying in Benson, they didn't have a future.

But he wanted a future with her, he was sure of that now, and maybe there was some slight hope for him. Jenna *fit* here in Benson. She'd charmed his family, a near impossible task, and she was obviously enjoying herself this weekend. He couldn't believe the way she'd hopped right up on Peanut and ridden as though she'd been doing it her whole life. She also appreciated his secret spot on the gym roof, and she was crazy about line dancing. Maybe if he could make her see *all* that Benson had to offer, she would consider a life here with him.

Sandro wondered if he could make her happy. He'd build her a dance studio. There was an old barn on his aunt and uncle's property, off behind the restaurant, that they could convert. Some drywall, insulation and a dance floor would transform it. He could build dressing rooms where the old tack rooms were. But there was more to a successful dance studio than just a cool old building. She'd need students. He looked around the packed dance hall. Surely some of the people here would want to learn a few of the classic ballroom dances?

Who was he kidding? As much as he wanted to convince her, and himself, it would be really hard for her to continue as a dancer out here. Unless she just wanted to teach stuff to kids.... That might work out.

Sandro cut off his own wishful thinking and held Jenna tight, relishing the way they moved across the floor together. She followed the slightest nuances of his movement—he'd never had an easier time leading. Dancing had always been just a social skill his mom had drilled into him along with *please* and *thank you*. When he got older, he'd realized how much women liked a man who could dance, so he made sure he had enough basic knowledge to get by. With Jenna, for the first time he felt the magic of it, the wonder of having someone's body connect with your own so you truly moved as one.

SANDRO OPENED THE kitchen door and cautiously poked his head in. "I think they all went to bed!"

Jenna followed him into the dim room, walking as quietly as the creaky floorboards allowed. "I can't believe we outdanced your parents!" she whispered. "And your brothers!"

"I know. By the end I think I was just staying there so I wouldn't be outpartied by the old folks. They were really into it. I haven't seen them have that much fun in years."

Sandro carefully opened a cabinet, took out two glasses and filled them with water from the tap. He handed her a glass and took a sip from his own.

"Thanks—I'm parched." Jenna sipped the icy mountain water gratefully. "You Benson folks really know how to dance!"

Sandro smiled at her over his glass. Then his eyes went beyond her and he walked over to the kitchen table and picked up a piece of paper. Turning, he held it out to her. It was Paul's permission slip for the dance contest, signed.

"Oh, my gosh, they signed it!" Jenna squealed.

"Shhh…" Sandro handed her the paper and took her glass, setting it in the sink with his own.

Jenna stared at the signature—it was proof that miracles happened. "I can't believe we did it!"

Sandro picked her up, swung her in a circle and kissed her firmly on the mouth as she landed. "*You* did it!" He kept his voice quiet but Jenna heard his gratitude. "I guarantee this would never have happened if you hadn't come out here, Jenna. I don't know what you said to them, but you deserve a medal."

"And are you really okay with Paul doing this?" Jenna asked. It was hard to reconcile this joyful man with the scowling chef who had been so furious with her in another kitchen not very long ago.

"As okay as I can be. Of course I'm worried that he'll get teased. But he looks happy and hopefully he'll stay that way."

"You know, there's a pretty big ballroom-dance scene in Reno. Do you have any family there he could stay with? It would be a lot closer than San Francisco."

"Actually, we have an aunt. Maybe I'll ask her."

Jenna felt their celebration cooling quickly. Here they were making plans for Paul that didn't involve her and didn't involve Sandro coming to San Francisco. It all suddenly felt very real and for an instant she tried to picture what it would be like once she was back home, knowing that whatever had happened between them was completely over. Her mind backed away from the image, not wanting to deal with it yet.

Instead she stood on tiptoe, pushed his hat back

farther and kissed him softly and slowly, savoring the way his lips felt under hers. Her worry about the future faded into the background where she could ignore it, for now. His arms came around her waist and he pulled her against him, and she felt the lean muscle of his frame and the steel of his arms. She knew beyond a doubt what she wanted—to feel his skin on hers. He ended the kiss with a shudder—he felt the same way.

"Did I mention," he whispered, the breath behind his words caressing her lips, "that I have my own cabin on this ranch?"

"You did mention it, yes," Jenna whispered back, smiling at his ridiculous attempt at a pickup line. "I suppose this is where you ask if I'd like to see it?"

His smile hovered over hers, their lips almost touching. "Well, since you *mentioned* it, I am open to giving you a tour."

She felt like a high school kid, sneaking out of his parents' house hand in hand. It was dark under the trees and the night was crisp and chilled and Jenna shivered. Sandro unzipped his jacket and tucked her under his arm, pulling the leather and flannel around her so she could feel his warmth. She walked in step with him, as close as she possibly could to his heat.

Then the pines cleared and there was a cabin with a wide porch along the front of it. An old wooden rocking chair sat by the front door. In the glow of the bright porch light, she saw a hammock attached to the posts where the porch rounded the cabin.

"It's adorable. So homey!" she said.

"Adorable. Great." She could hear the smile in Sandro's voice. "How about rustic? Manly and rustic?"

Jenna laughed. "Sure. A very rugged and manly cabin. I'm sure only the toughest, most dedicated rancher would live here."

"Thank you. I've been working hard to improve my cowboy credibility."

"Too many years in New York, huh?" Jenna giggled.

"You've heard the phrase 'cowboy up,' right? I'm living it." Sandro led her up the steps and through the door. He switched on the light, revealing a simple three-room cabin. They were in the living room, which had a stone fireplace, a small sofa and a few armchairs in front of it. Through a door framed in pine, Jenna could see a kitchen with an old-fashioned stove and a table and chairs that served as the dining area. She looked to her right and a small hallway led to a bedroom. She could just see the corner of an old four-poster wood bed.

"Let me just go get out of this shirt," he said.

"Dancer's etiquette," she said.

"What?" He threw the question over his shoulder as he walked to his bedroom, unbuttoning his shirt as he went.

"Dancer's etiquette," she called. "Never stay in a sweaty shirt." He disappeared from view for a moment and when he came through the door, he was pulling a plain white T-shirt over his head.

"So you're saying I'm a natural."

Jenna got a quick view of his abdomen, the muscles defined, before he pulled the fabric down. She looked away quickly, suddenly very shy, which made no sense since they'd already had sex. But that had been so rushed they hadn't even taken off their clothes. It had been unplanned.

"Something like that." She managed to blurt the answer out over the noise her heart was making as it banged in her chest. It was as if her heart were anticipating the future heartbreak that sleeping with Sandro practically guaranteed. Was it worth it?

Sandro went to the fireplace and struck a match from a box on the mantel. He knelt on the hearth and lit the wood already laid there. He lit a couple candles on the mantel, as well. His skin looked golden in the candlelight. She loved the way flickering shadows highlighted the sculpted muscles of his arms. The answer came in a rush. Yes, it was worth it.

"Come sit down?" he asked her. "Would you like something? A drink? Tea?"

An offer of tea was not what she would have expected from Sandro Salazar, notorious womanizer. She thought about all his phone calls last week.

The way he'd waited for her at dawn in front of the ballroom to plead his case. He really did seem as if he'd changed. The funny thing was, as much as she'd hoped this was true, now, with so much evidence in front of her, she kind of wished he hadn't turned into quite such a good guy. It was going to make it a lot harder to say goodbye.

If she was going to sleep with him, it had to happen now. Before she could think herself out of it. And knowing how amazing their night by the bay had been, she didn't want to miss out on this chance.

This was dangerous. She was deliberately stepping off the cliff and she was pretty sure there was no safe landing for her. But as a dancer, she knew well that some things of great passion and beauty were worth the risk of pain. She'd lived that concept every day in the ballroom, and there was something exhilarating about living it now, with the man she'd fallen in love with.

"No tea," she said.

"Water? Wine?"

Jenna took a deep breath and went to Sandro. "No water. No wine. Just this." She put her hands on his shoulders, went up on her toes and kissed him softly. "And this," she murmured against his mouth, and kissed him again.

He kissed her back, gently. "I want to do this right, Jenna."

"I think you will," she whispered back. Then she

pulled back. "Do you still have all those regrets from before?"

"No. Not anymore." Sandro bent down and touched his mouth to hers. "Jenna, when I'm with you, everything seems so much lighter."

She reached for him, and a thought floated through her. *Love does that.*

But right now she didn't want light. She wanted the darkness of his mouth, the weight of his body covering her, holding her down and somehow containing the need she felt building inside. She put her mouth to his, no more featherlight touches but a greedy kiss, with her two hands woven into the silky black of his hair, her thumbs outlining his cheekbones, her eyes wide-open so she could watch the expression in his deep, dark eyes.

She saw surprise there, and then heat and desire. Sandro's arms wrapped around her and she knew he was struggling with his self-control from the way they clamped so tight around her ribs, banded like iron across her back. It made it difficult to breathe but right now she didn't care about breathing—she just wanted him closer.

His mouth left hers and was kissing her neck and ear until she was squirming under him. It was too much sensation. She could feel the length of him all down her body, his arms holding her up.

"Bed," she managed to gasp somehow.

Sandro pulled back and put his hands lightly on

her shoulders, resting his forehead gently on hers and taking a deep breath. She was surprised to see that he was shaking, too. He kissed her, just a brush with his lips.

"You do me a pretty big honor, you know. Staying here with me."

Earlier today he'd threatened to talk dirty, but these courtly words were even hotter than anything naughty he could have come up with. Jenna threw her arms around Sandro's neck and he lifted her as if she were nothing. She clung to him while he walked them carefully down the narrow hallway and into his bedroom.

Jenna had impressions of a tall pine dresser and an old wooden chair in the corner with faded blue paint. Then Sandro sat her gently on the bed. She kicked off her boots. She had on black stockings and when his hands slid up her thighs and found the garter belt under her skirt, his eyes went wide.

"This thing you have with all things vintage..." he breathed, sliding her skirt up and staring at her exposed thighs. "I like it. I like it all, the dresses, your makeup, all of it." He finally tore his eyes away and looked at her face. "But I especially like this." His hands ran up her legs and his fingers followed the tops of her stockings.

He kissed her mouth, a long, lingering kiss that promised so much heat in its own time. Jenna tried to sit up to prolong the kiss, but he gently pushed her back so she was leaning on her elbows on the bed. He found the hook of her skirt and slid it off, taking all of her in with his eyes.

"The other night was incredible," he murmured. "But I wanted to be able to see you." And he stood and looked again for a long moment, both of them watching as his big hands covered most of her thighs, his fingers circling the pale skin of her hips before sliding down to the tops of her stockings. And then his thumbs slid along the edge of her panties and she moaned low in her throat.

His expression was worship and pure hunger and when the tips of his fingers slid under the fabric, Jenna's heart raced. It was so incredibly intimate, watching this, feeling this. And then he brought his mouth down and replaced his fingers with his mouth, his touch with kisses, and she fell back on the bed, surrendering. Surrendering to his touch, to their situation, to the finite moments they had together.

She closed her eyes and let herself get lost in the dark heat of him, his mouth fiercely exploring, his tongue finding every spot she'd ever wanted to be touched. He took his time until Jenna felt as if she were going to incinerate, just break into ashes and disperse. But she didn't. She shook and bucked under his mouth and he stayed with her, his hands on her stomach softly holding her down so she didn't break or float away, until she settled and came to her senses slowly. And only then, when she was quiet, did he pull away, kick off his boots and remove his jeans.

He came onto the bed, kissing her mouth so she tasted herself when she tasted him. He lay across her, supporting himself on his arms above her. His muscles held him rock steady, and she reached up to trace the definition with her fingers. He closed his eyes, as if trying to better feel her touch, and when he opened them, he looked completely dazed as he leaned down to find her mouth again with his. His legs found the space between her thighs and when he slid inside her, it was so much more than what they'd had before. She could feel all of his skin on hers—all of his weight on her. He was inside her, above her and around her. The air was laced with the salty scent of him, and her ears were full of his rough breathing.

She didn't think she could want him more than she had, but need made her wild. She pushed her hips to him, seeking still more contact. He gasped her name and his fingers wove into her hair and she pushed up to him one more time, clutching him deep within her. And that was all she needed. Her whole body released and she held on to him tightly as she let go of any last bit of control, feeling the waves of energy ripple through her as she clung to his shoulders, burying her face against his chest and letting her feelings take her where they would.

He stilled, and when she opened her eyes, his were crinkled in a self-satisfied smile. "I helped do that," he murmured. "Twice." And it was so unexpected that Jenna laughed.

And then he was moving inside her again, powerful thrusts that she took and met gladly. He kissed her deeply, then moved to her neck, his caresses so fierce they hurt and aroused. With a harsh breath, he pulsed deep within her and it seemed they might really have become one being. She held him as he finished. He said her name in a ragged whisper again and again. And his silly words came back to her, meaning more now. *I helped do that.*

They might not have much time left, but they had this. They had done this for each other.

CHAPTER SEVENTEEN

THE WOOL BLANKET was scratchy under Jenna's hand. She ran her fingers over it and the unfamiliar texture finally registered in her sleepy brain. This wasn't the duvet in her apartment, and it wasn't the quilt she'd slept under the previous night. Her location came back to her in a jolt of shock and warmth. She was in Sandro's bed in Sandro's cabin on Sandro's parents' ranch.

She sat up and glanced around wildly. A tall window looked out into the pine forest behind the cabin and let in the first dim light. Next to her under the blankets was a long lump with a pillow over its head. Sandro. A quick peek under the sheets revealed more of him, and he wasn't wearing any clothes.

She put the covers back quickly and brought her hands to her cheeks, covering the grin that had started there. He was amazing and loving and strong and totally bold. He'd woken her up in the middle of the night and made good on his earlier promise—that when he talked dirty to her, she'd know it. She'd known it through every cell of her body. His words had traveled leisurely through her brain, moved across her skin, taken root deep inside, and when he'd followed through with his touch and his mouth, she'd gone over the edge to complete oblivion.

How had she not known about sex like this? She'd been with Jeff and Brent and a few boyfriends before them. But this was different.

"Hey, Red." The pillow was off and Sandro's tousled head emerged. He looked up at her from under his black mop of hair. His grin was leonine in its contentment and its greed. "Come back down here."

"Sandro, I can't! Your parents! What will they think?"

"Probably that their son spent the night with the most beautiful woman in the world."

"No! I'm their guest and they put me in the *guest* room. I need to get back there."

"Five minutes," Sandro bargained with a promise in his lazy smile. "Give me five minutes and I'll take you back there."

Jenna laughed. "You can get this done in five minutes?"

"Looking at you right now, Red, I could get it done in about thirty seconds. But I'd like to bring you with me."

Desire speared through her and she sank beneath the covers. His body was so warm, his lean muscle corded around her, making her completely vulnerable and absolutely protected all at once.

"Five minutes," she whispered, and he turned her over and pulled her against him so he was lying along her back. His hand was on her hip and his fingers were touching her, waking her desire until she was rocking back against him. And when he took her that way, holding her close, whispering in her ear, a hand in her hair and a hand on her hip, she lost all track of the minutes. All her awareness was of him and what it felt like to push back onto his length, to move forward into his touch.

They lay silently after. Sandro held her close, his arms wrapped around her and Jenna sensed him drifting off. She realized that in about ten more seconds she'd be asleep, too.

"Sandro..."

"Four and a half minutes."

"What?"

"That's how long it took. Four and a half minutes."

"You timed it?" It was too ridiculous. Jenna glanced over at the clock on the bedside table. "Really?"

"I keep my promises." She felt his smile against her shoulder.

"Even the one about getting me to the house so your parents don't know I slept here?"

He sighed heavily and sat up, taking his warmth

with him. "Yup. Even that one." He reached for his jeans and yanked them on and Jenna rummaged under the covers, blushing as she tried to remember what on earth had happened to her underwear.

"Here." Sandro picked up her black lace bra from the bedpost.

"Aha." Her panties were tangled under the sheets at the foot of the bed. She slid them on and then added the bra, trying to ignore Sandro's very appreciative look as the black lace covered her breasts.

"Can we take that off again later? Or actually, maybe leave it on?"

"I have to go home today, Sandro." Jenna felt the loss even as she said it. She didn't want to say goodbye, but she had a bunch of private lessons scheduled for this afternoon. There was no way she could take more time off. Marlene would never forgive her and Nicole would be more than happy to take over her students.

Jenna pulled her shirt over her head and when she emerged, Sandro was looking at her with the same sadness that she was feeling.

They walked back to the house hand in hand, the air chill, the sky just barely light. Sandro let her into the kitchen and she was thankful that no one was up and about yet.

"Go upstairs and shower, start your day. I'll make a big old breakfast down here and when you come down, you can look surprised to see me."

"Sounds perfect. Thanks, Sandro."

"No." He leaned over and kissed her gently on the mouth. "Thank you, Red."

WHEN JENNA EMERGED from her room, there were voices downstairs. A happy buzz and the smell of coffee—the bustle of a family weekend morning that she'd only read about in books. When she was growing up, breakfast in her house had been served by the maid. She stopped by the hallway window for a moment just listening to the sounds.

"Pancakes!" That was Paul's voice, sounding so carefree that Jenna realized he'd been feeling more guilty about deceiving his parents than she'd known.

"Only if you help, you runt." Sandro had laughter in his voice. "And I think there's something on the table you might want to see."

A moment of silence and then Paul's voice. "No way! They signed it! Mom! Dad!" His footsteps careened through the big old farmhouse in search of his parents and Jenna hugged herself in delight. Maybe, just maybe, she'd played a small part in bringing some peace and acceptance into this family. And maybe that peace would be healing for Sandro, too. Now she just needed someone to show up at her parents' home and work the same magic for her.

She looked out the window and watched Paul

racing across the grass to the chicken coop where his mother was coming through the gate. Paul threw his arms around her and she almost dropped her bucket of eggs. They were both laughing.

Even if she never got to have Paul as her student again, he now had the confidence to move forward and the acceptance of his family. And that was the *real* purpose of all this.

There was a dull thud inside her, as if her heart had just slid into her stomach. It was time to go. She had at least six hours of driving ahead of her. She stepped back into the guest room and quickly shoved all of her things into her duffel bag. Shouldering it, she started down the hall toward the stairs.

Halfway down, she heard the thump of boots by the back door and the rumble of Mr. Salazar's voice. He was asking Sandro for help with moving sheep later today. Sandro said something about the merits of moving them to a different pasture with more shade but, apparently, less accessible water. This part of Sandro was like an alien to her. What did she know about sheep or ranches? It was as though he were speaking a different language.

The screen slammed as Mr. Salazar went back outside and Jenna walked into the kitchen and set her bag and purse on one of the chairs. Sandro looked up from the enormous bowl of batter he was mixing and gave her a long, lazy smile that made it clear he was remembering every detail of their night, and morning, together. She blushed.

"Morning, Red." He set down the spoon and walked toward her, leaning down and kissing her mouth. "Again."

They both jumped apart as Sandro's mother came through the door with Paul behind her, carrying the bucket of eggs. Mrs. Salazar's brows furrowed when she saw Jenna's bags. "Oh, you're leaving now? Wouldn't you like to stay for breakfast?"

"I have to get back for work," Jenna explained. "But thank you very much for having me. I had a lovely time."

Mrs. Salazar's eyes were kind. "We had a lovely time, too. Thank you for getting us all dancing last night. And thank you for all that you've done for Paul."

"Mom says that I can perform at the talent show!" Paul's grin was so wide it made Jenna smile in return, despite how sad she was to say goodbye. "And if Sandro has another cooking class in the city, I can take more classes with you."

"I'd love that, Paul." She was going to miss being his teacher. "I am so happy for you. Truly happy. And, Barbara, I think you'll be very impressed with your son's performance. Paul, call me if you need help with the choreography."

Sandro's mom smiled ruefully. "I wish we'd been

a little more supportive in the past. Thank you, Jenna, for opening our eyes."

Paul came forward. "Thank you so much, Jenna, for everything."

She held out her arms and he stepped in for a hug. Setting him apart from her, she looked him in the eye, suddenly fiercely protective of him now that she wouldn't be able to keep watch over him. "You have my number and my email. Use them. And if you can get to San Francisco, even for a day, come dance with me."

There were tears in his eyes that matched her own. "Will do."

"I'll walk you to the car." Sandro turned off the stove and crossed the kitchen with long strides. He picked up Jenna's bag for her before she could protest, and despite her anxiety about their impending goodbye, she smiled slightly at his insistent chivalry.

She followed him down the hall, admiring his broad back tapering to his narrow waist, the perfect fit of his faded jeans. She tried to connect this gorgeous stranger with the man she'd been so intimate with last night.

They walked out the front door of the old house. Mr. Salazar was doing something in the front garden and he gave Jenna a friendly wave. She knew she should go say goodbye, but she was afraid she'd start crying. Her car was her safe haven and the only place she wanted to be at the moment.

Once at the Mini, Sandro stowed her bag in her backseat. She had no idea what to say. "I'm really glad your parents agreed to Paul's dancing. I feel like I can drive away and say *mission accomplished.*" Her attempt at lightness sounded completely lame and her voice echoed hollow in the thin mountain air.

"Thank you again for that. For changing my mind *and* theirs. For changing all of us."

"I think you all did most of it on your own." She couldn't take credit. She'd just been the catalyst.

Sandro took her hands in his. "Jenna, last night was incredible. Everything. This morning was incredible, too. Then you come downstairs and insist on leaving, looking at me like I'm a total stranger. What's going on?"

"We have to say goodbye. Your classes in the city are over, so this is it. And I'm trying to be okay with it, but I'm sad." Tears welled up and she attempted to blink them back. She didn't want Sandro's last sight of her to be all red-eyed and puffy.

"It doesn't have to be goodbye," he said quietly.

She looked at him in surprise. Faint hope flared. "What do you mean?"

"We could try to meet up. Do the long-distance thing."

The hope fizzled. "It would take up all your free

time, which you need to get your restaurant open. And I rarely have two days off in a row."

"Then I have another idea." He took a deep breath. "Stay here with me."

Shock washed over her, paralyzing her brain for a moment. "Excuse me?" was all she could manage.

"You were amazing with my family. You completely turned them around. And they like you so much. Didn't you love the dancing? The riding? The mountains? Stay here, with me."

For a moment she pictured it, just dropping everything and starting again. Getting to be with Sandro. Creating a life together out here. And part of her wanted to say yes.

"Sandro," she started, "I…"

"Samantha is here. Your best friend." He paused, biting his lower lip in a very uncharacteristic gesture of insecurity. "I'm here and I want you with me, Jenna." He leaned down and kissed her gently. She kissed him back, loving the way his mouth felt over hers. Wanting so much to have more of this chemistry between them.

"My whole life is dancing," she said.

"Open a studio here! I bet there are a lot of people who'd like to learn to dance in this area. More kids like Paul. Maybe you could coach the drill team…."

Jenna thought about her dream studio. The old ballroom shrouded in dust, waiting to come to life. The dances she wanted to host—Lindy Hop dances complete with live bands and the Latin nights she'd already planned. There was the scholarship program she hoped to build. She was so close to making it happen.

"I just can't. I could never do out here what I do in San Francisco. Nothing close to it. And I don't think I could be truly happy if I don't try for my dreams."

He looked away, his jaw clenched, and when he looked back, she saw a new reserve in his eyes.

She'd promised herself that she wouldn't ask him, but now the question she'd been avoiding felt like her only hope. "What about coming to San Francisco? It's a city that practically worships food."

Sandro shook his head, but Jenna wasn't ready to give up yet. "The whole city is being overrun by Silicon Valley techies with large salaries to spend on great food. There's so much opportunity.... You could make the wildest, most innovative cuisine and people would love it."

"You're right," he said, and Jenna felt a stab of relief, which he banished with his next words. "But I can't do it. It's been proven—I don't do well in cities."

"But, Sandro, you've changed so much...."

"I've changed a little, Jenna. But not enough to move back to the city. Neither of us wants me to be that guy who ran out on you at Marlene's party."

Jenna's heart sank slowly, deflating in the complete absence of hope. She turned away and pulled open the car door, willing herself to get inside and drive away before she begged.

Then she realized she had one more thing to say. She turned to face him one last time. "You can run into temptation anywhere, Sandro. Hiding in Benson won't make all the alcohol in the world go away. In fact, your restaurant will be full of it. And I'm sure there are people around here who do drugs and offer up easy sex to other people. And you might end up meeting some of them."

He was looking away again—studying some horizon over her head. Was he even listening? "I respect that you want to stay in Benson. And I can even see why you do—there's a lot to love around here. But if you're staying because you think it will keep you safe? Well, I'm no expert, but I think that kind of safety has to come from *inside* you."

She reached up and kissed his cheek. He looked at her then and cradled her face in his big hands and kissed her gently on the mouth. Jenna wanted so much more. She pulled away.

"Goodbye," she told him.

"Jenna, wait."

"I'm right here." She stopped, that little piece of hope coming alive again until she heard his words.

"I'm sorry I can't be the guy you need. The guy you deserve."

She wouldn't cry. She tried to keep her voice

steady but it trembled anyway. "Maybe you *were* the guy I needed…at the time."

He smiled slightly. "Sent by the universe, you mean?"

"Well, you sure taught me a lot of lessons, so yes, maybe." Although right now all those lessons, the ones about letting go of expectations and living in the moment, weren't providing her with a single scrap of wisdom or perspective. Instead a voice inside of her was screaming that she couldn't possibly let go of this man. That she wasn't strong enough to say goodbye.

Jenna took a deep breath. *Accept,* she commanded herself. Accept that he was on his path and she was on hers. They were lucky and blessed to have run into each other on their journeys.

"Take care, Sandro, and thanks—I have no regrets about any of it."

He didn't stop her. She wanted him to. She wanted him to call out for her, to run after her and jump into her tiny Mini and zip off with her to San Francisco to live happily ever after. But he didn't, so she drove away, allowing herself one glance in the rearview mirror to see him standing there, hands at his sides, fists clenched, staring after her.

She was barely able to follow the long driveway back to Highway 395 because of the tears pouring down her face. Finally she gave up, pulled over on the gravel shoulder and cried. She sat with her sobs almost doubling her over and the massive mountains looming above her tiny car, completely indifferent to her insignificant suffering.

Part of the loss and sadness was for herself, knowing she'd never be with him again as she had last night. And part of her sadness was for him. She could see that deep down he still had so much ambition, so much joy in cooking. She'd seen the envy on his face that night at Oliva. The wistful look that came when you saw someone else living your dream. What if he was never truly happy in Benson?

She'd thought she could handle this. She thought it would be worth the heartache just to have more time with him. But right now the scales of love and heartache just wouldn't balance.

She got out and leaned on her car, sniffling and watching the mountains, noticing the way they rolled so abruptly into the high desert. Eventually she noticed the smaller things, the way the last chill of the night was gone and the world was warming around her, the way a lizard had crawled out from under a rock and was sunning itself just below the verge of the road, and the way the higher peaks lost their pinkish morning color and became pure gray.

Calm enough to drive, Jenna got back into her car and opened the sunroof, hoping the bright light would keep her spirits high enough to get her back to San Francisco.

CHAPTER EIGHTEEN

JENNA HIT TRAFFIC outside of Sacramento, which meant she wouldn't have enough time to go home and change before her lessons started. Instead she pulled over at a convenience store and asked for a cup of ice, which she held against her eyes as she navigated her car along the crowded highway toward San Francisco. By the time she got to the Bay Bridge, her eyes had depuffed a little and she willed herself to think only positive thoughts so the tears wouldn't start up again.

Praising the parking gods as she grabbed a miraculous space right in front of the ballroom, Jenna grabbed her bag of emergency dance clothes from the back of her car and hustled inside. She had five minutes to get changed before her first lesson.

"Oh, Jenna," Marlene said as she rushed through the ballroom door, "didn't Nicole call you? Your three o'clock student canceled."

This was why she hated private lessons, and this is why she was starting to hate Nicole. "No, she didn't."

"Oh, I'm sorry, hon. She must have forgotten."

"Sure," Jenna said, weariness from the long drive and the emotions of the morning taking over. "I'm sure that's what it was."

Jenna glanced at the clock. Her next lesson wasn't until four. Maybe she'd just put her bag in the dressing room and go get a coffee and something to eat. She had private lessons until nine. It was going to be a long night—assuming they all showed up. This was why teachers coveted group classes. The lesson went on, and you got paid, no matter who attended and who didn't on any particular night.

Well, it was just a rough day. Her heart felt as if it had been torn out and left behind in Benson. In comparison to that, a canceled lesson was nothing.

She pushed open the dressing room door with her shoulder and turned to go in. And stopped in her tracks. Brent was in the women's dressing room, shirtless, and his hands were roaming over a half-naked Nicole.

"Ugh!" The noise escaped before she could muffle it and they both started and turned, catching sight of Jenna before the door swung closed between them. She walked in a fog over to the DJ booth and sat down heavily. The main ballroom was empty and she stared out over the dance floor trying to figure out what to do next. And what might erase that image from her head.

She was just picking up her bag again to drop it in her car while she went to get her coffee when the dressing room door opened and Brent came out, fully dressed now, thank goodness.

"Hey, sorry about that," he said. "I guess we got carried away. You know what it's like when you're first dating someone."

"You're dating?" Jenna tried to hide her surprise. Brent had always laughed at Nicole's attentions and treated her like a little kid. Obviously he considered her all grown up now.

"I guess so." He practically scuffed his feet, he looked so sheepish.

"For how long?" *Were you seeing her when you were flirting with me?*

"A couple weeks now. Ever since the competition."

Well, at least there was that. He'd stopped flirting with Jenna after he'd come upon her and Sandro plastered up against the hotel wall that night. *Ouch.* She didn't want to think about that.

"Well…" Jenna tried to muster up some enthusiasm. "Great!" she said, and it sounded as fake as it felt.

"Look, there's something else I want to talk to you about. It's sort of related." Brent sat down in the chair next to her.

"Okay," Jenna said, mystified. Brent wasn't exactly the heart-to-heart-talk kind of guy.

"I want to partner with Nicole."

There were moments in life when everything

froze. When a person truly was that proverbial deer in the headlights. A marriage beginning or ending, a life starting or ending—moments that were so big people counted time from them. This day was one of her big ones. The day she lost Sandro *and* her dance partner. Her calendar would start again from here.

Even while Brent sat there waiting for an answer, the words *from this moment on, everything will be different* whispered and echoed off the hollow shell where Jenna's brain used to be. She hadn't seen this coming. They'd danced together for almost a decade.

"Jenna?" Brent finally asked. "Are you okay?"

She took a shaky breath. Then another. And finally trusted herself to speak without losing her composure. Because at any moment, Nicole would walk out of that dressing room with a smirk of triumph on her face, and there was no way Jenna would be a mess when she did. "Are you sure? Just because you're dating Nicole, doesn't mean you have to give up what *we* have!"

He looked uncomfortable and understanding dawned. "Nicole insists?" she asked.

"Well, she wants it, and it makes sense." He leaned forward in his chair, elbows on his knees, and looked at his hands, not her. "We really like each other and we want to spend more time together."

"But you've dated other dancers before and never wanted us to end. Why now?"

He sighed. "I guess I really like her. I want to try to make it work."

It made sense in a way. Nicole worshipped him. She'd pursued him for ages, and Brent loved that. Until he got bored and moved on. But maybe this time would be different.

If he wanted a new partner, she couldn't make him stay. Her heart hurt. Despite their difficulties, she'd loved dancing with Brent. It was the end of an era and she wasn't ready for it.

She tried to keep her voice steady but there was a lump in her throat—an enormous sticky lump that was part Brent, part Sandro and part panic that her world was changing so much in one small weekend. "How soon do you want to do this?"

"Well, it's the beginning of the month. We've got our group classes organized already. So I figure we'll see out this month, and Nicole and I will work with Marlene to figure out how to schedule next month."

How could she be upbeat with Brent and teach as well as she always did, knowing they were just going through the motions until the end of the month?

One month. The full extent of this disaster hit her. One month to find a new partner or face the bleak fact that she'd have to eke out a living giving private lessons. With no partner, Jenna would be stuck without group classes—stuck watching Brent teach their classes with Nicole. *Her* classes—the ones she'd worked years to build.

Her stomach tightened and Jenna thought she might throw up.

Maybe she could find some other ballroom to work for. The Golden Gate was the biggest, most popular ballroom in the city. Where else could she go? Her own studio was the obvious answer. But she didn't have enough money yet.

There wasn't really anything else to say to Brent, who was sitting there looking at her quizzically. Innocently? As if he hadn't just dropped a bomb into her life and blown it to a shambles. "I'd better go get some coffee," she mumbled, and left the ballroom.

But she didn't get coffee. She got into her car, drove a few blocks to an empty parking lot and stopped. And sat and cried for the second time that day, feeling as though life had just taken away all that she valued most. She hadn't thought she had any tears left after leaving Sandro this morning. But it seemed that when it came to love and dance, she had an endless supply.

CHAPTER NINETEEN

"What's going to happen with you and Dad?"

Jenna's mother looked out the window of the small visiting room and Jenna followed her glance. The open hillsides that surrounded the rehab center were golden-brown after the dry summer. Oak trees stood out as oases of bottle-green shade. A few cows clustered under the branches of one of the biggest.

"I told him it was over."

Jenna thought she'd feel sad when her parents' marriage finally ended. She wasn't expecting a sense of peace. "Are you okay, Mom?"

Her mother's smile was sad but also less tense than Jenna could remember. "I am. I mean, it's one day at a time, right? I'm sure I'll have a lot of feelings to get through. But all his lying and all those affairs just ate up my self-esteem. I wish I'd left him years ago."

It was liberating to set down the burden of anxiety Jenna had been carrying. Of course there was a chance her mom would relapse, but at least now, in this moment, she was safe and doing well. "I ran into him, you know. A few weeks ago, at a hotel with someone else." As soon as the words were out, Jenna doubted the wisdom of saying them.

Her mom suddenly looked a little more frail. "You're kidding."

"I'm sorry, Mom. I should have told you. I was trying to get up my nerve, but I was also trying to give him time to tell you himself."

"You mean you spoke with him?"

"Told him off. Yelled. In the middle of the lobby." Jenna still didn't know if she should feel embarrassed or triumphant about that moment.

Her mother closed her eyes briefly, as if looking for composure. When she opened them, she looked surprisingly serene. She was obviously learning some coping skills here. "I kind of wish I could have seen you do it." She smiled as if imagining the scene.

"It wasn't pretty," Jenna assured her.

"What he was doing wasn't pretty. Thank you for standing up to him. But I wish you hadn't had to. We've set such a terrible example for you, Jenna. I'm sorry."

"You tried to work it out with the person you love, Mom. That's an admirable thing."

"To a point, I suppose." Her mother sighed. "I just feel like there's all this time I wasted, and I'll never get it back."

Jenna didn't know what to say. She resented that

wasted time, too. And the stress she'd lived with for so long. But all they could do was go forward. "You're doing something about it now, Mom. And I'm proud of you." She stood up and went to sit beside her mother on the old sofa. It had probably seen a whole lot of family drama over the years. She hugged her mom. "I have to go. I teach tonight."

"Can you come again next weekend, Jenna? For family day? I hate to keep asking, but Shelley and Daniel… Well, they won't come."

Jenna made a mental note to call her siblings and give them a piece of her mind. "I can try, Mom. But I can't afford to miss too many of my classes right now." Because she was losing her partner and a huge chunk of her income. Tears started. She looked away quickly but her mother noticed.

"What is it? Jenna, is all this too much? Your dad? Me? I'll pay for as much therapy as you need." That was one of the problems with a sober mom, Jenna thought cynically. She actually noticed things. And wanted to help.

"No, Mom, it's just work stuff."

"What happened?"

She didn't want to tell her. Didn't want to hear the *I told you so* she knew her mother would think, if not say. But they were being honest now, so she spit it out. "My dance partner ended our partnership a couple weeks ago."

"Brent?"

She was surprised her mother remembered his name. She'd seen so little of Jenna's dancing. "Yes. He's gotten involved with another dancer. She's a very ambitious girl who's been really competitive with me at the ballroom. And the owner of the ballroom is her aunt, which doesn't help, either. I'm going to lose all my classes."

"Oh, Jenna, I'm so sorry."

Jenna scrutinized her mother's face, trying to tell if her words were genuine. Looking for the relief and the triumph. All she saw was sympathy.

"What about your plans for a studio of your own?" her mother asked. "You've mentioned that a few times."

Jenna could almost see her beautiful ballroom fading away. "I was really close, but I needed a few more months, at least, to get the money together. Now I'm going to need what I've saved just to pay my bills until I find a new job or another partner."

A shrewd look crossed her mother's face. Jenna had seen it before when they'd gone shopping or her mother was making plans to redecorate. "Do you have a business plan for this ballroom you want to open?"

"Yes, of course. But—"

"What about a location?"

"There's a place I love, but I can't—"

"Jenna." Her mother turned to face her on the sofa and took both her hands in her own. "I've been terrible about your dancing. Most parents would be so proud to have a daughter as talented as you, and I've done nothing but discourage you. I was talking about it with a therapist here, and she said that maybe I was jealous. I was so stuck, and you were pushing forward, pursuing your dreams. I think maybe she was right."

Her mother *had* discouraged her. She'd been mean and condescending. Jenna couldn't say that it was all okay now that she'd apologized, but her mother didn't seem to need her to say anything.

"I'd like to help you. Call it making amends, call it me realizing what an idiot I've been. I've got tons of money—family money, separate from whatever your father makes. Let me help you get your studio off the ground."

Jenna swallowed. Of course she wanted money. It would mean everything to her career. It would turn this despairing time into a triumph. But she'd always refused to take money from her parents. There were way too many strings attached. "I can't, Mom. It would make things complicated between us." It almost physically hurt to say it, even if it was the right decision.

Her mother sighed. "I can see why you'd feel that way, but it makes me sad." She paused, then continued. "It's my fault. Your father's fault, too. You've had to do absolutely everything on your own with no support from us."

Jenna stared down at her hands, twisting the small silver ring she wore on her pinkie, wondering how to respond.

"We sent your brother through medical school and your sister through law school. We spent thousands of dollars on them and gave you nothing. We had money set aside for your college. As far as I know, it's still in an account somewhere. Why not use it?"

Jenna felt her resolve faltering. She could lease the studio tomorrow and start cleaning, decorating and advertising immediately. It would give her time to find a new dance partner—the right partner.

"Just a minute." Her mother got up and left the room. Jenna heard her footsteps growing fainter along the corridor. She stared back out at the bucolic view. Her mother felt guilty. Was this her way of buying herself out of that guilt? Because if it was, Jenna should say no. The only way for her mom to get healthy was to actually deal with her feelings.

Her mother came back in and sat down. She handed Jenna a check for $50,000. "Will this help?" she asked softly.

That was an insane amount of money—at least for a broke dancer, it was. Jenna had a feeling that for her parents, it was petty cash. "Why are you doing this, Mom?" she asked, not reaching for the check.

"You're my daughter. I should have been helping you all along. I want to help you now."

"That's just guilt talking."

"Maybe a little. But if you think this is going to make my guilt go away or is going to allow me to forgive myself for all that I've done wrong, then you can't possibly understand how devastated I feel."

Something in Jenna still hesitated. Over the years, she'd coped with her parents' disapproval by nurturing a stubborn pride. She hadn't taken a dime from them since she left home. Could she start now? It felt like a threat to everything she'd worked so hard to create on her own.

"You could take it as a loan if it makes you feel better," her mother said. "Please? This is your big dream, Jenna. Let me help make it happen?"

Jenna reached out and took the check. Her hopes were right there on that piece of paper. She'd never felt despair as she had in the past couple weeks. Her life had fallen apart and she didn't know how to pick up the pieces. Yet somehow thc universe was giving her what she needed. It was just so odd that it was providing it via her mother.

"Thank you, Mom. I appreciate it—I really do. It's hard to say how much." She felt as if she was in a daze, her mind jumbled with so many conflicting emotions. Gratitude, excitement, fear.

"Go teach your classes now. And hold your head up high around Brent. He is going to rue the day he left your partnership when he sees the wildly successful ballroom you are going to create."

Jenna hugged her mother and stumbled out the door. At her car she stood, inhaling the hot baked smell of the dry earth, taking in the bright blue sky patterned by the oaks that grew over the rehab center's driveway. *Thank you,* she said silently, turning her face up to the sky, to the universe—mind-boggling and endless—so far out beyond the blue. She closed her eyes and felt a beam of sunlight fall across her face. *Thank you*.

Driving back to San Francisco, across the Golden Gate Bridge, Jenna tried to fathom the events of the day. She pressed the button to open the sunroof and let the fog swirl through the car, cranking the heat to lessen the cold and damp. With the music turned up, she glanced above her to see the rusty red towers coming in and out of view with the incoming fog. Misty air blasted her face and sent her hair flying upward.

Her mom was in rehab, starting to heal. Now it was Jenna's time to heal herself. But she had no idea how. When she thought about Sandro—which she did often—her heart felt vacant, like a fragile shell webbed with cracks.

In her worst moments, she wondered if she'd made an enormous mistake. Brent ended their partnership right after she'd left Sandro behind in Benson. What if that had been a sign that she never should have said goodbye to Sandro? Maybe her destiny was to stay in Benson with him, and she'd taken a wrong turn? In the worst moments, she ached, mind, body and soul, for Sandro, feeling as if she'd easily give up all of her dreams for just one more day with him.

But there were glimpses of healing. In her best moments, Jenna thought of falling in love with Sandro as a short-term, beautiful gift that she could be grateful for. Like those gorgeous pears wrapped in gold foil and tucked into a fancy box that her great-aunt always sent her mom at Christmas. They were lovely but not meant to last. Just savored and enjoyed for a week or two.

Jenna slowed for the tollbooth. She was striving to feel a little better every day. To cultivate a good attitude. To be grateful for what she had rather than mourning her losses. To trust that she would be okay, eventually.

But she wasn't there yet. Despite all her good news today, she still missed Sandro. Hopefully, she'd get used to living without him. But for today, she'd just have to put one foot in front of the other and inch her way forward. Thanks to her mom, she now had a destination.

CHAPTER TWENTY

His MOM HAD organized a barbecue and put Sandro in charge of the grill. At least it gave him something to do, since he didn't feel like socializing. He hadn't felt like doing much since Jenna left two weeks ago.

Sandro flipped a burger and it went sailing through the air and landed on the grass nearby. With a word he shouldn't have uttered at a social occasion, he stomped over and picked it up, tossing it into the trash.

He couldn't figure out what was wrong with him. Everything was fine. Great, actually. He'd finished building the bar. The wood had varnished to a gorgeous gold that brightened the room. He was almost ready to order the kitchen appliances. He'd been working on his recipes and Joe and Gabe had actually liked a few of his test meals.

Sandro was even getting along pretty well with his dad. They talked often these days, and his dad was a little more appreciative of the time Sandro put in on the ranch. When Sandro talked about his plans for the restaurant, his dad stuck around to listen—he'd even asked about them once or twice.

His entire family seemed happier now. It had been like that since Jenna's visit. It was as if she had shown up in Benson and waved her wand, or sprinkled her fairy dust, or whatever hocus-pocus she got up to, and his whole family was different. His mom was actually trying to give Paul advice on his choreography! Paul complained, but it was obvious he loved the attention. And his parents had gone out dancing the past couple weekends, coming home late, with a new spark between them.

Everyone was happier but him. Thoughts of Jenna and their last conversation were making him crazy. How had he allowed her to leave like that? The sadness in her eyes had been clear even while she'd held her head up, trying to be so brave.

He'd been keeping himself busy every waking minute trying to forget her, but at night the memories haunted him. The way her ivory skin had felt like satin under his hands. How her body curved in such outrageous ways, muscled from dance but soft and pliant in his arms. How free she'd been with him. How generous. She was beyond beautiful in his eyes.

A few of his parents' friends came up for burgers and Sandro forced himself to greet them cheerfully, reminding himself that everyone at this barbecue was a future customer at his restaurant. He couldn't afford to be distracted or brusque; he had to put his thoughts of Jenna aside. But it seemed as if no matter what dark, dusty corner of his brain he tried to shove his memories in, they just popped out again, bright and dancing in a swirl of sparkly skirts and red hair. He wished he could see her again. Wished that she'd agreed to move to Benson.

Burgers served, Sandro leaned back against the stone wall behind him, waiting for the next order. Across the lawn, he and his mom had set up long tables covered with all kinds of appetizers and salads—mostly Sandro's creations. He watched as people wandered along the buffet, helping themselves. He couldn't help but notice that standard fare like deviled eggs and his mom's Jell-O salad were disappearing rapidly. His dishes had barely been touched.

Jenna's words about San Francisco came back to him again. *You could make the wildest, most innovative cuisine and people would love it.* He thought of Gavin's success with Oliva and the fun they could have working together again. For the millionth time he imagined opening his own place in San Francisco. It would be a bistro, the best of French and Spanish rustic cuisine, filled with fresh ingredients from all the organic farms within a few hours of the city. It would be incredible to visit some of those farms and cultivate connections with those farmers. If his restaurant succeeded, he could commission crops—heirloom tomatoes, exotic tubers and rare greens.

"Can I get a burger, man?" He looked up to see a guy he knew from high school, whose name he couldn't remember, holding out a paper plate.

"Sandro?" The man stuck out his other hand for a shake and Sandro took it, trying not to wince in the meaty grip. "Blake Henson. Remember me?"

Sandro had a sudden memory of being fourteen years old and shoved up against a locker with Blake's pale eyes squinting into his while he asked what the hell Sandro was doing in his math class. *Shouldn't you be in home economics where you belong?*

He's a future customer, Sandro reminded himself. Just hand him the burger and move on. He slapped the burger onto the paper plate just a little too hard, so that the ex-bully had to scramble to keep it from falling. "Yeah, I remember you, Blake. Enjoy the party."

Sandro turned off the grill and walked toward his cabin. With every step, he left the noise of conversation and laughter farther behind him and his relief grew. At the cabin door he stopped. It held memories of Jenna now, incredible memories, and he couldn't face those at the moment.

Sandro walked back down the steps and around behind the cabin to a tiny trail through the woods that zigzagged up the steep hill. Each muffled step on the pine-needled forest floor soothed him. He inhaled the clear air, only faintly tinged with bar-

becue smoke now. After a few hairpin turns, he left
the trail for a smaller one, following it as it wound
up the mountainside, meandering along a stream.
At the top of the hills, he came out of the trees and
into open granite spaces and there was the boulder. The same one he'd visualized when Jenna had
made him think peaceful thoughts while she dealt
the tarot cards. He scrambled up to sit on top.

It was just as he remembered it. From here he
could see the entire valley, past Benson and out over
the high desert beyond, shining gray and brown
in the late-summer heat. So dry and dusty and yet
covered in shrubs and plants that were quietly im-
pressive for their toughness, their ability to survive
extreme conditions.

Sandro wished, suddenly, to have some of their
strength, their ability to weather stress by digging
their roots down deep to find their own sources of
water and nutrients. He'd never figured out how to
do that. He'd always sought something outside of
himself to give him sustenance. He'd pressed forward, to the next job, to the next party, to the next
good review of his cooking and, finally, to Benson.
When he couldn't run somewhere new, he ran away
in his head with alcohol, drugs and all that casual
sex. He'd never learned to just stand still and deal
with whatever life threw his way.

*I'm no expert, but I think that kind of safety has
to come from inside you.* Jenna's words were so

clear, as if she were sitting right there next to him. She'd been right. She'd been right so damn often he was starting to think she *did* have some kind of psychic powers.

She'd certainly gotten it right with those crazy tarot cards. The knight in black on the white horse. Death. Rebirth. He remembered how she'd explained it. *The end of an old phase of life that's served its purpose and the beginning of a new one.*

Insight hit him so hard that Sandro stood bolt upright on his rock, jumped off the back and was heading back down the trail before he was even conscious of moving. He'd mourned long enough. This phase had served its purpose. He'd come home to mourn his dream of New York and the mistakes he'd made. He'd come home with a corpse of regret slung across his shoulders. But somehow he had to set that burden down and move on. He had to find the courage and inner strength to put down his roots where they belonged. Just as those plants out in the desert did.

He was running down the trail, feet pounding into the soft turf. He rounded a sharp corner and almost crashed into his dad. Swerving to avoid him, Sandro skidded on the pine needles and went off the path, landing hard on the steep hillside below.

"Son!" His dad's face was a confused expression of alarm and humor.

"Hey, Dad." Sandro slowly swiveled his legs

around until he was upright, then scooted back a few inches until he was sitting with his back against the copper scaled trunk of a huge pine. "You looking for me?"

And then they were both laughing, huge peals that rang out through the quiet air. His dad gasped for breath. "Hell, son, I thought I'd lost you for a minute there."

Sandro thought of Jenna—she'd laugh if she were here right now, and he'd love to see her laughing again.

"Were you coming to find me? Do you need more burgers?"

John Salazar sat down on a piece of granite that bordered the trail. "I saw you leave the party all of a sudden. Just wondered if you were okay."

Sandro envisioned his eyes bugging right out of his head—he was that surprised. He tried to remember if his dad had ever sought him out to see if he was all right. When he was a little kid, sure. But not since.

"I'm okay. Better now. I think I've got something to tell you."

"That you're leaving the ranch?"

"Pops, what the…?"

"I guess I can see how the land lies now, Sandro. It's obvious that you belong in the city."

Sandro stared at his father, speechless.

"I'm starting to understand it a little more. Your mom's been talking to me a lot about how I need to start accepting that my sons are all different. That I need to appreciate it." He paused, picked up a pine needle and rolled it in his fingers, studying it. "To be honest, I'm not sure I've gotten to the appreciating part yet. But I think I'm at least ready to stop fighting it."

"That's great, Dad."

"I know one of the reasons you came back here was to try to make things better between us. And I appreciate it, more than I can say. It was a bad day for me when you left. It was hard every day that you were gone."

"I wish I'd done it differently. Not hurt you all so much."

"I wish *we'd* done it differently. I'm pretty sure the blame for you leaving sits squarely on my back. But you came home, and you threw your heart into the ranch and into this family and I'm glad you did."

Sandro braced himself. His revelation was so new it was hard to figure out how to voice it. "But my heart's not really in it."

"I know." His dad leaned forward on his rock, bracing his elbows on his knees, feet planted firmly in the dust of the mountains he loved. "I think I realized it when Jenna was here."

"I realized it just now."

His father laughed, a guffaw that echoed on the quiet hillside. "It's a rare moment that I've ever been a step ahead of you, son."

"Well, maybe times have changed." Sandro picked up a pine needle of his own. It was dry and he snapped it into pieces. "I sure don't feel on top of stuff these days."

"Welcome to adulthood." His dad smiled ruefully, the deep web of lines around his eyes crinkling. "You're officially a real man when you realize you have no idea what the hell you're doing."

He stood from the rock and held out a hand. Sandro grasped it and let his dad's iron strength help haul him up from the base of his tree. "Just do me a favor, son. Don't tell your mom you're leaving until after the party today. You know how much she loves her annual barbecue."

"Will do, Dad."

"And don't spit on anyone's burger."

"Pop, I wouldn't!"

"Well, when I saw that bozo from your high school was here today, I figured you'd be tempted."

"I sure was. But, hey, I'm a professional, don't forget."

"I won't, son. Honestly, eating your food the past few weeks, I've felt damn proud of your talents."

They walked back to the party in silence. Sandro didn't know what his father was thinking, but he was busy replaying his dad's last comment, filing it away in his memory under the category of Miracles.

SANDRO'S TRUCK WAS packed and all that was left were the goodbyes. Joe and Gabe had clapped him on the back earlier and disappeared out in the hills on horseback for a day out checking on the sheep. His mom, dad and Paul had stuck around to say goodbye.

"Take care of yourself, Sandro." His mom hugged him hard. "Keep your focus. Don't let the city dictate your choices."

He'd sat up late with his parents last night and finally told them about what had really happened in New York. Not everything, not the women, not the Dumpster, but all about the drinking and drugs. They deserved to know.

"I won't, Ma. Nothing like that will happen again." His heart thudded like a sickly thing in his chest. He wouldn't *let* it happen again. He'd found a way to be sure of that. It was called Alcoholics Anonymous and he had his first meeting tonight. As soon as he put his stuff down at Gavin's apartment, he was headed there.

He hoped it would do more than keep him sober. He wanted that inner strength and resilience he'd realized he lacked. Hopefully, the Twelve Steps would teach him some of that.

"Can I come stay with you? After you get settled?" Paul's face was alight with hope and eagerness. "There's a performing arts high school in San Francisco. Some of my friends from Jenna's class go there. It's public—you don't even have to pay for it."

"Hush now, Paulo." Sandro's mom tucked Paul under her arm firmly. "You told me yourself that auditions aren't until the spring. Don't ask your mother to think about losing her baby today, too."

Sandro's dad pulled him in for a rough hug. It was awkward but also heartfelt and golden. "Come back and visit as often as you can. Bring Jenna with you."

To Sandro's surprise, his own voice came out gruff. Too much damn emotion. "If I'm lucky, Pops, I'll bring Jenna. If not, you'll have to settle for only me."

"You just tell her that your mom and I have a few more dances to teach her."

Sandro grinned. There was so much surprise in this new version of his parents. "I'd better get going. I have that meeting tonight."

He got in his truck and slammed the door. Then he leaned out the window for one more look at his family. "I love you guys. Thanks for giving me a place to get my head on straight."

"It's called home, son." His mother smiled gently at him. "And it will always be here when you need it."

He blew her a kiss. Heading down the driveway toward the valley, he remembered the last time he left home for San Francisco. He'd been a kid and he'd left before dawn. He'd hitched a ride out of town with a trucker.

Both departures had been sad, but this time there was a whole lot more peace in his heart. That scared kid had faced a rough road ahead. Hopefully, if Sandro followed the steps he needed to, his road would be a lot easier this time, and he'd get a much happier ending, as well.

CHAPTER TWENTY-ONE

"IT'S COMPLETELY TRANSFORMED!" Jenna couldn't decide what to admire first. The forgotten ballroom was alive again with sparkling chandeliers, clean windows, new drapes and carpets, and the refinished, polished dance floor.

"It's going to be wonderful." Emily gave the top of the reception counter one last wipe with her dust cloth. Her entire cleaning crew stood with them at the edge of the gleaming dance floor, admiring the results of their hard work.

"Well, you and your crew made it happen," Jenna told her. "I can't thank you enough." She wanted to hug the woman she'd gotten to know as they'd labored side by side. She handed her the check instead. "So you'll come back for the weekly cleaning? Once I get my programs under way?"

"It will be our pleasure," Emily assured her.

Jenna said goodbye and waved to Emily and her crew as they headed down the marble stairs to the lobby below. Then she went back into the ballroom—*her* ballroom. She walked to the middle of the dance floor and caught her reflection in the wall of mirrors that she'd had installed last week. She looked tiny and alone in the huge sheet of glass.

Well, she *was* alone. She was making peace with that fact slowly, day by day. Working on her ballroom for the past couple weeks had been a good distraction from her heartache, but she still missed Sandro constantly.

Watching herself in the mirror, Jenna did a pirouette, then another. Maybe she'd offer some ballet classes here. It would be a good idea to have classes she could teach on her own while she searched for a new dance partner.

A noise from the lobby stopped her midturn. Somebody was coming up the stairs. The cleaning crew must have left the door to the street ajar. In the future she'd have to make sure it was locked when she was here by herself. Jenna quietly walked to the side of the dance floor until she was in the shadows behind one of the old columns.

A man paused by the reception counter at the entrance to the ballroom. The light in the entry was off and Jenna couldn't see his features. Her heart thumped as adrenaline kicked in. Who would come here in the evening like this?

"Jenna?" the man called softly.

His voice was electric current in her system. "Sandro?" She stepped out from behind her pillar. "What are you doing here?"

He moved into the light of the dance floor and

hesitated, waiting as she walked toward him on shaking legs.

"I came to see you. Marlene told me where you were."

She was pretty sure her heart did a backflip. "I can't believe you're here!"

"I've missed you."

Jenna stepped close enough to see the details of his face—his mouth tilted up but not quite smiling, his dark eyes studying her intently. "I've missed you, too," she said softly, still not fully able to absorb his unexpected presence.

He looked around, taking in the room. "This place is incredible. You did it!"

She was still having trouble absorbing his presence. Sandro was in her ballroom! "I did. Well, with a little help from my mother, in the end."

"Your mother helped? I thought she didn't approve of your dancing."

"Apparently she does now." Jenna couldn't stop staring at him—at his strong jaw, his broad shoulders under the familiar leather jacket, the dark waves of his thick hair. She wanted to run her hands over him to make sure he was real.

"It's incredible to see you again." He brought his fingers up to her face and smoothed a curl along her forehead. "You look beautiful. It suits you—this fancy old ballroom." He glanced up at the ceiling. "Especially the cherubs."

"I'm trying to think of names for them." Jenna pointed to the chubbiest one, who was sitting away from the others, looking a little miffed. "I'm pretty sure that one is Cosmo."

Sandro laughed. "It fits him."

Jenna had to ask, though she wished his answer didn't matter so much. "So how long are you here in San Francisco?"

"Forever, I hope." He stepped forward until he was inches from her, looking down into her eyes. "I want to make a life here, Jenna, with you."

Jenna's heart was in the air before her feet left the ground. She jumped and landed in his arms. He chuckled, soft and low, as he staggered back under her sudden weight.

"Are you serious? You want to be here? With me?" Jenna wrapped her arms and legs around him and he held her close, burying his face in her hair, spinning once around with her.

"I don't want to be away from you again, Red."

Jenna didn't think there was a name for the emotion she felt. Excitement, relief, joy, gratitude, all mixed into one overwhelming sensation. She pulled back a little so she could kiss him softly. A welcome-home kiss. A kiss he responded to and took deeper with one hand woven into her hair, pulling her into him.

When it ended, happy tears blurred Jenna's vision. She put her head on Sandro's shoulder, her arms around his neck as he held her easily in his strong arms.

Neither of them spoke, just held on tight to each other until finally he set her down in front of him.

"Sandro." Jenna looked up at him and took his hands in hers. "Tell me everything! Why did you decide to come? Did you just get to San Francisco today?"

He smiled at her interrogation. "I came because I realized that you were right, Jenna. I *should* be here. I want to be with you. And there isn't a better place to open my restaurant—to cook the way that I want to.

"When I looked down the road at what my life in Benson would be like, I realized I'd be missing out on so much, just because I was scared to trust myself again."

"I'm so proud of you, Sandro. So happy for you." Jenna stood on tiptoe and kissed him on the cheek. "I know that wasn't an easy decision."

"And as for the second half of your question…" He hesitated slightly. "I've been here for two weeks."

At first Jenna thought she couldn't possibly have heard him correctly. "You've been here for two weeks and didn't let me know?" All of her buoyancy at seeing him seeped away.

"I wanted time to make sure I'd be okay living in

the city—that I could handle it here without making poor choices."

She tried to understand his logic. But all she could think was that he'd been here two weeks and hadn't called. She'd been so sad, she'd missed him so much, and almost the entire time, he'd been right here, not missing her enough to pick up the phone. "Where have you been staying?"

"I crashed at Gavin's for a few nights, but then a studio apartment opened up in his building. I'm renting it. I'm in the Mission District—at Twenty-Fourth Street and Guerrero."

"The Mission District?" she repeated in disbelief. "I live four blocks from you."

"It'll make it easy to spend time together." Sandro was looking at her hopefully.

What did he want from her? A pie and a card saying welcome to the neighborhood? He'd been here two weeks, four blocks away, while she'd been mourning him. "I don't understand why you didn't get in touch earlier." She moved back a few steps, putting some space between them.

"Jenna, you saw how I was. Totally stuck. Unable to move forward because I was so afraid I'd end up like I was in New York. But then I remembered what you said, that the safety I was looking for had to come from inside me. And it hit me that I *could* live in San Francisco, as long as I make sure that I'm a much stronger person than I used to be.

"So I drove here a couple weeks ago and started going to AA meetings. I've been at a meeting every night since I arrived, just to get in the habit. I want to do this right, Jenna. I've been spending my free time reading their literature, learning about the Twelve Steps and finding a sponsor."

Anxiety pitted Jenna's stomach. "But you're not an alcoholic! You told me yourself that you never really craved it. Did you start drinking again? In Benson?"

"No. But I do have a problem with alcohol. I might not crave it the way some people do, but when I was drinking, I didn't drink to enjoy it. I *used* alcohol to fill a void inside me. I used it to numb my emotions and take away all the stress that I didn't know how to deal with.

"If I want to be with you and have a restaurant here, then I've got to figure out how to handle stuff without drinking, or doing drugs, or sleeping around, or running off to Benson, or any of the other things I used to do because I didn't know how to stand still and face whatever I was feeling."

She tried to take in his words. Everything he said made sense, but Jenna was unable to reconcile the Sandro she knew with this self-described addict.

Jenna shivered—the ballroom seemed cold suddenly. Tears stung her eyes. This dream she'd had, of her and Sandro together, suddenly seemed like just another one of her dead-end relationships. She used to pick men who cheated. Now she'd fallen in love with an alcoholic? Someone who'd be going to AA meetings all the time, who'd be uncomfortable at parties, who would never be able to just enjoy a glass of scotch with her? And he worked in restaurants, constantly surrounded by the temptation of alcohol—what if he relapsed?

She'd tried to have faith in him when he told her he was no longer a womanizer, like her dad. But now he was an alcoholic, like her mom—she wasn't sure she had enough faith left to handle this latest revelation. She tried to plaster some kind of smile on her face. "Sandro, it's so good to see you again, but I've got a lot to do."

The hope in his expression dimmed. "Can I see you later? Take you out?"

Jenna's entire image of him had been knocked askew. She didn't want to think that he was like her alcoholic mom. Not after her mom's drinking had caused so much stress. And honestly, after a few weeks of family meetings at her mom's rehab facility along with her regular Al-Anon meetings here in the city, she was sick and tired of twelve-step programs and alcoholism.

She shook her head no and grabbed at the easiest reason for a fight. "Why do you want to date now? You obviously didn't miss me! You were here for two weeks and didn't tell me!"

"Jenna, I did miss you. I left Benson for you.

Maybe it was a bad decision, but I didn't stay away these past two weeks to hurt you. I was trying to make sure that I could come to you with my head held high, knowing I was healthy and strong. Knowing I was the kind of guy you deserved!"

"But what if you're not the kind of guy I want?" It wasn't until she saw the stricken look on Sandro's face that she realized she'd actually said the words out loud.

"Jenna." His eyes were dark with anguish. "I love you."

"I'm so confused." Jenna rubbed her hands over her eyes as if it would clear her mind. "I love you. I fell in love with you. But you can't just announce you're an addict and that you've been going to AA every day and expect everything to be instantly normal between us! I know this is going to sound horrible, but I don't know if I can handle more than one alcoholic in my life!"

Sandro ran his hand through his hair in a gesture so familiar it made Jenna's heart hurt. But she had to voice her fears and the anger that made no sense but was boiling inside her.

"Can't you see? I've already got my mom to worry about—now I have to worry about you, too? What if you and my mom both relapse at the same time? Though I guess—" her voice was more bitter, her words more hateful than she'd planned "—I'm already spending a few nights a week at Al-Anon, thanks to my mom. So I guess if you and I are dating, I can multitask. The two-for-one alcoholic special."

Shame that she'd say something so poisonous hit her like nausea. The hurt on Sandro's face didn't help. "You'd better go," she said abruptly. "I'm not handling this well. I'm sorry."

"I'm working with Gavin right now," he said softly. "At Oliva. If you need me."

"Okay," she said, blinking back tears. How was it that she had missed him, craved him, been so miserable without him, and now that he was here in some kind of twisted miracle, all she wanted was to be alone?

Sandro turned and walked out of her ballroom. She heard the thud of his boots on the stairs and the slam of the door as he left the building. There was an extra click when he pulled it a second time, ensuring that it locked behind him.

That last tiny gesture of caring for her was her undoing. Jenna walked over to the beautiful floor-to-ceiling windows, where the lights of the city were glimmering in the gathering dusk, and sat down heavily on the floor. She'd tried to be so strong ever since she'd said goodbye to Sandro in Benson. She'd tried to find comfort in the idea that Sandro was a life lesson in loving and letting go—in trusting that the universe would provide and she would be okay.

Now the universe had provided exactly what she wanted most but in such a flawed and faulty package. *Addict.* Logically, she knew that it was just a word. He was still Sandro. He'd told her about his past—his addiction shouldn't come as a surprise. But somehow that one label changed her perception of him.

And then the tears came. Tears for her mother, for Sandro, for how much everything had changed and was still changing. She cried because she missed the Sandro she'd fallen in love with, the beautiful, troubled man she'd known in San Francisco and the cowboy in Benson who had completely captured her heart. She cried because she wasn't sure she recognized the man who'd walked in the door just now. *An addict. A life spent in AA.* It wasn't how she'd dreamed it when she'd dreamed that Sandro might come find her in San Francisco.

THE SKY OUTSIDE went from dusk to dark and eventually she had no tears left. The anger was gone. The shock of everything Sandro had told her tonight had a softer edge to it. It was night now, but many of the windows in the buildings surrounding the ballroom had their lights on. A few weeks ago she'd looked at the view from Dolores Park, seen these lights in the distance and promised herself that someday her ballroom would be among them.

Now here she was, in the window of her own ball-room, right in the middle of the city. She'd made that dream come true.

Was there a way to make the rest of her dream a reality? Was there a way to go forward with San-dro?

God grant me the serenity to accept the things I cannot change. The words of the prayer she'd re-lied on that night in Dolores Park wafted through her whirling thoughts. But serene was the last thing she felt right now. She'd been so horrible to Sandro tonight and he hadn't deserved it. He'd been an idiot not to call the minute he'd arrived in San Francisco. But he'd thought he was doing the right thing.

Even with no serenity in her tumultuous mind, could she find acceptance? Because she couldn't change who Sandro was—she couldn't change him into a non-addict. She had no doubt she loved him, but could she accept him?

A new calm filled her, along with the rest of the prayer. *The courage to change the things I can...* She certainly hadn't shown courage tonight. She'd been petty and selfish. Banging her head up against the things she couldn't change instead of focusing on the one thing she actually had control over—her re-action. Her last words to Sandro had been brutal—definitely not the reaction she'd go with if she could redo that conversation.

The wisdom to know the difference. Who knew what would happen in the future? Her mom could relapse, or Sandro might, or maybe neither of them would. She could stare at her tarot cards for days and they wouldn't be able to predict that. She just had to go forward, live her life and do her best to be happy.

She could do it alone, cut off from the man she loved, in an attempt to avoid potential pain from things that might or might not happen. Or she could jump in and pursue all the happiness that was there, trusting that she was strong enough and wise enough to handle whatever might come.

And then the irony hit her. She'd gotten upset at Sandro for needing AA. And yet the prayer that was the base of all the twelve-step programs had just brought her hope, insight, clarity and, possibly, a way forward.

Jenna jumped up and ran to the reception desk for her purse and coat. Flipping off the ballroom lights, she raced down the dark marble steps to the lobby and out into the street, tugging the doors shut behind her. A rare empty cab was waiting at the stoplight on the corner of Sutter and Hyde. "The Mission District!" she told the driver as she settled into the torn backseat.

Jenna watched the city lights flash by and caught herself smiling. Love had walked through her ball-room door tonight. The universe was offering up its most precious gift. But it came as is, with quirks and flaws and no guarantees that it would last or always stay the same. And that meant she should cherish it even more.

CHAPTER TWENTY-TWO

IT WAS A Tuesday night, but the sidewalk in front of Oliva was crowded with people waiting for tables. Jenna wove her way through the throng to find the hostess stand.

"Two hours for a table," the young woman told her without looking up from her wait list. She tapped the pencil clutched in her tattooed hand on the paper in front of her. "Want me to put your name in?"

"No, thank you. I'm looking for Sandro Salazar?"

The hostess looked up immediately, revealing a pierced nose and eyebrow. "The new guy? He's hot. Is he a friend of yours?"

"Um, yes. He is. A friend." Jenna shifted uneasily. This was the restaurant culture that Sandro had been so steeped in before. Would he be able to resist all the young women like this one who would be enamored of their gorgeous new chef?

"I don't think he's here right now, but let me go check." The hostess winked at Jenna and turned on her heel to stroll through the crowded room toward the kitchen.

She didn't come back for a while. Jenna stood awkwardly as patrons tried to get around her in the small foyer to put their names on the list. It felt way too familiar, as if she were still Jeff the musician's girlfriend, waiting around for him to pack up his gear after a show.

"Sorry 'bout that." The hostess was back, peering at Jenna from under her thick black bangs. "He's not in yet."

Where could he be? She'd left the ballroom after he had and come straight here.

"Jenna!" It was Gavin, parting the turbulent activity of his restaurant, people whispering and pointing in his wake. The head chef of Oliva was a local celebrity. "When Eloise here told me there was a redhead asking after Salazar, I thought it might be you!"

He swept Jenna up into a hug as if they were old friends. "Have you made up your mind to leave that lout and be mine forever?" he asked when he set her down.

"Well, we should probably get to know each other a little first," she teased, and Gavin roared with laughter.

"Sandro, that lucky dog, is out right now. We're expecting him soon. You'll wait, right? Can I get you a drink or something to eat?"

She couldn't do it. She couldn't stand around waiting like a groupie tonight. "Thank you, Gavin, but I have to go. Would you mind telling him I stopped by?"

"Of course," he said. "And come in for a meal soon, okay? We'll have wine together. Sandro's no fun now that he's sober." But he said it with a grin and a wink that told Jenna he was proud of his friend.

Jenna thanked Eloise and headed out into the street, glad to be out of the crowded restaurant. She turned down Valencia, ready to get home, take off her heels and run a steaming-hot bubble bath after such an emotional evening.

The wind was getting stronger and she'd forgotten her coat this morning, lulled by the September weather that was San Francisco's real taste of summer. Jenna clutched her thin cardigan around her chest and put her head down, willing her legs to go just a little faster.

She passed the local dive bar. Light spilled out into the street through the open door, jukebox music following it. The melody was familiar and Jenna stopped abruptly. It was one of the songs she and Sandro had danced to that night in Benson—one of the happiest nights she'd ever spent.

"Brings back memories, doesn't it?" Sandro was standing beside her, taking off his leather jacket and handing it to her. "Put this on—you're freezing."

"What are you doing here?"

He grinned. "We're neighbors, remember? I was on my way to Oliva."

Jenna pulled his coat on—it was still warm from his body. "I don't know if I can get used to running into you."

"Well, if you spend a lot of time with me, you won't have to worry about running into me. You'll know where I am."

She laughed. "That's true." Then her horrible words from earlier came back to her. "Sandro, I feel awful about what I said. I was surprised, but it's no excuse."

"No, I get it. You're already dealing with alcoholism. You've gotta decide if you're up for taking on a work in progress like me."

"I think it's obvious after today that I'm a work in progress, as well."

"I should have let you know I was here. I was selfish. I didn't consider that you might be having a hard time. You seem so grounded, Jenna. Like you were going to be just fine without me. Like you've got it all figured out."

She stared at him. "You're kidding me. Sandro, I've got *nothing* figured out. But I think I realized after you left this evening that I don't need to have it all figured out. I just have to trust that I'll be okay, no matter what happens in the future."

"I want to be in your future," Sandro said, and his expression was solemn now. He took her hand

and Jenna marveled that it was still so warm in the cold air. The man was like a heater. "I love you, Jenna. You are the most important reason that I moved here. I know it's early days for us but I also know that I'm completely crazy about you. I want to spend all my spare time with you."

Jenna put her hands up to his cheeks, stood on tiptoe and kissed him slowly on the mouth, filling her kiss with all the emotion in her heart. "I love you, Sandro," she whispered against his lips. "And I want to spend my spare time with *you*."

His arms wrapped around her, pulling her in tightly to his warmth, and he kissed her back, his mouth strong and sure against hers. It felt like home in the best possible way—languid, comforting, promising. Then she felt his lips curve into a smile under hers and he slowly pulled away, looking down at her with the knee-weakening smile she loved and feared. She kept her arms on his shoulders just in case she started to fall over.

"Don't you think it's a little strange that we ran into each other like this? In front of a bar that's playing what might be the only country-western music in this entire city?"

Jenna grinned, realizing where he was going. "And playing a song we had such a good time dancing to in Benson?"

"You know what it means, don't you?" He tilted his head to hers so their foreheads touched.

"It's a sign!" She didn't mind the teasing. Not when the sign had led her to him.

Sandro pulled her in close again. His laughter blended with hers. Then he pivoted, tucking her under his arm in the way she'd come to love. "Let's get you inside before we both freeze."

"What about Oliva?"

"If there's one excuse Gavin will accept, it's that I've just convinced the woman I love to love me back. He'll understand why I have to skip work for the celebration."

Jenna stopped and looked up at him. "What celebration?" she asked.

Sandro turned, and there on the dirty Valencia Street sidewalk he went down on one knee. Jenna's hands went up to her mouth and she looked down at him in a mixture of wonder, excitement and pure terror. He pulled a black velvet box out of his pocket and flipped the lid. The rubies on the woven gold band glimmered in the streetlight overhead.

"Red, I am the worst bet. I'm an alcoholic who doesn't really know much about having a real relationship—since I've never actually had one. And I'm a guy crazy enough to try to open a new restaurant in a city that has great food on every square block."

Jenna smiled at his humor, though her mind was racing right along with her heart, trying to absorb what was happening.

"You are the first woman I've truly loved and it's clear to me that I will love you forever. You are this magical person who can talk anyone into just about anything—and now I've got to somehow convince you to take a chance on me."

"I think I already have," Jenna answered, trying to breathe and keep her feet on the ground.

"I can't ask you to marry me right now—there's too much in my life that I have to straighten out first. But I want you to know, without any doubts, how much you mean to me. Jenna Stevens, will you be a work in progress with me? Will you love me and dance with me and cook with me and let me love you?"

Jenna just nodded. It was hard to speak with such deep feelings caught in her throat.

"And in a year or two, when I've proven to you that I really can be a healthy, somewhat normal guy, will you at least hear me out when I get down on my knee one more time, to ask you to marry me?"

Jenna looked down at the gorgeous, complicated man kneeling in front of her, and at the beautiful ring he offered. She loved him. She *would* be with him, but she couldn't help teasing him, just a little, about his offbeat proposal. "That's a whole lot of questions, Sandro. Are you looking for an itemized response?"

A small crowd of people had gathered around, watching the romantic tableau they'd created. "Just say yes!" someone shouted.

"You heard the guy." Sandro gave her the cocky smile he knew she could never resist. "Just say yes. To all of it."

Jenna took a deep breath. "Yes."

Sandro let out a whoop and slipped the ring on the third finger of her right hand. "I'm not kidding about the next proposal," he explained. "You have to leave your ring finger bare for the real thing."

"*If* you play your cards right, cowboy," she said.

"Oh, I will, Red. I will." He stood and swooped Jenna up, swinging her around as he kissed her. Their audience clapped. And once he'd set her down and they'd finished shaking hands with everyone who'd stopped to listen to his not-a-proposal, Sandro took Jenna by the hand and led her into the bar. They snaked past the barstools and into the space back by the jukebox where an old Johnny Cash song was playing.

"Love is a burning thing," Sandro sang softly into her ear as he held her close and danced her around in some freewheeling version of a two-step.

Jenna closed her eyes and let him lead her around the tiny dance floor. He was strong and steady and made it easy for her to know where to put her feet. She loved him, and he loved her, and they were going to figure it all out, together. Her happiness was mixed with an awe that somehow, through all the twists and turns their lives had taken since they met, it had come round to this moment, this love that truly did burn inside.

Sandro stepped away and she opened her eyes. He let go of one of her hands and raised the other so she turned beneath it, coming back around into his arms. She couldn't stop smiling. He was looking at her with a combination of tenderness, desire and joy that exactly mirrored how she felt inside.

After all her worry and all her attempts to think things through, suddenly everything seemed very clear. Love was like being a follower in a dance. You had to give up control and just see where it took you. And trust that you could keep your balance, no matter what happened next. It was that simple, and that beautiful.

* * * * *

LARGER-PRINT
BOOKS!

HARLEQUIN *Presents*

PASSION
GUARANTEED
SEDUCTION

GET 2 FREE LARGER-PRINT
NOVELS PLUS 2 FREE GIFTS!

YES! Please send me 2 FREE LARGER-PRINT Harlequin Presents® novels and my 2 FREE gifts (gifts are worth about $10). After receiving them, if I don't wish to receive any more books, I can return the shipping statement marked "cancel." If I don't cancel, I will receive 6 brand-new novels every month and be billed just $5.05 per book in the U.S. or $5.49 per book in Canada. That's a saving of at least 16% off the cover price! It's quite a bargain! Shipping and handling is just 50¢ per book in the U.S. and 75¢ per book in Canada.* I understand that accepting the 2 free books and gifts places me under no obligation to buy anything. I can always return a shipment and cancel at any time. Even if I never buy another book, the two free books and gifts are mine to keep forever.

176/376 HDN F43N

Name	(PLEASE PRINT)

Address	Apt. #

City	State/Prov.	Zip/Postal Code

Signature (if under 18, a parent or guardian must sign)

Mail to the **Harlequin® Reader Service:**
IN U.S.A.: P.O. Box 1867, Buffalo, NY 14240-1867
IN CANADA: P.O. Box 609, Fort Erie, Ontario L2A 5X3

**Are you a subscriber to Harlequin Presents books
and want to receive the larger-print edition?
Call 1-800-873-8635 today or visit us at www.ReaderService.com.**

* Terms and prices subject to change without notice. Prices do not include applicable taxes. Sales tax applicable in N.Y. Canadian residents will be charged applicable taxes. Offer not valid in Quebec. This offer is limited to one order per household. Not valid for current subscribers to Harlequin Presents Larger-Print books. All orders subject to credit approval. Credit or debit balances in a customer's account(s) may be offset by any other outstanding balance owed by or to the customer. Please allow 4 to 6 weeks for delivery. Offer available while quantities last.

Your Privacy—The Harlequin® Reader Service is committed to protecting your privacy. Our Privacy Policy is available online at www.ReaderService.com or upon request from the Harlequin Reader Service.

We make a portion of our mailing list available to reputable third parties that offer products we believe may interest you. If you prefer that we not exchange your name with third parties, or if you wish to clarify or modify your communication preferences, please visit us at www.ReaderService.com/consumerchoice or write to us at Harlequin Reader Service Preference Service, P.O. Box 9062, Buffalo, NY 14269. Include your complete name and address.

LARGER-PRINT BOOKS!

GET 2 FREE LARGER-PRINT NOVELS PLUS
2 FREE GIFTS!

◆HARLEQUIN®

Romance

From the Heart, For the Heart

YES! Please send me 2 FREE LARGER-PRINT Harlequin® Romance novels and my 2 FREE gifts (gifts are worth about $10). After receiving them, if I don't wish to receive any more books, I can return the shipping statement marked "cancel." If I don't cancel, I will receive 4 brand-new novels every month and be billed just $4.84 per book in the U.S. or $5.24 per book in Canada. That's a savings of at least 19% off the cover price! It's quite a bargain! Shipping and handling is just 50¢ per book in the U.S. and 75¢ per book in Canada.* I understand that accepting the 2 free books and gifts places me under no obligation to buy anything. I can always return a shipment and cancel at any time. Even if I never buy another book, the two free books and gifts are mine to keep forever.

119/319 HDN F43Y

Name _____ (PLEASE PRINT)

Address _____ Apt. #

City _____ State/Prov. _____ Zip/Postal Code

Signature (if under 18, a parent or guardian must sign)

Mail to the **Harlequin® Reader Service:**
IN U.S.A.: P.O. Box 1867, Buffalo, NY 14240-1867
IN CANADA: P.O. Box 609, Fort Erie, Ontario L2A 5X3
Want to try two free books from another line?
Call 1-800-873-8635 or visit www.ReaderService.com.

* Terms and prices subject to change without notice. Prices do not include applicable taxes. Sales tax applicable in N.Y. Canadian residents will be charged applicable taxes. Offer not valid in Quebec. This offer is limited to one order per household. Not valid for current subscribers to Harlequin Romance Larger-Print books. All orders subject to credit approval. Credit or debit balances in a customer's account(s) may be offset by any other outstanding balance owed by or to the customer. Please allow 4 to 6 weeks for delivery. Offer available while quantities last.

Your Privacy—The Harlequin® Reader Service is committed to protecting your privacy. Our Privacy Policy is available online at www.ReaderService.com or upon request from the Harlequin Reader Service.

We make a portion of our mailing list available to reputable third parties that offer products we believe may interest you. If you prefer that we not exchange your name with third parties, or if you wish to clarify or modify your communication preferences, please visit us at www.ReaderService.com/consumerschoice or write to us at Harlequin Reader Service Preference Service, P.O. Box 9062, Buffalo, NY 14269. Include your complete name and address.

HRLP13R